The Warmest December

by Bernice L. McFadden

This is a work of fiction. All names, characters, places, and incidents are the product of the author's imagination. Any resemblance to real events or persons, living or dead, is entirely coincidental.

Published by Akashic Books
Originally published in hardcover by Dutton in 2001; followed by a trade paperback edition from Plume in 2002
©2001, 2012 Bernice L. McFadden
Introduction ©2012 James Frey

ISBN-13: 978-1-61775-035-9
Library of Congress Control Number: 2011923102
All rights reserved

First Akashic Books printing

Akashic Books
PO Box 1456
New York, NY 10009
info@akashicbooks.com
www.akashicbooks.com

Also by Bernice L. McFadden

Gathering of Waters
Glorious
Nowhere Is a Place
Camilla's Roses
Loving Donovan
This Bitter Earth
Sugar

For me,
those daughters,
and their fathers

Photo by Vivian McFadden, circa 1967

*. . . And every time I see him put the bottle to his mouth
he don't suck out of it, it sucks out of him . . .*
—Ken Kesey, *One Flew Over the Cuckoo's Nest*

Introduction
BY JAMES FREY

I met Bernice L. McFadden at a spelling bee. It's a charity spelling bee where a group of well-known writers sit on a stage and pretend we're in sixth grade again, and a crowd of people laugh at how poorly most of us spell without our computers. Although I do it every year, I don't really enjoy it. I'm not friends with any of the other writers, and I always get knocked out in the first round. I show up, say hello to the organizers, misspell a word I should know, I leave.

This past year, though, it was a bit different. Shortly after I arrived, a beautiful African American woman walked up to me, a huge smile on her face, and said hello. She was smart, funny, warm, radiated kindness and serenity. We chatted for a few minutes and exchanged e-mail addresses. The bee started and I got knocked out in the third round. Bernice lasted longer.

She and I stayed in touch. We became Facebook friends. I had not read any of her work, so I did, starting with *Sugar*, moving to its sequel *This Bitter Earth*, and finishing with her masterpiece *The Warmest December*. She's an amazing writer. Her work can be brutal and heartbreaking, but is full of heart and emotion. Stories of family and love, violence and abuse, struggle and redemption. All of it is filled with a spirit of grace and forgiveness. In many ways it was easy to connect the work to the woman I had met and who became my friend. In other ways it led to questions.

We live in a peculiar time in the publishing industry.

Publishers are obsessed with categories, and being able to place things within them, usually for marketing reasons. The categories themselves—fiction, nonfiction, memoir, etc.—tend to pigeonhole books, many of which defy them, and impose rules on them which might not have been part of their creation. People read memoirs and nonfiction and ask questions about what in the books isn't real. They read novels and short fiction and ask what in them is. Ultimately, none of it matters. Good writing is good writing, and a story well told isn't beholden to issues of fact and fiction, and moves beyond wherever it is shelved in a bookstore. Any author, and every author, regardless of how their book is categorized, draws from their own life and their own experience in shaping their narrative. Writing a book is an act of subjectivity, and this subjectivity is what separates literature from journalism or academic writing. It is also what makes readers love certain authors. They connect, for whatever reason, with the author's perspective, believe in it, learn from it, grow and change because of it. It is why, in this age of digitalization, writing will survive. No other medium does this in the same way.

In reading Bernice's work, particularly *The Warmest December*, which, unlike her other two books that I've read, is set in contemporary times, I wondered how much of it came from her actual life. On her own website, there is banner across the top that says, *I write to breathe life back into memory*. The book tells the story of a woman named Kenzie sitting at her father's bedside as he slowly dies. She relives, through memory, the horrific childhood she experienced at his hands, a childhood marred by alcoholism and extreme physical abuse. The narrative moves back forth between Kenzie's memories and her present life, one in which she has survived, but is struggling with, her addiction to alcohol. It is a beautiful book, and my words about it don't do it justice.

What I can do, though, is think about how it was written, how it came to be, how Bernice L. McFadden was able to give her readers the gift of *The Warmest December*. There are certain emotions, deep, profound, often brutal and sometimes beautiful, that can only be written about if the writer has actually lived through them. This is what I suspect the case is with Bernice. She goes so deep, and it feels so real, that it just couldn't have been done if she hadn't lived some version of it. Names have probably been changed, maybe settings, certain details to either enhance the narrative or protect someone's identity, but art can't be created in a vacuum, and a book like hers can't be written without the years required to build it, make it great, and bring it to life.

I hope you love the book as much as I did, and I hope it moves you as much as it did me, changes you as it did me. I am fortunate to have access to the great woman who wrote it, which has only bolstered my belief that it comes from her direct experiences. Certain people glow. They glow because they have survived things most of us could never have imagined living through. They glow because hardship gives them the gift of wisdom, and kindness, and grace. They glow because they've figured out how to take those experiences, as horrific as they may have been, and turn them into something beautiful.

James Frey is originally from Cleveland. He is the New York Times *best-selling author of* A Million Little Pieces, My Friend Leonard, Bright Shiny Morning, *and* The Final Testament of the Holy Bible. *His work is published in thirty-nine languages.*

Chapter One

Now and then I forget things, small things that would not otherwise alter my life. Things like milk in my coffee, setting my alarm clock, or Oprah at four. Tiny things.

One day last week I forgot that I hated my father, forgot that I had even thought of him as a monster, forgot the blows he'd dealt my body over the years and the time he called me to him and demanded that I show him my hands. "Are they clean?" he asked as I slowly raised my arms. "Yes, sir," I said and shook my head furiously up and down.

They were clean, in fact still damp from my having washed them. "Come closer," he said. "Come closer so I can see better," he said. I moved closer and closer until my small hands were right beneath his chin. "I see a speck of dirt," he said and stifled a laugh. I smelled the whiskey. It was whiskey then.

"A speck of dirt . . . hmmm . . . right there," he said and smashed the hot tip of his cigarette down into the soft middle of my eight-year-old palm. I'd forgotten that day, the broken ribs, and the feel of the hard leather belt that held his Levi's up and left black bruises on my lower back and the underside of my thighs.

I forgot how the sound of my mother crying ate holes inside of me and ripped a space open near my heart. But worst of all I forgot about Malcolm, and for some reason I woke up early one cold winter morning and boarded two buses, traveling over an hour to sit by his bedside in Kings County Hospital.

By then he looked nothing like the beast I imagined from my childhood. The hands that had caused so much pain and left so many bruises were now shriveled and black, the fingers curled under like the ragged claws of a vulture. The fingernails were long gone, having decayed months earlier until finally flaking off and turning to dust as they hit the floor.

I sat for a long time watching him, while the winter sun fought to be seen through the dirty, cracked glass windows of his hospital room.

The room was heated but I did not remove my heavy jacket or the thick rust-colored wool hat that covered my head. Being this close to him made me shiver despite the warmth, and I dug my hands deep into my pockets, where my fingers were going numb at the tips.

He had less than half of his liver left, and bad blood circulated through his body, turning his once warm cinnamon-colored skin an inky black. The veins in his arms and legs were weak and thin; the only good vein left was in his penis, so that's where they attached most of the tubes. Delia thought that was funny and had smiled smugly when the doctor shared that piece of information with her.

Dozens of tubes ran in, out, and through every part of his body, like translucent tentacles, and I half-expected them to stretch out and enwrap me in their plastic grip.

Most of his teeth were gone and the ones that remained were the color of butter, buried in tobacco-brown gums. Never a big man, his small frame had withered so that his skin draped on his body.

I watched him, and to my surprise my heart pulled in my chest as I remembered a Saturday a few years earlier when we still owned the house. The rain and wind were pounding at the windows, ripping away the petals of the tulips that filled the garden and tearing at the black phone lines hanging above the two-family homes that lined the neighborhood.

It was Saturday and no matter the rain and the gray of the day, the sheets needed changing and the laundry needed to be done.

Delia's hands were hurting. The damp weather was aggravating her arthritis, her fingers refused to bend, and her knee swelled and bulged through her pants leg.

I told her not to worry, I would change the linens on her bed and wash her clothes. "Leave my underwear alone," she said as she half-walked, half-limped her way to the kitchen. "I'll wash those tomorrow when I'm feeling better." I just smiled and shook my head and then began stripping the sheets from the bed.

I picked up Delia's pillow first, removed its case, and then went for Hy-Lo's, but I dropped it back down to the bed just as quickly as I had snatched it up. I stood staring at it for some time, trying to distinguish what I thought were tiny blooming roses camouflaged among the green-stemmed daffodils that sprinkled the mauve canvas of the pillowcase.

I scratched my head in confusion and checked Delia's pillowcase. No blooming roses there. I looked at the matching top sheet and bed ruffle. Again, no blooming roses.

My heart began to race and I could feel panic taking hold of me like a vice grip. The air became thin, and all at once I knew that the crimson rose-shaped figures were not roses at all, but splatterings of blood.

That dried sanguine fluid dragged me toward a knowledge I had been sidestepping for some time. Two, maybe three years at least. I had managed to ignore Hy-Lo's bloated stomach and swollen face, disregarding the stench that seeped from his pores and hung thick in the air like smoke and settled deep into the upholstery. I chose instead to smile away the smell and his physical appearance rather than offer an explanation when a visitor raised his or her eyebrows in surprise.

He was ill. More than ill at that point. My Grandma

Mable said he was wiping his feet on Death's doormat.

I collected myself best I could and gathered the soiled linens and carried them down to the basement. He was there; he was always there, sitting in his recliner in front of the television surrounded by old lamps, boxes that held long-forgotten items, and dusty, rusting gym equipment that hadn't helped a body in years.

The washing machine was to his left and he rarely bothered to acknowledge anyone who came to use it; he would just lean forward, remote control in hand, and increase the already earsplitting volume of the television.

But for some reason, on that windy, rainy Saturday, he turned and looked at me and I forgot I hated him and smiled. He did not return my happy face with his own, but gave me a queer sort of look before turning his attention back to the television.

I looked at his balding head and the tiny sores that had begun to fester there, and I pitied him. A pity so deep and blue welled up within me like the sea, misting my eyes and blurring the image of the tiny blooming roses on the mauve pillowcase just before I dropped it into the soapy water of the washing machine.

He moved a bit. His head turned left then right, and he squeezed his eyes so tightly that milky tears ran out and onto his hollowed cheeks. I looked away from him, past the other three beds and the sick men they held, toward the open door of the room. I wanted so much to get up and leave, escape back into the bright winter sunlight. I wanted so much to reach over and pluck a Kleenex from the box on the nightstand beside his bed and gently wipe the sick tears away from his face.

Instead, I pulled my chair closer, hiding myself behind the green curtain that surrounded us.

These were his last days and he would spend them on

his back, tubes running in, out, and through his body. Orderlies would come in once a day to give him a sponge bath, maybe fluff his pillow, and make sure the sheet was tucked tight beneath his mattress. Visitors would look at him when their conversations waned, allowing their eyes to travel over his face, and maybe they would wonder who he was or who he had been. They might whisper, "Who's that? What's wrong with him?" but the people they confided in would not be able to give a response. Instead, they'd just shrug their shoulders, dismissing my father over their food tray.

I blinked back the tears that I could not understand and focused on the beige wall behind his bed. There were bits of tape that still clung there, yellow and brittle reminders of a Get Well card or a banner from a relative of the patient who'd lain there before my father. Someone who got better, got up, and checked back into the world.

Hy-Lo would never get better. Never stand up and stretch as if just awakened from a long nap. Never smile at the rosy-cheeked nurse as he signed his release papers or check the nightstand drawer a second time to make sure he was not leaving his Father's Day watch behind.

Hy-Lo would leave the hospital almost exactly the way he came in: on his back with his eyes closed. Except this time there would be no heartbeat, not even the faint one that kept him alive now.

I shivered again and pulled my collar up around my neck, folding my hands beneath my armpits and repressing the urge to stamp my feet for warmth. The sun was setting and the thermostat in the room rose five degrees. But my memories were cold and I was closer to him now. The heat would do me no good. Leaving would be best. Leaving would mean warmth, but I stayed until the streetlights glowed and the rosy-cheeked nurse placed a small soft hand on my shoulder. "Ma'am, eight o'clock," she said with a smile.

I looked stupidly at her.

"Visiting hours are over," she said with an air that made me think she felt this was something I should know.

"Oh," I said, and gathered myself to leave. I moved the chair back to its place beside the wall. I would remember just how close I'd gotten and perhaps tomorrow I would get closer.

I walked briskly up the street and away from the dark, looming brick walls of the hospital. I walked with my head down, cussing my feet for having carried me there to begin with. I hated Hy-Lo and had for most of my life. The other part of my life was lost deep inside of me in a place where I was not yet able to reach.

I had hated him so desperately that as a child I prayed for his demise more times than I care to remember. I'd even plotted to poison him by spraying his favorite drinking mug with Raid roach spray. In my mind Hy-Lo was a treacherous two-legged insect that made sudden and unwelcome appearances.

I hated him so desperately that I cried it into my pillow when I was five and mumbled it beneath my breath at ten. By the time I was thirteen I was screaming it into his face and catching the callused palm of his hand across my cheek for doing so. He was a stone wall and my hostility was nothing more than paper tossed against it. Or so I thought.

For years I believed, as I had as a child, that his absence would wipe the memories of him clean away. "That would be impossible," a lover of mine had once suggested, his hand moving across an inch-long battle scar from a belt buckle gone wild. "Hmm," was my only reply. He never saw me in the nude again.

I hurried past a woman wrapped in colorful cloth and newspaper. Her hair was thick and matted and hung down to her neck in brown turds of filth and grime. She was bent over a garbage can, both of her hands deep into the waste and filth, rummaging through it as if sorting through her sock drawer.

Walking past, I turned slightly to look back at her and realized that I was right where I had started, in front of the hospital. The concrete stairs lay before me, the silver specks they held shimmered beneath the streetlamps, reminding me of a summer day in 1970 and the way the sun gleamed through the warm air that glided around me, setting the stage for the hate I would develop at the tender age of five.

At that age life just was. It wasn't what it would become: black hours, and days on end when the only thing that mattered was the next drink, and then later, the next meeting. No, life was supposed to be sweet at that age and the only thing you would have to count were the hours before the sun rose again, allowing you to lose yourself in the happy world of Crayola, cartoons, and blue Italian ice.

In 1970 I was five years old and summertime was a playful woman-child who kept watch over me in the daytime and rocked my mother through her lonely nights. She was the intense heat and long sweltering nights that kept people out late, fanning themselves on the stoop of their five-story walk-up or sometimes forcing them out onto the rusted fire escape, where they would lie, half-naked on a bare mattress, and watch the heavy yellow moon until sleep stole their eyes away.

That was where my first real memory took place, right there in the midst of summer, beneath a rain of clothes that fell from the fifth floor and landed around the small feet of Glenna and me. We were not yet friends, but would become the best of friends in time.

Glenna and her mother had moved in just as spring slowly took winter's place. Our eyes had locked in the halls of our building during our daily comings and goings. Our mothers had traded nods and polite hellos, but no formal introduction had been made.

On that summer day Glenna stood less than five feet away from me, her hair plaited neatly in six long cornrows that began at the top of her forehead and ended in ropes that hung down her back. She had a yellow yo-yo that she held tight in the palm of her hand, allowing it to fall to the end of its string only when my eyes grew tired of watching her and moved to scrutinize something other than her clean white Keds and green jumpsuit.

We should not have been there, but it was hot in the house and Delia had sent me outside to play beneath the oak tree, where the shade was cooler than beneath the steady whirl of the fan. I was lining up milk crates for a game of train, while Hy-Lo, my father, washed and waxed his car. His transistor radio sat cradled in the driver's plush green seat, spilling out the Jackson Five's song about love and the alphabet. Glenna had also been ordered outside.

In only three short months Glenna's mother, Pinky, had become the talk of the building. She was infamous for her loud two-person parties. They all began and ended the same. Pinky coming in from the Blue Bar around midnight, stockings torn and wig akimbo; some man, some good woman's husband, behind her, his hand beneath her dress before she even got the key in the door. She'd put on Marvin Gaye and open her window, filling the courtyard with his sexy lyrics until someone hollered out, "Turn that shit down! Some of us have to get up in the morning!" But she never did.

Her laughter would come in spurts, sailing above the music, reaching its own crescendo and then falling into a deep groan. Something would happen, perhaps a misplaced word or a denied carnal request, that would ignite an explosion of filthy words and flying fists that snatched Glenna and the rest of the tenants from their sleep.

But there was no one sleeping on that day, not at three in the afternoon. This man did not stumble in from the Blue Bar in the middle of the night. This man had driven up to the apartment house, rung her bell, and greeted her with a kiss that caused my mother's face to heat and her eyes to drop. An old friend in town for a night. The night turned into twenty-one sunsets, ten matchstick covers holding simple names and seven digits, lipstick-stained collars, and two women too many ringing Pinky's phone and boldly asking, "Pablo there?"

That afternoon he left quickly and on foot, Pinky's screams at his back violently shoving him forward. His lip was busted and bleeding and his cream silk shirt was ripped at the cuff. I blinked as he moved past me like the wind and around the corner to the Blue Bar. I looked at Glenna but her head was tilted back, her small hand shading her eyes as she looked up at her mother. The curse words came first, a string of indictments in Panamanian Spanish and broken Brooklyn English. Passersby either stopped to stare up at her or lowered their heads and hurried on. My father stopped his waxing, turned off the transistor radio, and leaned against the side of the car. He lit a Camel cigarette and inhaled the coarse smoke. When he exhaled, he laughed and shook his head.

The clothes came next.

We stood there, Glenna and I, our hearts beating in quick unison as polyester bell-bottomed pants and knit shirts came down around us. Then the shoes came flying down like grenades, sending us scurrying into the street for safety. We did not look at each other; our eyes remained on the boxer shorts and black silk socks that flew from the window like wingless birds.

"He ain't never coming back in here! *Never!*" Pinky's affirmation could be heard from Nostrand Avenue all the way down to Bedford Street. It was a refrain every woman in that neighborhood had heard or said more than once.

The clothes stopped coming and then she was on the stoop: Pinky, with her milky brown skin, carrot-colored hair on top and black roots on the bottom. She was wrapped in a red silk robe that barely covered her thick thighs and broad behind, and to make it worse, she had forgotten to knot the belt. Her breast, heavy and bruised, but still beautiful to the men who stopped to stare, played a swinging peek-a-boo with the audience that was gathering on the sidewalk. She did, thankfully, have on underwear; black nylon that barely covered her privates, lending onlookers a glimpse of the wild, black Panamanian hair that grew there.

Glenna gasped but didn't move. Pinky was leaping down the stairs like Spider-man, cussing with each step she took.

"Fucking asshole!"

Step.

"*Pendejo!*"

Step.

"*Maricón!*"

Step.

"Bastard!"

She hit the sidewalk and snatched up one of my milk crates all in one motion. I took another step backward, anticipating the outcome of that action. Pinky ran over to Pablo's cream-colored, four-door Cadillac and brought the crate down hard into the front window. It shattered and buckled beneath the impact. Then she ran to the rear window and repeated the deed, with increased force and intensity. The men who watched forgot about the swinging breast and scrunched their faces against the destruction that was unfolding before them. She smashed each side window and then pulled an ice pick from the pocket of her robe and bent over, revealing her tight broad behind to the world, and sliced, stabbed, and jabbed at each of the four tires, until the air whistled out of them and they were dead. Then she crumpled into a heap of female ruin on the pavement.

The crowd moved on.

Delia approached, at first with caution and then her

steps quickened. Hy-Lo stood up and cleared his throat. Delia shot him a quick unsteady glance but kept moving. I looked at my father and his mouth was hanging open.

Delia was also wrapped in a robe. Pink and white terry cloth patched in noticeable places hung open in order to accommodate the child that was growing inside her. Her hair was pulled back in a messy bun that had not seen a Saturday wash 'n press appointment in over a month.

She knelt down beside Glenna's mother and coaxed her with soft words, until Pinky raised herself up from the pavement and pulled her robe closed around her body. They sidestepped the clothes that littered the ground, making their way up the steps and into apartment number A5.

Our apartment had seen its own days of wrath. The white kitchen wall was tinged yellow in spots where no amount of scrubbing could completely lift the bloodstains away. That was the night Hy-Lo had come home from work early and found Delia chatting on the phone, the sink piled high with dishes and the food still sitting in cold pots on the stove. There were few words passed between them before he hauled off and slapped her, breaking the vessels in her nose and splattering her blood, thick and red, across the wall.

But for the moment apartment A5 was quiet and would be a place for Pinky to sit and cry.

My father laughed at their backs as they walked inside. A loud, long laugh that chilled me and I shivered. He had a can of beer in his hand, his fifth for the day. He tilted it up to his mouth and finished it in one long swallow. He never looked at me, not directly, but he knew I was watching him and that my young eyes were filled with disgust.

I blinked back that summer and saw that the old woman was staring angrily at me. "Fucking bitch!" she yelled and then gave me the finger before bending over to show me her behind. "Kiss my ass!" she screamed.

I moved on, feeling more insulted by the long-ago laughter of my father than the revolting invitation from the old woman.

Chapter Two

Anurse with dark eyes looked back at me through the glass at the visitors' check-in. The gold beads that graced the elaborately braided hairstyle she wore would have made her appear regal if not for her heavily shadowed eyes and bright white lipstick. Looking at her hurt my eyes and so I looked down at the metal shelf.

She'd repeated herself a few times, but each time she spoke into the microphone her words came across in distorted shreds of syllables that made no sense to me and further agitated her.

"I'm sorry, I—I just can't—" I started to say again.

The woman turned her eyes up and cocked her head. She pushed the mike aside and cupped her hands around her painted white lips. "What room?" she yelled. I saw that she had a gold tooth and a missing molar.

"Oh," I said, and thought that a foolish smile should follow, but I had no smiles left in me to offer.

"201," I said. "D building," I added. *Dead dog building*, I wanted to say, but bit my lip instead.

I pressed my forehead against the glass and watched as she scrawled my destination on a large green sheet of paper. I turned my head a bit hoping that the words she scrawled there said *Go home*, because I needed some other forces besides myself to help me get out of this thing I had started to do.

"Thank you," I said as she shoved the paper through the open space and shook her head.

"Next!" she yelled.

I looked down at the paper and my name was written there, as was my destination and time of arrival. I kicked at my ankle with the heel of my boot. If I could not be trusted to remember or control my feet and the places they led me to, then my ankles should suffer for not maintaining some sort of authority. I kicked the other ankle before moving on.

The elevators in that building frightened me. They smelled of sick people and despair and reminded me of the months before I found Hy-Lo half-dead in the courtyard, his lungs pulling so hard for air that his chest looked as if it would explode.

I took the stairs, avoiding the faces that moved past me as I made my way up, up, up.

I walked into the room and the rosy-cheeked nurse stepped out from behind the green curtain. She was close to my father's age and she smiled brightly at me before she whipped the curtain around the bed, exposing Hy-Lo. He looked the same as he did yesterday. Broken and bent.

"Hello, dear," she said as she walked past me, snapping off her plastic gloves as she went. Her name tag said D. *GREEN*, and her eyes reminded me of someone, but I did not know who.

"Hi," I responded as she passed me, but I didn't move closer to Hy-Lo. I swallowed hard and waited for my feet to make a decision.

I couldn't do it. Not again. Maybe it was too soon. Two days in a row was a bit much. After all, who was gaining from this? Not Hy-Lo, he didn't even know I was there. Not me, all it did was conjure up unhappy memories.

I gained control and forced my feet to carry me in a wide circle that placed me back at the door, and then I walked out of the room and down the hall toward the stairway.

The closer I came to the exit sign, the warmer I became.

I pulled at my wool scarf and wiped at the perspiration that formed on my brow.

"Shit," I said as my hand came to rest on the doorknob of the staircase entrance. I stood there for a long time staring at the red letters that told me this was the way out. *Exit.* But I couldn't open the door. Or maybe, looking back, I wouldn't.

I tucked the scarf around my neck and started back toward the room. Nurse D. Green looked up at me as I passed the nurse's station and smiled.

I pulled the chair to the spot I had left off at. I was parallel to Hy-Lo's covered feet. The bare wall behind Hy-Lo mocked me, and the lonely nightstand dared me to make his space homey and bright with a slash of purple and bit of green in a vase shaped like an egg or maybe one of those oversized cards with glittering words that said, *Get Well Soon,* signed by everyone he knew.

I ignored the challenge because he did not deserve any warm wishes, flowers, or cards. None at all, not after what he'd done to Malcolm, my mother, and me. "Humph," I grumbled aloud. I straightened my back and my lips began to move. Words escaped. Mere whispers really, not even loud enough for the other patients to hear over the game show contestants' squeals of joy emanating from the mounted wall television.

"Remember, Hy-Lo," I began with a little disgusted laugh. "You were standing over me, breathing down on my head. I didn't hear you approach but I knew you were there. Not because of the wide-eyed, frightened look that stole Malcolm's smile away as he sat across the table from me, but because the air grew heavy and it became hard for me to breathe."

We always ate alone, my brother and I. Delia was usually ironing clothes for the next day or busy trying to wake my father from his drunken slumber so that he could make it into his night job on time. Family dinners were reserved for special holidays only. I was glad holidays were few and far between.

My brother dropped his eyes and began to tremble. I held my breath and stared down at my peas.

Thwat! The first strike came in the form of a rolled-up newspaper. Malcolm jumped and his cup of Kool-Aid fell over into his plate, drowning his food in purple sugar water. My body slumped and my head dipped forward from the blow.

"Sit up," Hy-Lo commanded in his low, hard voice.

My eyes filled with water and I fought to keep the tears from spilling down my face. I pulled my body erect but kept my head down. I wanted to reach up and rub the spot on my head he'd attacked, but that would show weakness, that would mean he'd won this round. I wouldn't do it.

"Malcolm?" Hy-Lo temporarily turned his attention to my brother. "Pick that cup up out of your food now." Malcolm slowly, carefully removed the cup from his plate. He kept his eyes fixed on the peas that floated lazily around his plate.

"Eat it," Hy-Lo's voice came again and I knew he was smiling. Malcolm's mouth opened and then closed. I saw the first tear escape from the corner of his eye and drop off the side of his cheek to mingle with the purple Kool-Aid in his plate. He picked up his fork and scooped up a small hill of dawn-tinted mashed potatoes. He swallowed twice before he put it in his mouth and then he gagged.

"Boy, if you puke it up you'll be eating that too!" My father's voice became deeper, meaner, but I knew the smile was still there.

Malcolm slapped his palm over his mouth and swallowed hard. He was sobbing now.

"What's going on?" Delia's shrill voice came from behind my father. There was a pause as if she actually required an answer and then she sucked her teeth long and hard.

"Mind your business, Delia." Hy-Lo's voice remained

the same but I was sure the smile was gone. I dared not turn around to confirm my suspicion.

"Get up and empty that plate, Malcolm." Delia's voice was firm but Malcolm did not move. His fear of my father was too severe. Malcolm's sobbing increased and he dropped his fork to the floor.

Delia tried to push past Hy-Lo but he caught her by the wrist and twisted her arm backward. "Pick it up, you little crybaby." His voice was labored as he tried to keep my mother back. Delia moaned in pain and her knees began to give way. I quickly reached up and rubbed the burning spot on the back of my head.

"Pick it up!" He barked his command this time and Malcolm jumped from his chair and onto the floor to search for his fork. My mother's moans graduated to screams. I clasped my hands over my ears and began to cry.

The buzzing sound of the doorbell ended everything. Malcolm's head popped up from where he was searching for the fork and his expression said, *We're saved*. I nodded back at him in grateful agreement. Hy-Lo released Delia's arm and she fell back against the wall massaging her wrist and whimpering to herself.

Hy-Lo walked to the door and looked through the peephole. He stepped backward and drew in a deep breath before he unlocked and opened the door.

"Mother," he said in his driest voice.

"Hyman," came the response, and my grandmother Gwenyth stepped in.

Gwenyth was a thorn in my mother's side from the first time Hy-Lo brought Delia home to meet her. Gwenyth had looked her up and down, snuffed at her, and declared that she did not much like Southern girls and that she would have no son of hers eating pig intestines and corn bread for breakfast, lunch, and dinner.

Later she had accused Delia of getting pregnant on purpose and did not even come to their wedding.

She remained mean and cold-hearted toward my mother even when she came to live in the same apartment building Hy-Lo and Delia had moved into after they got married.

245 Rogers Avenue was a small, five-story walk-up that held two apartments on each floor. We were on the fifth floor and my grandmother lived on the first floor. It seemed as though the neighborhood started to change before the ink had dried on my parents' lease. They were the first blacks in the building and the third black couple on the entire block. The Ackermans and Epsteins did not keep secret their unhappiness at my parents' presence. They would rush past my mother and into the building ahead of her, letting the door slam in her face as she struggled with groceries and her swollen belly.

They moved far out of her way when she passed them in the street, as if being black were a catching disease, and they mumbled Jewish vulgarisms beneath their breath whenever they found themselves standing behind her in line at the A&P.

By the time I was born there were only two Jewish families left in the building and they were living out their security. No one ever saw them leave. They moved when the night was in its deepest darkest stages, leaving the doors to their apartments swinging wide open on their hinges.

Gwenyth moved in when the last Jewish family moved out. She had waited because she said she did not trust people who did not appreciate a good pork chop or celebrate Christmas.

She'd come to be closer to her son. Delia would say she came to make her life more miserable.

My Uncle Randy, Gwenyth's youngest son, lived with her in between shacking up with whatever woman would have him. She kept a hide-away bed for him in the hall closet and there was always a plate of food warming in the oven.

Charlie, the oldest of her three sons, lived two blocks away. He and his common-law wife, Carol, rented the first floor of a private house. Gwenyth called her the rabbit because she made babies like it was going out of style. They had two children and one on the way.

I was thankful she had rung the bell when she did and maybe in my juvenile mind I had looked on her as a savior, but that would change.

Gwenyth stepped into the hallway of our apartment. From there she could tilt her head to the left and see the kitchen; a tilt to the right would reveal the living room and the two bedrooms that sat at the back.

She pushed Hy-Lo to the side and walked into the kitchen. Gwenyth was a thick woman with large shapely legs, broad hips, and a behind that sat up high on her back. Her lips were small and delicate, but the words that lived behind them were razor sharp like her laugh.

It was warm and she wore a light blue sleeveless dress that showed off her wide shoulders and beefy arms. The material hugged her hips and sat a little too far above the knee for a grandmother. A small patent leather pocketbook dangled from her wrist and her favorite imitation gold and sapphire ring sparkled brightly beneath the sixty-watt kitchen bulb.

"Children." That was how she greeted us.

"Goodnight, Grandmother," my brother and I responded in unison.

She surveyed the mess at the table and shook her head. She did not immediately acknowledge my mother, who pretended to busy herself at the kitchen sink. She did not like Delia because she had taken her prized son away from her. And instead of attending the small wedding that took place in the backyard of my Grandma Mable's home, she called the house twenty times (ten times during the ceremony) crying and screaming for my father to come to his senses and return home. "That woman is trash, Hyman! A whore!"

Back then Delia put Gwenyth off as crazy and looked into her husband's eyes and said a loud and happy "I do!"

She had no idea what she had committed herself to.

"Malcolm, why are you on the floor?"

Malcolm, still on his knees, fork in hand, peered at her over the edge of the table and shrugged his shoulders. His tears were gone, leaving behind salty tracks on his dark brown cheeks.

Gwenyth laughed. "Get up from the floor before the roaches get you."

My mother dropped a glass into the sink. I knew that last remark had unnerved her. Delia kept the house spotless—Hy-Lo would have it no other way—and roaches were rare visitors in our home.

"Oh, Delia, how are you, dear?" Gwenyth barely turned her head in my mother's direction. "Careful, you could cut yourself and bleed to death." She giggled and then looked down on me. "Kenzie, dear, how are you?"

"Fine," I mumbled, not looking at her.

"Hmmm," she sounded and touched the top of my head.

"Mother, I have to go to work." My father's voice was irritated. Gwenyth's presence had sobered him right up.

"I know that, Hyman," she snapped at him. "I need to talk to you about something."

"But—"

"Now, Hyman," she demanded and walked past him, through the living room, and into my parents' bedroom. Hy-Lo followed like a puppy with his tail between his legs, closing the door behind them.

I looked at my mother. She was crying again.

My own tears rolled down my face and I turned toward the windows of the hospital room. The sun was gone, leaving only a black backdrop outside. I could see my reflection as clear as if I were looking in the mirror. My face was absent of makeup and I had bitten away the mocha-colored lipstick I had applied before leaving the house that morning.

I stood up and began to pace back and forth across the brown and beige tiled floor. I didn't have to go all the way there to remember the bad times; there were so many of them that they left little room for any other memories.

I could kill him, I thought to myself. Pull the tubes from his body or the machine plugs from the wall. Everything would stop working and he would die and I would not have to ride two buses to figure out why.

Yes, I could release both of us from our miseries.

I stopped myself, suddenly aware that my thoughts were spilling out of my mouth. I sat back down and pulled my coat tighter around me.

I could see the old man in the bed next to my father; he had propped himself up on his pillow and was staring at me. His hand held the emergency call button; his thumb was poised for attack.

I cleared my throat and smirked. I wanted to smile, but those had been hard to come by for months, years. So I just turned my attention back to Hy-Lo.

Nurse D. Green approached. Her soft-soled white shoes squeaked against the gleaming floor of the hospital room. I watched her reflection walk toward me. The smile filled the windowpanes with each step she took until she blocked out the night and only her grinning lips remained.

She checked the machines that monitored Hy-Lo's heart and blood pressure and then she changed the intravenous bags. Hy-Lo stirred but didn't wake and I waited.

"How are you doing today?" Her words startled me and I jerked a bit as if she'd tapped my shoulder instead of spoken.

"Fine," I replied meekly and then quickly averted my eyes. I did not want to invite any further conversation.

She read my actions and nodded. Her eternal smile never wavered and then she walked out of the room. She walked like my grandmother, hard and heavy, the soles of her shoes slapping against the floor.

Looking at Hy-Lo, I wondered if he would be there tomorrow when I arrived. Maybe I would come in and find an empty bed, the few belongings he'd checked in with stuffed into one of those large manila envelopes with his last name written across in thick black Magic Marker: *LOWE.*

Chapter Three

God, I miss America!" Glenna's voice came over the phone lines in choppy waves. She was on layover in Berlin. She was doing Europe this month and hating it. "Oh, I hate these long trips," she complained each time she got a new transatlantic schedule from the airline. Glenna held a master's degree in child psychology and had worked two jobs to put herself through school. When she graduated she decided she wanted to spend a year seeing the world before settling down to pursue her career. Twelve years later she was still flying the friendly skies, serving tea and coffee to overbearing passengers twenty-two days out of the month. "God, I hate this place," she said again as a bus rumbled noisily through her background.

"Then quit," I said, balancing the phone between my cheek and my shoulder while I tried to put my coat on.

"How is everything?" she asked. I knew the *everything* either meant my drinking or Hy-Lo. She wanted to know if I was still clean or if we'd gotten the call yet. The call that would say he was finally out of our lives forever and for good. "Okay, I guess." I was avoiding her. "Listen, I was just on my way out," I added, hoping that would put an end to her questions. I hadn't had a drink for more than six months and didn't want to discuss the toll it was taking on me, the visits to Hy-Lo being the main evidence.

"How is everything," she repeated, sounding annoyed.

"I saw him," I said abruptly and held my breath so I could hear the surprise in Glenna's voice. There was nothing for a long time except for the harsh, brassy street sounds that emanated from across the Atlantic.

"Glenna, I said I saw him—"

She cut me off and her response was just as sharp as her interruption. "I heard what you said, Kenzie. I just don't understand why."

"Maybe if you knew *your* father, you would understand," I said, and then I couldn't believe that I had said something so hurtful to her.

"What?" Glenna screamed back before the line cracked and went dead.

"Glenna, I'm sorry . . . I didn't mean it," I said into the emptiness that listened at the other end of the line. My words echoed back and said: *Yes, you did.*

I didn't know why I kept coming to Hy-Lo's bedside. Not the first time, not the second, and not now. Maybe it was the same reason why Delia kept going back, even after the beatings that sent her running in the first place were still fresh in her mind, the bruises still fresh on her behind.

Mable didn't understand why Delia kept going back either. All of those years, all of the times he tore her skin and blackened her eyes. It was always the opening question to their long and turbulent discussions about Hy-Lo.

"I don't understand why you keep going back to him." My Grandma Mable spoke in a hushed tone. "He ain't gonna stop drinking. He always promising, promising. Don't you know his promises don't mean shit?"

I sat at the top of the stairs, barely breathing, my tiny knees pressed tightly together and my arms hugging my shoulders as I eavesdropped on their conversation.

"He ain't shit. I told you that before you got married. But you know what I say: experience is the best teacher." She leaned back in her chair and cocked her head so she could watch Delia sideways.

There was the cracking sound of a walnut shell giving

way and I could hear the pop and fizzle of the Pepsi-Cola as it covered the ice cubes in their glasses.

"How much experience you need before you decide you're an expert at getting your ass kicked? When you're dead and I'm raising your children?"

"Mama." Delia's voice was tired. She had been sitting at the dining room table with Mable since ten o'clock. It was near two in the morning now. Delia stretched and rubbed the small of her back. She winced at the pain there and wondered if her spine was cracked. Hy-Lo had kicked her way across the room. His foot had landed so hard in her back that she saw stars before she even hit the wall. That's how she got the black eye.

"Mama *what*?" Mable waited, but Delia said nothing else. "Let me tell you something, Delia. You my daughter and I love you, but you disrupting my life too. I gotta leave my job and come and get you and my grandkids so that Hyman doesn't kill you."

I winced at her words.

"Now, I got plenty of room here for you and the kids. You can stay until you get yourself together and get your own place or you can stay forever, whatever is best for you. But whatever you do, don't go back to that man!"

Mable's fist came down hard on the wooden table and my mother's quiet agreement followed, "Okay, Mama."

I could see her face reflecting off of the china cabinet that sat in the corner of the living room. It was swollen and bruised, sabotaging the beautiful Cherokee-African features she'd inherited from her mother. Her eyes were turned down in shame, their deep black color clouded with tears.

We found ourselves escaping to Mable's house at least twice a month. Us three with only God and the stars to watch over us. Delia running for her life, dragging us along by our tiny hands. Sometimes we tripped and fell over our untied laces, but she would snatch us up by our collars and brush at our knees all in one motion and then we'd be moving again.

Most times we took the bus, dried sleep in the corner of our eyes, our hair helter-skelter on our heads, coats and scarves wrapped around our thin pajamas.

Thankfully, the majority of the time the bus would be near empty. A late-night passenger or two might be on their way to work or home, but it was the bus driver who seemed most interested in us. He would watch us so hard and for so long through the rearview mirror that I thought he would run the bus up onto the sidewalk or go careening into oncoming traffic at any moment. His eyes made me feel naked, as if my whole life had unfolded before him.

I would untangle myself from my mother's embrace and take a seat far away from her and my brother. I was better than that life the eyes in the rearview mirror saw. I stuck my tongue out at him and closed my eyes.

If there was money, we would take a cab, but that was a luxury. Sometimes we would call Mable at work and she would jump in her car and pick us up at the meeting place. The meeting place was a small all-night diner four blocks away. We would huddle into a booth and Delia would let us order french fries and grape soda.

Delia would have black coffee. She'd sit and sip it in between puffs on her Newport. Her hands would shake and fresh tears would well up in her eyes.

Mable would come in and pay the check and then we would be on the Belt Parkway doing seventy all the way to her house.

Once, Delia tried to take us to Gwenyth's apartment. It was right downstairs and it was three in the morning. I had to go to school and Delia had to go to work in the morning. "We'll just go to your Grandma Gwen's house and let Daddy sleep it off," Delia had whispered to us. Malcolm was almost two. He lay sleeping in Delia's arms, his skinny legs swinging with every step she took. We tiptoed down the stairs to the first floor.

Delia kept pushing her hair to the right side of her head in an attempt to try and cover the bald spot. "I didn't mean it, Delia!" he had screamed at her as he followed her around the house with the tuft of chestnut brown hair in his hand.

No, he hadn't meant to pull it out, but what did he think was going to happen when he tried to drag her across the floor by her hair?

Delia knocked softly on Gwenyth's door. She looked over her shoulder to see if this would be the night Hy-Lo broke tradition and followed her out of the apartment. We stood there staring at the gray door with its brass knob. We could hear the low hum of the television coming through from the other side. The hall was drafty and we shivered in our pajamas. I looked at my mother. "I'm cold," I said, and the tone my voice took on was much older than my seven years. Delia ignored the anger that came across loud and clear in my words and knocked a bit more loudly. Still no one came.

Someone was coming through the front door of the building. We heard keys jingle and then drop onto the marble floor. "Shit," a man's voice mumbled. Delia knocked again, this time more urgently. She shifted Malcolm so that his head could rest on her left shoulder and then leaned in close to the door, pressing her mouth into the space where the door and doorjamb met. "Gwenyth.Gwenyth," she whispered.

The man turned the corner and my mother froze. We stood stock still and held our breaths. His back was to us and he stared down at some mail he had retrieved on his way in. It seemed as though he stood there forever before he started up the stairs whistling to himself.

After the man entered his own apartment on the third floor, Delia began knocking again. "Gwenyth."

The door was at least a good half an inch off the ground. I

peered down and saw a shadow there. My heart began banging in my chest and I looked up at the silver square with the clear eye that sat in the middle of the door. The peephole. She was there watching us shiver.

The shadow moved away and the volume on the television increased. Delia stumbled backward as if slapped. "C'mon," she said and took me by my shoulder, leading me back up the stairs. "He's probably asleep by now." She glanced over her shoulder once more in pure disbelief. I'll never forget the look of abandonment that came across my mother's face.

She never sought help from Gwenyth again.

"So what are you going to do?" Mable was asking Delia for the fifth time, and Delia still did not respond.

"I guess that means you're going back."

There was a long silence and then the sound of chairs being moved. I stood up and crawled into the bedroom, easing myself back into the bed I shared with Malcolm.

"We going back?" His breath was hot on the back of my neck.

"Yeah, I guess so," I said and curled my knees into my stomach.

"Just like always." He shifted his body into a comfortable position, taking a breath, and then the sucking sounds came.

"Yeah, just like always," I said and didn't bother to reprimand him about sucking his thumb.

It was barely eight when I heard my father's voice sailing up from Mable's living room. The sun was beaming in through the window sending red rockets across the inside of my eyelids. I pulled the covers up over my head and prayed it was all a dream. I had begged God to kill him while he slept. I wanted the whole building to collapse on top of him. But God had ignored me and there he was in my grandparents' living room, alive and well.

I removed the covers and opened my eyes. I surveyed the room. It had been my mother's bedroom before she got married. The walls were a soft pink. It was practically bare except for the twin bed and white dresser. A picture of my mother sat in a silver frame on the top of the dresser. That was my favorite picture of her. She was on the back of a truck, surrounded by watermelons, her legs crossed beneath her, her bare feet covered in dirt. She was smiling and waving at the cameraman. Her hair was piled high atop her head in wild loose tresses and watermelon juice shone wet on her chin.

She was seventeen in that picture and it was the last time she ever smiled that way. Hy-Lo was the cameraman and married her six months later, five days after her eighteenth birthday. He took her hand in marriage and took away, forever, that easy joy of her youth.

I turned over on my side and hugged myself. I felt safe there at my grandmother's house. There was never any yelling, screaming, or fighting. When Sam, my grandmother's second husband, laid his hands on Mable, it was always an affectionate caress, not a punch or slap. Their disagreements were settled quietly behind closed doors and they always went to bed friends.

I wanted to stay there forever.

The smell of pancakes and bacon pulled me from my bed. As much as I didn't want to go downstairs and look into the sorry eyes of my father, I had to quell the hunger pains in my stomach. I tippy-toed to the bathroom, quietly closing the door behind me. I quickly washed my face and brushed my teeth. I smoothed my hair down and adjusted the large T-shirt my grandfather gave me to sleep in. I looked at myself in the mirror and saw that I looked so much like my mother in the picture, minus the joy. I guess I looked exactly how she looked now. Worn, tired, and miserable.

I opened the door, took a deep breath, and started down the stairs.

They were already at the table: Delia, Mable, Sam, and Malcolm.

"Good morning," I said as my eyes searched every corner of the dining room for Hy-Lo.

"Good morning, baby." My grandmother smiled and began to fill my plate with Sam's down-home blueberry pancakes.

"Grandma, can I have soda?" Malcolm asked, his mouth filled with food.

"No," Delia said sternly.

"Oh, Delia, please. Of course you can, baby." Mable patted him on the head and Malcolm jumped up from the table and ran to the refrigerator to retrieve a can of Coke. Delia rolled her eyes and shook her head, but said nothing. It was Mable's house and she had the final word.

Sam smiled, but said nothing. He paid the mortgage, but knew that didn't mean a thing in this house. What Mable says goes.

I avoided my mother's eyes and focused on my food. I was tense; I didn't know where Hy-Lo was.

"Sleep okay, Kenzie?" Delia was trying to make breakfast conversation. Trying to fix her voice to sound like June Cleaver. I nodded at my food.

"Look at your mother when she's talking to you, Kenzie." Mable's voice was pleasant but stern.

I glanced at Delia and saw the blue half moon beneath her eye. "Yes," I mumbled my reply.

The back door opened and my heart jumped in my chest. I looked up and Hy-Lo looked back at me. His face was expressionless. He took one long last drag on his Camel and then flicked it outside. My mouth went dry and the blueberries began to back up in my throat.

He wiped his feet on the brown rug and walked over to the table. All the time his eyes never left mine. He stood over Malcolm and pulled the can of Coke from his hand just as he was about to drink from it. Delia's mouth twisted but she said nothing.

"Hey, man, don't you think it's a little early in the morning to start a commotion?" Mable's voice rang out.

Sam grunted and sat back in his chair, folding his arms across his massive chest. He licked at his lips and grunted again.

"Mable, it's too early in the morning for this boy to be having soda. And to make it worse, with pancakes," Hy-Lo said as he walked over to the sink and emptied the bubbling, caramel-colored liquid into the sink.

"Well, I said he could have it," Mable replied and shoved a piece of bacon in her mouth. Sam grunted again and scratched at his chin.

Hy-Lo didn't say anything for a long time. He'd released my eyes, but I couldn't stop staring at him. Him in his white T-shirt and clean blue Levi's that held a crease so sharp it could cut steak. That's when I noticed the butter knife, the dark blue handle resting against the cream-colored lace of the tablecloth and the shiny silver tip resting on the edge of my plate.

I could do it, I thought to myself. I could jump up, run across the table, and stick the butter knife right in his heart. I could. I could.

My body began to shake at the thought and my hands trembled in my lap as I ran the image over and over in my mind.

"The boy is already hyper, Mable." Hy-Lo was done talking. He threw Delia a look that promised her a beating for not supporting him. He pulled out a pack of Camels from his back pocket and started walking toward the door again. He whistled "Stand by Your Man" as he went. I looked at Delia and she was trembling.

Chapter Four

My heart stopped as I walked into the room. The chair was not against the wall but pulled close to the bed, past Hy-Lo's toes, closer to his knees. The thought of coming that near to him sent shivers up and down my spine.

"Uh-unh," I said and shook my head back and forth like a disagreeable two-year-old. "Uh-unh," I said again as I moved forward. "That is too close," I voiced to no one in particular.

I stood a few inches away from the foot of the bed and looked from the chair to Hy-Lo. Had he done this? Was it a cruel joke he was playing on me? Maybe. He was an expert at being cruel. Jokes weren't his thing though.

I glanced toward the open door. Visitors, doctors, nurses, and patients dressed in green pajamas with *Property of Kings County* stamped across their chests moved up and down the hallway. Perhaps one of them had done it. Perhaps Nurse D. Green had done it.

I snatched at the raised back of the chair and dragged it noisily across the floor back to the spot by the wall. I would have to start all over again, from the beginning, from the wall, where the temperature was the warmest. No one would force me ahead. My whole life had been an acceleration. No more. I sat down.

The morning news came across the television and a wide-eyed blond woman with braces smiled through the dusty glass. She seemed glad to advise her viewing audience that a cold front was coming down from Canada and would be here by early Thursday.

I snuffed at her and tugged at the hem of my gloves. Thursday. That was tomorrow. I looked at Hy-Lo and then back at the wide-eyed weather reporter. "That makes today Wednesday then, I guess?" I said to the television.

"Uh-huh," someone replied from behind his green curtain.

I'd hated Wednesdays for a long time. From age ten to thirteen to be exact. Those were the years I attended Catholic school, and during those years every Wednesday we had half a day of school. Most children chalked that up as a plus, as if it made up for the ugly plaid skirts and clunky black shoes. Malcolm and I hated it.

Our schoolmates hurried past us, leaving a knotty stream of laughter behind them as they giggled their way through plans for their afternoon. Malcolm and I turned the normal ten-block walk into fifteen or twenty, going out of our way to stretch the time between the 11:45 bell and the moment we stepped over the threshold of apartment A5.

Glenna was always with us. Her wide bright ribbons bounced against her cheeks as she slapped at the back of Malcolm's head and teased his ears. "Stop," he'd yell at her, but she would keep harassing him; she knew he had a crush on her.

Glenna was a latchkey child and spent every afternoon, Wednesday or not, stationed in front of the television, a bag of candy in her lap, waiting for her mother to walk through the door at six. She was lucky if Pinky walked through the door before midnight.

"You gotta go to the bank today?" she asked as she nibbled on a Twizzler.

"Yep," I said. That was Wednesday protocol. The bank and the A&P. I hated both places. But I think the A&P was worse. Hy-Lo did all of the shopping for the family. He bought what he liked, Delia cooked it, and we ate it.

He always used two shopping carts, one for food and the other for household supplies. Malcolm and I would trail along behind him, up and down the wide, white aisles with shelves that dwarfed us. We would struggle with our cart of toilet paper, detergent, and cleaning supplies, often rolling into a display or jamming into Hy-Lo's heels.

"Meatheads," he'd sneer at us and maybe pop us upside our heads or pinch us on the underside of our arms.

After we came home and unpacked the brown paper bags and put the food and supplies away, we had to fold the bags. Not just any old way; there was, according to Hy-Lo, an art to folding a paper bag.

Bag after bag, crease after crease—we folded until our fingers ached, and if we didn't do it right Hy-Lo would throw all the bags to the floor and make us fold them again.

Yes, I hated Wednesdays.

"You want me to go with you?" Glenna always asked.

"He might see," I said as I kicked over a bottle someone left standing in the middle of the sidewalk. It fell on its side and rolled into the street.

Hy-Lo made it clear every week that I was to go straight to the bank and then come directly home. No stopping, no socializing. I was to do this alone. And if he found out otherwise, my behind would be his.

"Oh, that's right," Glenna would say as if she'd forgotten that it had always been that way.

No matter how many blocks out of our way we went, we always seemed to make it home by twelve-thirty. My stomach turned as we rounded the corner and started toward the apartment building.

Maybe he wouldn't be there. Maybe today would be the day his truck jackknifed on I-80 and he was lying dead on the highway somewhere. Maybe today would be the day I would walk through the door and there would be two nice policemen comforting my mother. She would look up at me with her red eyes and tell me, "Your daddy is dead." I would hold my smile back, for her, so she could have her grief.

I would hug her and tell her it was going to be all right, offer the policemen something to drink, and then show them to the door. "Thank you," I'd say. "We'll be fine."

I'd tuck Delia into bed, make her some tea, and close the drapes. Maybe call Gwenyth and his brothers, Charles and Randy, with the news, and then I would go to my bedroom, close the door, and scream with joy into my pillow.

The car was there.

"Well, he's home," Glenna said and gave me an apologetic look.

My stomach turned over and I grabbed Malcolm's hand.

I rang the bell and waited. I didn't have keys like the rest of my friends; Hy-Lo wouldn't allow it. Wednesdays were the only days we didn't have problems trying to get into the house. He would still be wide awake and only a quarter of the way into his vodka. All of the other days we stood in the hallway ringing the bell for such long periods of time that the round black dot left its impression on the tips of our index fingers.

Many times, Delia would come home to find us sitting on the floor in the hallway, our books spread out around us as we struggled to do our homework amidst the traffic of our neighbors and the squeals of playing children that sailed in from the backyard.

We dared not move from the hallway. We never knew when he would wake up from his drunken slumber and open the door, and if we were not there, it would be the belt for sure.

Delia would slam open the apartment door and rush into the bedroom to find Hy-Lo fully clothed and sprawled out across the bed. His mouth would be open, drool sliding down the side of his face, as he snored loud enough to drown out the curses my mother unleashed above him.

"The pillow," I stated timidly one day as I stood behind my mother while she called out my father's name in between the *Damn you*'s and I *hate you*'s.

Delia turned to look at me. "What?" she asked, perplexed. "What did you say?"

"Pillow," I repeated and pointed at the pillow that lay at my father's feet. Her eyes opened wide and a look of disbelief spread across her face, but just for a second, long enough for me to know that she understood what I was suggesting.

"Go take off your school clothes," was all she said before she pushed past me.

I didn't have to ring the bell today. The door was propped open by Malcolm's baseball bat. Jimmy Smith's "Midnight Special" sailed out on the seasoned scent of mashed potatoes and baked pork chops. Malcolm shot me a worried look and we stepped hesitantly inside.

Our apartment was always dark. Hy-Lo kept the drapes drawn and the shades down. Looking back now, I think maybe he needed his dwelling to match his emotions. Black. The only parts of the apartment that held any natural light were the kitchen and bathroom. He hadn't figured out a way to keep the sun out of those rooms yet.

When we walked in we saw that Hy-Lo was in the kitchen, sitting at the table, his body hunched over, hands clasped together, forearms resting on his lap. This was his thinking position. An empty pint of Smirnoff sat ominously on the table. I rolled my eyes and braced myself.

"Good afternoon," Malcolm and I mumbled.

We stood there waiting for the first order of the afternoon. It was early fall and we wore heavy cable-knit navy blue sweaters. On our backs we wore book bags heavy with textbooks and binders.

Hy-Lo said nothing.

Ten minutes turned into twenty and still we stood there waiting for an order. The apartment was warm and it fed the heat that was building up beneath our clothes. Sweat trickled down our armpits and tickled our sides before dissolving into the cotton material of our shirts. Our backs ached with the weight of our book bags and our legs began to wobble from standing in one place too long.

"Midnight Special" had ended long ago and the needle made a steady scratching noise on the black nothingness at the end of the album.

Hy-Lo sat and stared at his hands.

I looked at the clock and it said one. Malcolm's bladder was full and he stepped to cross his legs.

"Stand up straight." The sudden sound of Hy-Lo's voice startled us and we jumped.

"Daddy, I—" Malcolm tried not to whine, but he was only seven and that was hard not to do when you had to pee.

"Shut up," Hy-Lo said in a low voice.

"But—" Malcolm began again. His hands were between his legs holding on tight to his penis as he hopped from foot to foot.

"I said shut up!" Hy-Lo yelled and finally turned to look at us. His eyes were bloodshot and I suspected that he had consumed more than the one pint of vodka that sat on the table.

He got up from the table and moved to open the door of the oven to check on the meat he had cooking there. I looked at Malcolm: he had stopped dancing, a dark stain was spreading across the front of his pants, and his eyes were filling with tears, his bottom lip trembling uncontrollably.

Hy-Lo closed the oven and stared back at us. He saw the wet stain on Malcolm's pants and began to laugh. He laughed until he coughed and then he wiped at the tears that formed at the corners of his eyes. "Idiots," he muttered and took a jerky step toward the sink. He turned on the faucet and filled a glass with water. Lifting the glass, he stopped before his lips touched the rim and slowly turned his head toward us and said, "Malcolm, go take off those pissy clothes and go into the drawer and choose the belt you want to be beaten with." He finished the glass of water in one swallow.

In the bottom drawer of Hy-Lo's dresser was a bottle of Old Spice aftershave, a small jewelry box that held his wedding band, a deck of cards, ten pairs of black nylon socks, and three belts that were coiled like sleeping snakes. Two were black and one brown. The width and length of the belts were identical, but still whenever Malcolm and I were sent to the drawer to choose, we agonized over which one would hurt the least.

Malcolm began to bawl as he stumbled toward the bedroom; his wails filled the tiny apartment and tore at my insides. I did not look after him; my eyes remained ahead of me, on my father.

"You eyeballing me, Kenzie?" Hy-Lo's tone was loose, almost jolly.

"No," I said loud and clear.

"No, who?" he asked, raising his eyebrows.

"No, D-Daddy." I hated the word; it always seemed to stick to my tongue like peanut butter when I said it.

"No, sir!" he bellowed and my heart skipped two beats.

"No, sir," I said.

There was a time before Malcolm was born, up until he took his first steps, when I had to refer to Hy-Lo as "sir." "Daddy" was not used in our home. Hy-Lo was proud of the service he rendered his country during the Vietnam War in the early '60s. He spent three years in the army, two of which were served in the Philippines.

During those years, uniformity, discipline, and respect shaped his character while alcohol hacked away at his mind and undid his soul.

"This is not the army, Hyman," Delia would say in a soft,

chastising tone she usually used on us kids. "You are their father, Hyman, not their sergeant."

Delia had won those long-ago conflicts because they were still young and so was his disease.

"No, sir." My response was meek. I was putting great effort into hiding the anger that was building within me. I did not want to choose a belt today.

He mumbled something I could not hear and then dug into the front pocket of his pants. He still wore his blue work uniform pants. He pulled out a wad of bills and shoved it at me. "Count it," he said and sat back down at the table. He reached for the bottle, but his hand stopped in midair, suddenly remembering it was empty.

I started to count.

Malcolm's sobs kept coming from the bedroom. The agony of waiting for a painful act could drive you mad, and Malcolm sounded like he was on his way there.

I started over again placing the tens, twenties, and fives in neat little piles on the table as I counted out the four hundred and twenty dollars. It was the same amount every week.

"Go straight to the bank. Don't stop. Don't talk to anyone, and come straight back home." Hy-Lo spoke slowly, methodically. I blinked twice and then nodded. He stared through me and waited for the proper response.

"Yes, sir," I replied as I curled the money tight into the palm of my hand.

"Don't come home if you lose it," he said with a thin smile that made me think he really wanted me to lose it, to give him an excuse to send me to choose a belt.

He stood up and his body swayed a bit. "Go on," he said, waving me away. I looked over my shoulder and saw Malcolm, stripped down to his briefs, standing in the doorway of my parents' bedroom, brown belt in hand. His body was shaking and his bottom lip was glossy wet with spit and tears.

I walked out the door and Hy-Lo closed it behind me.
I stood there in the hallway awaiting the sound of the first
stinging lash. When it came I ran, Malcolm's long wailing
cry pushing me forward.

Even as I sat there in the hospital I could hear Malcolm's
wail just as clear as if it was 1978 again. I looked up from
my tightly clenched hands and half-expected to see a young
Malcolm tear around the corner and into the room, his pants
down around his ankles, Hy-Lo hot on his tail, eyes like fire
and the belt swinging in the air above his head.

The wail got louder even though I was sure it was 1999
and I was in a hospital room and not apartment A5 on Rogers Avenue. I turned and looked at Hy-Lo to make sure he
was still there, still dying—but the wail swelled around me,
pulling at me. My heart thumped harder in my chest, my
mouth went dry, and I opened my arms in preparation for
Malcolm to run into them. "I'll protect you. Come on, run,
Malcolm, run," I whispered, leaning backward, arms spread
wide like angels' wings. I closed my eyes, bracing myself,
and then the wailing stopped.

I opened my eyes to find a young man with a long ponytail and two gold loops in each ear looking back at me.
He had come to a stop outside of the room, a large laundry
hamper before him. It was the ancient wheels that cried,
not Malcolm, as they turned over and over against the cold
marble floor.

The man's face twisted in wonder and he raised his
hands to his mouth to cover the smile that surfaced there.
"Pssst," he called over his shoulder to someone I couldn't
see. "Look at this nut case." He beckoned the person to hurry
with a quick wave of his hand.

I dropped my arms to my side, cleared my throat, and
tried to make myself look sane.

A small bald-headed man peeked quickly around the

doorway, considered me, and then pulled back. I could hear his laughter from behind the wall.

The man with the ponytail laughed again but this time he did not hide his amusement behind his hand. He laughed raucously until Nurse D. Green came and shooed him on. He left taking Malcolm's cries with him.

Chapter Five

I beat the stars this time and caught the sun just as it began slipping from the sky. The wind was picking up and the bare branches of the oak trees beat loudly against their trunks. The heavy thumping sounds followed me as I hurried away and down the block. I crossed at least three streets before I turned a corner, careful not to walk in a circle back to the hospital again.

The memory of Malcolm had been too much for me and I felt the hole near my heart stretch wider with a pain that began to burn. I clutched at my chest and tried to rub the want away, but my actions seemed to augment the process instead of quell it. The hole expanded and the need grew.

What I *needed* was to get to a meeting and share the pain; distribute it among the others, thinning it until it disappeared. What I *wanted* was a drink. I could pour the liquid down my throat and let it filter into the hole and extinguish the pain that lived there.

I walked two blocks and then turned left and walked three more blocks. There was a liquor store on the corner and I hurried toward it, almost broke into a run, but ended up doing a step-skip walk instead.

The closer I came to the door the worse the pain got, until a voice inside me told me to stop, and I did, smack dead in my tracks, right in the middle of the sidewalk. I stopped hard and someone bumped into me and then hurried around me cursing as he went.

"Oh God, please," I said beneath my breath as I stared at

the blue and white neon lights that blinked *Bacardi-Bacardi-Bacardi*.

"Oh God, please," I begged, and turned and bolted toward the open mouth of the subway.

I had had my first taste of whiskey when I was five years old. It came in a teaspoon guided by my father's hand. I didn't like that, but I loved the occasional Rheingold beer that he kept in the house when he was trying to lay off the hard stuff. It tasted like a thick ginger ale and tickled my tongue, leaving frozen icicles in my throat.

By the time I was ten, I was walking the four blocks between our apartment building and Beehive Liquors, buying fifths of rum or vodka for Hy-Lo and sneaking sips from his bottle when he'd finally pass out across the bed. It tasted disgusting and burned the inside of my stomach, but the benefits were well worth it; the floaty sensation my head took on and the carefree feeling that embraced me.

Back then the neighborhood was small and everybody knew one another within a ten-block perimeter. The owner of Beehive Liquors knew me, Hy-Lo had made sure of it.

"This is Kenzie, my daughter," Hy-Lo said to the tall, thin man with saucer-sized eyes behind the counter. It was a Tuesday afternoon. Things were slow for the moment; the working folk were still earning the dollar they needed to spend in his store.

"Hi," I said, barely lifting my eyes to meet his. I felt uncomfortable around the shelves and shelves of liquor bottles. Despite their different labels, each one reminded me of the one that constantly sat on the bottom shelf of our food cabinet, right next to the salt.

"Well, hello there," the thin man said and smiled at me, revealing a dark space where his front teeth should have been. He'd been watching the afternoon news on a small black-and-white television that rested on the wooden counter. He stood up and leaned forward, pushing his hand out to me. I looked up at Hy-Lo for permission. He nodded his head and grinned.

I moved my hand into his. It was soft and warm. It felt safe. We stayed that way for a long time, my hand wrapped in the security of his.

"This is Hal—I mean Mr. Hal." Hy-Lo's voice broke my trance and I dropped my hand back down to my side.

"Nice to meet you, Kenzie," Hal said. I looked briefly at his beak-shaped nose and then lowered my eyes again.

A brief exchange was made between my father and Hal, one that did not include words, just nodding and winking. At the time I did not know why my father brought me to that place, but I would know within a day.

"I have something for pretty little girls that come to visit me," Hal said in his scratchy voice. He reached underneath the counter, there was rustling, and then he pulled out a lollipop. It was bright red and seemed to glow beneath the fluorescent store lights.

Again I looked up to Hy-Lo for permission. He did not agree as quickly this time, but after a moment he nodded his head okay.

"Thank you, Mr. Hal," I said and took the lollipop from his hand.

My father and I left the store after he and Hal spoke of people I was unfamiliar with. People with names like Lonnie and Altamonte, who frequented the Beehive or the Blue Bar. My father's drinking buddies. The ones who sat beside him at the bar and talked sports, women, and work. The ones he passed coming in or out of the Beehive on a daily basis, offering an expression of cheer during the holidays or a cautious word about the weather that would lead to full conversations.

The walk home would seem too long and the conversation too good to move away from the storefront just yet, so they would remove the brown bags that were tucked neatly beneath their armpits, and carefully reveal the glass heads of their bottles. A hasty look over their shoulders while their fingers worked at removing the cap. Quick sips would follow and then a grateful exhale as the liquor hit the spot, filled the need, quelled the pain. The caps would be replaced and the bottle heads would vanish back into the brown bags while the conversation rolled on.

It was easier now; the words ran in steady streams, and during the lulls, scarce as they were, or the quiet considerations of words just passed, the act would be repeated— over and over again until the bottle was empty or the sun too hot, the wind too cold. But mostly, until the bottle was empty.

His drinking buddies.

Last names were a mystery between these men, phone numbers never changed hands, and invitations to a family barbecue or an extra ticket to the baseball game would never emerge. But they could share a bottle between them, wrap their lips around the glass circle and pass it on to the next man and the next man and the next man.

They would promise to do these things—the barbecues or baseball games—but a pen never seemed handy or the outing date unsure. It didn't matter; by the time the bottle was finished those promises had been long forgotten, brushed beneath the blackness of inebriation.

We reached the corner before he spoke. "Give it to me," he said and my heart sank. For a moment I thought of playing stupid, fluttering my eyes and cocking my head to one side in an act of idiocy. I started to do just that, staring at the callused palm of his outstretched hand.

I knew he wanted the lollipop. Hy-Lo only allowed us candy on Halloween and Christmas, otherwise he forbade it. "You think I'm going to spend my life savings getting your raggedy teeth fixed? You got another thing coming!" he would say whenever he caught us with candy. I'd find out later he had other plans for his life savings.

Delia felt sorry for us and would sneak bags of Now and Laters, SweeTarts, and Snickers bars into the house like contraband, warning us to keep it hidden until Hy-Lo was out of the apartment.

I slowly handed him the lollipop and watched hopelessly as he tossed it into the gutter.

The following day and many days after that I became his mule, walking the four blocks to Beehive Liquors, a five-dollar bill clutched tightly in my hand. I would lower my head as I crossed the threshold of the store, keeping my eyes fixed on my badly laced sneakers and far away from the wide-eyed stares of the adults I took my place behind in line.

Once at the counter Hal did not offer me his wide toothless smile or his hand in greeting like he did on the day of our introduction; instead he would snap his fingers impatiently at me until I raised my hand and dropped the crumpled five-dollar bill on the wooden countertop.

"What he want?" he'd ask, his back already turned away from me. I could hear the cash register bells go off and the loud clank of the drawer as it slid open.

"A fifth of Smirnoff," I would reply to my sneakers. I could feel the eyes of the adults behind me boring down on me. I could hear the quiet murmers of disapproval like the wings of a hundred butterflies at my back.

"Her parents oughta be ashamed sending her in here."

He would ignore the comments, maybe even throw the person a dirty look or snuff loudly and clear his throat. Their words did not stop him from grabbing the bottle from the shelf and shoving it into the brown paper bag.

Coins would rattle and the sound of paper dollars would rustle until Hal came face-to-face with me once again. He would place the bottle gently on the counter with one hand and slam the dollar-fifty change down with the other.

"Next!" he'd call out loudly, instantly dismissing me until I came to him again.

I was Hy-Lo's liquor mule for months before Delia finally became aware of what was going on. She'd left work early one afternoon and walked up on me as I made my way back home.

"Kenzie, what you doing down this side of the avenue?" she asked breathlessly. She had not noticed the brown bag tucked beneath my small armpit. I carried it the way I saw my father carry it. I had to squeeze my arm tightly to my side to keep it from slipping out and crashing down to the ground.

"I had to go the liquor store," I said matter-of-factly, as if this were the way of the world for a ten-year-old child. Delia's eyes opened in surprise, she stopped dead in her tracks, and her mouth dropped open so wide that the pedestrians passing her turned to look over their shoulders in an attempt to catch the sight that so struck her. All they saw was me, a little girl on her way home.

"What did you say?" She was behind me again; her hands grabbed hold of my shoulders and spun me full around, sending the package flying from beneath my arm and landing with a splattering, stinking crash to the ground.

I didn't need to repeat myself; what she'd thought she'd heard was apparently correct, the evidence lying broken and shattered on the ground before her.

"I can't believe you're ignorant enough to send a child to the liquor store! I can't believe you would do something like this!" Delia was in a rage. Her face was streaked from anger and her index finger became a dangerous switchblade slicing the air. She waved it in my father's face with reckless abandon, knowing full well that at any second he could reach out and snap it in two.

I had been sent to my room. Malcolm and I sat cross-

legged on the floor, our ears pressed against the closed bedroom door as we listened to our mother read Hy-Lo the riot act.

"She is a child, for God's sake, Hy-Lo. If you wanna
drink, *you* go get it!" We heard Delia walk across the floor
toward our room and we jumped up and scurried to our
beds. Halfway there she changed her mind and turned back
toward the kitchen, a new flood of angry words spewing
from her mouth.

She was winning this battle only because Hy-Lo had
not had a drink. If he had, Delia would have been blocking
punches by this time. In his sober state, Hy-Lo was quiet, almost mouselike. Now he stood staring out the kitchen window into the backyard, allowing Delia to scream her anger
in his face. It went on for more than an hour, until he got
tired of walking from room to room trying to escape her.
Finally he grabbed his keys and walked out of the house.

The bedroom door flew open and Delia stormed in. Her
eyes were red and her face was sad and tired like an overused dishtowel. "How long have you been going to the liquor store for *him*, Kenzie?" The *him* came out like snot; the
sound of it made my skin crawl. I shrugged my shoulders
and picked at my cuticles. Delia sighed and came and sat
beside me on the bed. She looked at me, long and hard, as
if she was trying to make a decision. She pulled at the barrette that hung at the end of one of my twisted ponytails and
sighed again.

Her eyes moved to Malcolm, who was lying on his back.
He had a G.I. Joe figurine in his left hand, sailing the toy
through the air above his head as he sucked frantically on the
thumb of his right hand. This was how Malcolm dealt with
the madness that was as constant as the air we breathed.

"Malcolm, I told you you're gonna end up with bucked
teeth." Her words were heavy but did not mask what was
really on her mind. "Kenzie." She said my name once and
waited for my eyes to look up into hers.

But I wouldn't, I just kept staring at my fingers and wishing myself far away. A long moment passed and then I felt her fingers fiddling with my barrette again, this in place of the embrace she knew I needed, but for some reason could not give to me. Delia stood and left the room, leaving the door open behind her.

After a while I could hear the pots clang against the metal burners of the stove, the squeaky oven door open and close, and then the apartment was filled with the good smells of baked chicken and simmering wild rice. My body relaxed and the knots in my stomach loosened and I was finally able to leave my ragged cuticles to their healing process.

Malcolm was asleep; his thumb hung loosely at the side of his mouth, the G.I. Joe doll rested at the base of his soft round cheek. It was only the quiet before the storm.

When the front door opened it was nearly eight o'clock. Dinner finished, the dishes washed and put away, my brother and I were scrubbed clean and in our pajamas sitting quietly on the couch in front of the television watching *The Muppet Show*. Delia was in her bedroom on the phone. Her soft words and easy laughter sailed out into the living room, mixing in with the Muppets' quick slapstick and odd laughter.

Hy-Lo walked into the living room and stood directly in front of the television. Neither one of us tilted our heads in an attempt to see around him; instead we straightened our backs and said, "Good evening," in our tiny, fearful voices.

Hy-Lo's eyes were red. We could smell the sharp scent of alcohol and cigarettes as it sailed off his breath, extinguishing the happy smells of dinner and Mr. Bubble that still lingered in the air. He said nothing for a long time and then he raised his hand and extended his index finger toward our bedroom and we understood it was time for bed.

The sound of my mother's voice disappeared as soon as Hy-Lo had walked in. I supposed then that the bubble that seemed to surround me whenever I was in my father's presence had locked out the sound. But I know, now, that my mother had uttered a quick and quiet goodbye to her friend and had hastily placed the receiver down in its cradle and waited for whatever was to be that night.

Without objection, my brother and I stood, turned, and walked quietly to our bedroom, each of us throwing a pleading look at Delia as we passed her open door. The show was not over and bedtime was a full hour away.

Delia shook her head, but said nothing. She had already fought her battle earlier that day.

We cried ourselves to sleep, weeping pitifully into the softness of our pillows, feeling angry that we could not delight in the make-believe world of Kermit and Miss Piggy.

We heard his shoes fall heavily to the floor and the sound of the bedsprings as they gave way against the weight of his body. I imagined that Delia must have been blue from holding her breath, bracing herself for the fight that she was sure would come.

I could hear him mumble something to her and then the low curling chime of the rotary as she dialed the seven numbers that would connect her to Pastalo's Trucking. "Yes, um—this is Mrs. Lowe. Fine, thank you. Um, Hyman—yes, no, I know . . . but he's very sick. Fever. Vomiting . . ."

Delia spilled out excuses, her voice sickeningly humble while Hy-Lo's boss screamed and threatened her husband's future with his company. They knew he was a drunk. He'd been sent home at least once every month.

"Yes, thank you," Delia said and then hung up. I could hear her swallow and the loud splash as her pride plunked down hard into the pit of her stomach.

My body tensed and the sound of my heart echoed in my ears. I remained that way until I heard the heavy snoring sounds of my father and the lonely words my mother spoke aloud to herself as she sat smoking in the kitchen.

Chapter Six

I sat huddled in a corner at the back of the room, a Styrofoam cup of bitter black coffee in my hands. Cigarette smoke loomed around me like a gray cloud and quiet chatter cradled the screeching sounds of chairs being moved and rearranged.

I wouldn't speak today. In fact, I hadn't spoken at all since the day I first stepped foot in this room. Six months and counting and not a word had I uttered. I just needed to be there with people who were like me.

I didn't even speak to Glenna about the time I spent in those rooms, among those people. She never really asked me how it was going; she was good about things like that. She didn't want to make me feel different, even though I was. Well, maybe not different, but definitely sick. It got so that whenever we were together Glenna would look straight into my eyes to make sure they stayed clear for the first time in years, and so she had her answer without ever having to ask.

This particular meeting took place in a public school, in classroom 316. Artwork and graded spelling tests that held large smiley faces or red metallic stars hung from the walls of the room. I eyed the scraggly letters and poorly painted flowers and was reminded of my own third-grade handiwork and my eighth year on earth with Hy-Lo.

I shuddered and wondered if these children had fathers that polished off a fifth of vodka while forcing them to sing—over and over again—the alphabet song because they just couldn't seem to get it right once they got to the L-M-N-O-P part.

I hated that damn song.

"Hello, my name is Joseph and I'm an alcoholic."

I tilted my head to see Joseph the alcoholic, but his face was blocked by someone who hadn't found a seat yet. "Hello, Joseph," the crowd replied. "Hello, Joseph," I said to myself and sipped my coffee.

Um, Joseph, do you think the parents of the children here make them sing the ABC song? Did your parents ever make you sing the ABC song . . . over and over again—Joseph? Joseph!

I tried to shake the words from my head. I bit down hard on my bottom lip, forcing my brain to concentrate on something other than my thoughts. I had had these episodes before, days when my mind just freaked out and ran amok. Days when I was sure I was insane.

Joseph, did he, Joseph, did he? abcdefghijklmn . . .

I was going to lose this battle, my mouth was going to open up and the nonsense running around in my brain was going to spill out and then everyone would think I was crazy.

I gulped the hot coffee until my tongue went numb and my throat closed up. My brain rattled on for a while, but my tongue was dead and my throat was swollen and finally my brain surrendered. I had won the round.

The meeting went on for almost two hours; it was almost ten-thirty by the time I stepped out into the cold black night. I felt better having spent time among others with stories so similar to my own. It felt good to know that I was not suffering alone and that so many others shared my fear.

I walked quickly past the bodega and Mei-Mei's Chinese takeout, trying to keep the pace the brisk fingers of wind had set for me as she pushed me up the street toward the bus stop. We danced there, the wind and I, until the bus came and I looked up and into the judicious eyes of the driver.

He watched me the whole time, his eyes shifting like a pendulum between the street and me. I crossed my legs and wished I hadn't taken a seat so close to the front. I looked out the window and then down at my hands. I uncrossed my legs and wished I had a magazine to flip through. I glanced up and his eyes looked dead into mine.

Did he know me? Did he remember me from those nights when Malcolm, Delia, and I climbed on board his bus, tired and beaten. I peered hard at those brown eyes and wondered.

He looked at the street and then back at me.

Was that shame I saw glistening there—pity in those swimming brown pools for eyes he had?

He looked at the street and then back at me.

I got up and rang the bell. I would walk the rest of the way home.

Home. A one-bedroom apartment in a housing project with shadowy halls that smelled of urine and whatever it was the woman on the second floor cooked that night.

I stepped over the garbage that someone had dumped in front of the doorway and checked behind me twice to make sure that I was entering the building alone. I laughed to myself, laughed at the irony of the situation; we had ended up in the very same place Delia had tried to avoid for most of her life. The projects.

Eastman Projects was just one step away from the state-run shelters. The families that lived in the Eastman Projects had lost more than their homes; they'd lost their spirit, dignity, and sometimes their sanity.

The accounting firm where Delia had worked for most of her adult life had been sold twice, finally management decided to reorganize, and no matter how they shifted their numbers, Delia just no longer seemed to figure into the budget. "I got two kids," she'd said when her boss pulled her into his office to give her the news. "Isn't there *something* I can do?" she'd asked and wiped at the tears that were forming in her eyes.

Her boss, he simply adjusted his yellow and green striped tie, shrugged his shoulders, and shook his head. Delia got six weeks' severance pay and a bouquet of flowers with a card that said: *Good luck, we'll miss you!*

Me, I just couldn't hold a job. I could hold a bottle, but I found jobs to be slippery, hard to hang on to.

When the bank foreclosed on the house, we had nowhere to go, and so Delia and I went to the welfare office, signed our names on long white sheets of paper, and sat among dozens of other men and women like ourselves, waiting for our names to be called. "Lowe, Kenzie!" "Lowe, Delia!"

Mr. Chang. He had only been a caseworker for three months. Fresh out of college. Clean-cut, straight teeth, nice nails. His desk was still uncluttered, the people who sat before him were still people and not just case numbers. He drank mineral water out of the bottle and listened when they spoke.

Delia and I left there with one hundred dollars in food stamps and a letter for emergency housing at Eastman.

We would see Mr. Chang six months later for recertification. I noticed his skin had lost its glow and his attention span was a bit short. He still smiled though, even if it seemed forced. The third time I saw him, his desk was a mess of papers and half-empty coffee cups. He smelled of cigarette smoke and something else I couldn't put my finger on. His eyes were bloodshot and he had developed a nail-biting habit. He still smiled, even though it was strained and looked more like a crazed grin than a smile. My fourth visit, I was assigned a new caseworker. Mr. Chang had gone to work in the private sector.

I rounded the corner and started toward the elevator. Two

men, boys really, stood huddled near the entranceway of the elevator. One boy was tall and dark with a long thin scar that ran the length of his cheek. He wore a bright orange baseball cap and an army fatigue jacket. He had one Timberland boot–covered foot cocked up against the door of the elevator, propping it open for the light while he counted the roll of five- and ten-dollar bills he held in his hands. The other boy was smaller, just as dark, and wore a tattered brown leather jacket that hung too big on his small frame; he sported two diamond studs in his ear. They both looked up as I approached.

"Hey, girl," Orange Baseball Cap called out to me.

I nodded and said hello and even forced a smile. I had to be congenial if nothing else. "Hey," I said back and tried to tear my eyes away from the money. I considered turning around and moving toward the stairway, but the risk was too great. "Hey," I said again and nodded my head toward the elevator.

"Take the fucking stairs," Brown Leather Jacket mumbled beneath his breath as he watched me out of the side of his eye. He was just a baby, maybe seventeen, if that old.

"Have some fucking respect, man!" Orange Cap yelled and slapped Brown Leather Jacket in the face with the roll of money. "Move the fuck outta the way," he said and shoved him backward.

"Here you go, miss," Orange Cap said and stepped aside, holding the door open for me. I heard the vials of crack clinking in his pockets as he moved.

"Thanks," I responded, still keeping my eyes away from the money and trying hard not to look at either of their faces. I stepped inside the small gray box and said a prayer.

Orange Cap didn't let the door close right away; he just stood there smiling at me, blinding me with the row of gold fangs that covered his top front teeth. I was looking at the buttons, trying to will my finger to stop pressing number 3 over and over again. *Idiot*, I called myself in my mind.

My heart was racing and I was sure he could smell my fear. Finally I looked up and into Orange Cap's face. He was cute, long lashes and nice thick lips. It made it easier for me. I smiled and said, "It don't work if you keep the door open," with just a sprinkle of street.

"Yeah, yeah," he said and laughed before letting the door close. The elevator jerked upward and I leaned into the graffiti-scarred walls and thanked God for getting me through . . . again.

The elevator came to a stop and I stepped into the corridor. My heart was beating so loudly I couldn't hear the sound of my footsteps as I hurried down the hallway toward my apartment. I moved quickly, careful not to kick over the empty beer bottles and crack vials that littered the black and white checked floor.

The lightbulbs had been shattered again; the soft white glass crunched lightly beneath my feet. I thanked God for the moonlight as I moved on.

I smelled pork chops and I could hear the crackle and pop of the grease as it raged against the flame. When I pushed the door open I was greeted by the blaring noise of the television; Delia kept it loud to drown out the sound of gunshots that rang in from the courtyard every night.

She was seated on the secondhand tweed couch, bent over as far as her round belly would allow as she tried desperately to paint her toenails.

"Hello," I said and let the tension of the hall slip from my shoulders.

Delia looked up, grunted a greeting at me, and went back to her toenails.

She was barely fifty-five, but the weight she'd gained over the past few years made her look ten years older. Her hair was a mass of gray and had only recently started to grow back in around the edges. "Nerves," the doctor had told her when it started dropping out in clumps. Delia's eyes were vacant and they made you feel sad just to look into them. Her skin was blotchy and dark in places where Hy-Lo's fists had visited often enough to leave behind marks that she would die with.

The heat of the apartment gathered me into its clutches, forcing beads of sweat to form on my forehead and above my lip. "It's hot in here," I exclaimed as I began to remove my coat.

"Uh-huh," Delia said absently and attacked her pinky toe with the tiny brush.

The couch tilted a bit with her weight. It had probably seen twenty different apartments by the time it got to ours. The left back leg was missing and so we substituted it with two encyclopedias. The cushions were thin and growing thinner by the day. That was how Salvation Army furniture was. Overused, broken down, and shabby, just like the people who purchased it.

Shabby. That was the word that always came to mind when I walked into the apartment, greeted by the dull beige walls and peeling paint that hung from the ceiling like cobwebs. I had to bite my lip just to keep the word from spilling out of my mouth in a loud angry scream.

Shabby. That's what would be on my tongue when I slipped the key in the lock and jiggled until the bolt slipped free. *Shabby* is what I saw when I saw my mother, her hair gray from worry and arms fat from Fritos and Pepsi-Cola. *Shabby* is what rested on the tip of my tongue, but "hello" is what I would say when I stepped in.

I sighed and came to sit beside Delia on the couch.

"I was thinking maybe next summer we could go down to Florida, maybe, um, visit with my cousin Anna and her family," Delia said, leaning back to admire her toenails.

"Uh-huh," I responded, not sure where she was going with this. We had not seen or spoken to Anna in about five years.

Delia lit a cigarette and took a puff between every three or four words. I looked on and listened intently. She did this when she was trying to avoid what she really wanted to say.

"Or maybe we could go on down to Sandersville and see Tessie and her husband Michael. They're always asking us to come down. Maybe next summer . . ." She trailed off as she lit another cigarette.

"Uh-huh," I responded again and went to the kitchen to turn the chops.

"Yeah, that'll be real nice. A vacation next summer," Delia said and reached for the nail polish again.

Do you think he'll be dead by then?

I heard the voice inside me pipe up and I turned to see if Delia had heard it too. She hadn't, she was focused on the second coat of red polish she was struggling to apply.

Well, do you think he'll be dead? the voice inside me was asking, pushing, demanding.

Where will we get the money for a vacation? I thought to myself, trying to ignore the voice in my head.

Well?

Public Assistance didn't give out enough money for plane trips and a new pair of open-toed sandals. Where would the money come from? I asked myself again, louder, way above the sound of the voice in my head.

Will he be dead?

The voice won out, its questions filling not just my mind, but every space in my body. "I don't know!" I said aloud.

"What?" Delia yelled from the living room. "What did you say, Kenzie?"

"Nothing, Mom," I said and bit my tongue. I felt the blood fill my mouth and I thought: Good, that's what you get!

The voice went silent.

We sat together on the couch and watched sitcom after sitcom until finally ten o'clock rolled around and the news came on.

"Oh, please," Delia huffed at the newscaster. She rolled her eyes and reached for the remote.

"It's ten o'clock, Mom, it's all that's going to be on now," I said and curled my arms around myself. "What's wrong with the news?" I asked, already knowing she would ignore the question.

Delia used to like the news. "You need a world view of things," that's what she used to say. The world view was the real view to Delia. But now things were different and she did not want to deal with any reality except her own, and her reality was right here on the couch in this shabby apartment, no more and no less.

She preferred to lose herself in the afternoon soap operas, evening sitcoms, and late-night talk shows. We spoke to each other during commercials. Three minutes of empty chatter that touched on nothing important and never, ever stumbled onto talk of Hy-Lo. He did not exist to her. He'd been dead to her long before he lay dying in a hospital bed across town.

"Summer in Florida, yeah, that would be real nice," Delia said again and flipped the channel away from the news.

Up until I was twelve, my summers were spent lazing beneath billowing white clouds that moved slowly over my grandmother's house. This was Foch Boulevard, South Ozone Park, Queens, where laughter was a daily tonic and hugs and kisses were always in great abundance.

Back then, that part of Queens was still rural. Only the main streets were black-topped. Foch Boulevard was a long, narrow dirt road where raccoons roamed in search of food during the early-morning hours. It was the North imitating the South, a slice of Augusta and a wisp of Richmond right in the middle of Queens.

Large oak trees shaded Foch Boulevard; they towered above the neat one-family homes that lined the block. In the summer their branches hung heavy with glossy green leaves the size of two hands. We children would stand on our toes and pluck them free, lacing them together with needle and thread and draping them along the backyard fences as decorations for our imaginary dinner parties.

Butterflies filled our days with all the colors of the rainbow while the night glowed alive with lightning bugs. We painted our lips with the juice from wild blackberries and gorged ourselves sick with the fat green grapes that hung heavy from the vines that wrapped and weaved their way along the brick walls of the backyards.

People left their front doors unlocked and sat out on their small porches late into the summer night telling down-home stories, not caring if the next workday was just a few hours away. Summertime on Foch Boulevard came but once a year and you only got one round at life—you had to make the best of both.

It was there among the salmon- and slate-colored stones that paved the patio and bordered the small green patch of grass that was my grandmother's yard, that I was able to be a child. For two straight months, my smile found my lips again and plastered itself happily across my face. My cuticles grew in thick and my stomach filled out round inside me.

For two months I was able to watch television until my eyes burned for sleep. For two months Malcolm and I stuffed as many Oreo cookies as we could into our mouths and then washed them down with cherry Kool-Aid. Two months of White Castle hamburgers, drive-in movies, and dancing in our underwear beneath the rushing cold water of the fire hydrant.

There were few rules in my grandmother's house and the ones she did have were normal ones that were easy to abide by: brushing your teeth in the morning, taking a bath at night, and saying grace before a meal.

Delia would come and spend weekends with us; sometimes Hy-Lo would bring her in his long green Oldsmobile.

Malcolm and I would spot it as it turned the corner and we would dash into a neighbor's yard and stay hidden there until he'd leave. Sometimes Hy-Lo would sit on the steps of my grandmother's front porch and smoke, his head turning left and right, his eyes picking through the children who ran and jumped their way up and down the block hoping to spot us among them, calling us out and ending our joy.

Mable always covered for us. "They went to the beach with Jacob and Lot," she would say, her eyes boring into Hy-Lo's, daring him to challenge her.

Jacob and Lot were Sam's sons from his first marriage. They lived in Dallas and would share our summers in Queens until they became too old to find sweet content on Foch Boulevard. By the time they were in their late teens, their summer visits decreased from two months to two weeks and then nothing at all.

Hy-Lo would look back at Mable, sometimes even holding her icy stare for a moment or two, but in the end he would just bounce his head and cluck his tongue. He didn't like to run up against Mable and had little to say against Sam's sons. He and they had come to blows once when the boys were just fourteen and fifteen. Even at that young age, they towered over Hy-Lo. They loved my mother dearly, as if she were their own flesh and blood, and protected her as such.

Hy-Lo had made the sad mistake of speaking harshly to her in their presence, and even worse, he'd snatched at her, ripping the seam of her blouse. Their assault on him was quick and furious. Hy-Lo's words had not finished tumbling from his mouth, his hand not completely loose of Delia's blouse, before Jacob and Lot were on him, pounding him with their large fists until he fell to the ground, where they kicked him until Sam appeared and pulled them off.

My mother had been screaming from the corner she found herself huddled in, begging for them to stop before they killed him. I sat solemn on the couch looking down on my father's head as it knocked against the top of my foot.

I wanted to join them and kick him until his blood left a dark stain on Mable's carpet, but instead I pulled my knees up to my chin and watched as tears of pain squeezed out from under my father's clamped eyelids.

Sam had sent him off with rough words that Hy-Lo did not have the strength to dispute. He walked bent over out the door and to his car. Delia tried to follow, but Sam used the same tone he had on my father and ordered her to stay put. "He'll be okay. You stay here and tend to your kids." Delia opened her mouth once and a small broken sound escaped before she ran up the stairs and disappeared.

Sam looked at me and his eyes softened. "Go on outside, Kenzie," he said and I obeyed immediately. He did not say a word to Jacob and Lot, but something passed between them, a vibration that I caught hold of that allowed me to understand that there would be no verbal chastising or physical punishment for their actions. The beating was a long time coming. Sam had steeled himself against being drawn into Delia and Hy-Lo's disputes but it was becoming increasingly harder to do so.

He sighed heavily and his body shook against what could have happened had he been the one to deliver the beating. Surely his fists would have done more than bruise Hy-Lo's ego or break his skin. His fists would have found Hy-Lo's heart and ended its even rhythm with one hard blow.

The spring before I turned twelve years old, white men with red pinched faces, cut off T-shirts, and hard hats came to Foch Boulevard. They brought with them noisy machines: trucks loaded with gravel and smoldering black tar. They spread the tar and gravel the length of Foch Boulevard as easily as my mother spread icing across a cake, and then they flattened it with a large silver rolling pin.

Things would be different from that day on.

The oak branches dipped in misery and the grapes turned gray and shriveled up black. Porches seemed smaller, more cluttered, as people began to long for down home's wide-open spaces. Houses went up for sale and children were ordered to stay close to home or inside all together. People walked quickly, lifting a hand in hurried greeting instead of stopping to talk.

A new element had followed the blacktop and they did not care if butterflies graced the day and lightning bugs stole the night. They laid out poison for the raccoons and chopped away the crooked limbs of the grapevines and blackberry trees.

I was different after that. I lost my taste for Twizzlers and M&Ms, my body curved in places that drew the attention of boys and men, and my mouth came loose at the sides, spilling out words that I had previously kept hidden beneath my tongue.

I had begun to openly challenge my father.

Chapter Seven

I was back at the hospital, standing at the doorway of the room, staring at the chair. It was where I'd left it, pressed against the wall beckoning me over. There was someone new in the bed next to Hy-Lo's, a white man who didn't look sick at all. His cheeks were rosy and his green eyes sparkled when I walked into the room. "Morning," he said cheerfully in a Brooklyn accent I'd only heard in the movies. I just nodded and walked past him toward my chair.

"That your father?" he asked and leaned forward.

I sighed heavily. "Yes," I muttered back at him and sat down.

"What's wrong with him?"

"What's wrong with you?" I shot back. The hostility in my voice was thick but did not seem to affect him.

He pulled at the sheet that covered his body; pulled it until it traveled up to his knees and all that was left below was the white bedsheet he lay on.

"Sugar," he said and smiled. "I love Hershey bars," he added and laughed.

I stared at the starched white sheet for a long time before I spoke. This time my voice was low and apologetic. "Oh, I'm sorry," I said and turned away.

"Uh-unh, don't be, it's my own fault, really. You get what you deserve, you know. They think they might have to take the rest of my right leg off. I guess they'll just keep chopping away until I'm just a head!" He bellowed with laughter that was as buoyant as the ocean. There were no secrets there. No pain, disappointment, or regret—just joy.

No feet, no calves, and now the thighs were on their way out? Where was the joy in that? I thought that he had been placed in the D building in error. He should have been in the G building with the other lunatics.

"So now your turn: what's wrong with your father?" he said after he wiped the tears of laughter away from his shining eyes.

"Everything," I said and got up and pulled the curtain along its thin rod until it blocked out his face.

I pulled the chair from the wall and set it parallel to Hy-Lo's toes. I shoved my hands into my pockets and stood staring at his drawn and ailing face. He would not last past Christmas. I could see it in the deep creases that crisscrossed his face like great chasms. He had sucked from the bottle and now the bottle was returning the deed.

I sat down and crossed my legs and arms. The wind howled frigid outside the window, but it was colder by his bedside than it was outside. I wrapped my arms around myself and watched as Hy-Lo's cracked and peeling lips moved silently while he spoke to someone in his dreams. I watched him and recalled my own nightmares.

"Were you on Montgomery Street yesterday?" Hy-Lo stood directly in front of me. My mouth stared at his chin, while my eyes focused on his inflamed cheeks. I was eight, maybe ten, not older than twelve.

We were alone in the apartment; Delia and Malcolm were at the store.

"No, Daddy," I said.

"Someone told me they saw you there. Are you calling my friend a liar?"

This was a game we had played since I was five. Hy-Lo would say *someone* saw me *somewhere* I wasn't supposed to be. When I was five I questioned my five-year-old mind. When I was eight I began to wonder if I had a twin. At ten years old I knew it was a game. By age twelve I was sick of the whole thing.

"No, Daddy," I said wearily.

He was silent for a long time. He just stood there breathing Smirnoff into my face. I rolled my eyes, held my breath, and turned my face away.

His cheeks flushed crimson at my act and he took a step away from me.

"Look at me!" he bellowed.

My body jerked at the sound of his voice but I did not allow my head to snap around at his command. I slowly, casually turned to face him. My face was bent in a smirk and my eyes were cold and black.

"Wipe that look off your face, Del— Kenzie!" he yelled and took a threatening step toward me. I almost laughed at his blunder. He had, for a split second, mistaken me for my mother. No two people could be less alike; I would never have married a man like Hy-Lo, not even if he was the last man on earth!

My mouth was drawn in a crooked line. I was trying to keep my composure but my eyes smiled smugly at him and he reacted.

Slap!

His hard palm came across my cheek with quick intensity. I heard bells in my head and the living room swam around me, as I crumpled to the floor. When I opened my eyes he was standing over me, looking down at me. "Get up," he said and stepped out of my blurry vision. I couldn't move, my face was on fire, and my hot tears only stung more.

I turned my head and watched his feet walk away and into the kitchen. I crawled into the bathroom and slammed the door behind me. I screamed that I hated him until my throat closed up raw and my legs grew tired of kicking the door. I sat whimpering on the cold tile floor until I heard the front door open, the brief exchange between Delia and Hy-Lo, and then my mother's soft voice floating through to me from the other side.

"Kenzie. Baby?" I could hear her fingernails tracing over the pearl-colored paint of the door. "Kenzie, come on out. Please, baby. He's gone." Her voice was shaky.

"I hate him!" I screamed in my hoarse voice and gave the door one last kick for good measure.

"I gotta pee, Mommy," I heard Malcolm whisper from behind her.

I swung the door open and tried to rush past my mother and brother. Delia caught me by the arm and pulled me close to her. "What happened, baby? What happened?" I fought against her embrace. I did not want to be cuddled and spoken to in soft tones. She held tight as I struggled against her chest. After a while I collapsed in my mother's arms, repeating my declaration over and over in her neck: "I hate him."

It was discussed with my grandmother before the idea was even presented to me. It was late, way past twelve at night. Malcolm was fast asleep in his bed and I was stretched out on the living room floor watching Wolfman Jack's *Midnight Special*. Tina Turner shimmied and shook her way across the stage as she belted out "Proud Mary." Delia was in the kitchen sitting at the table. Her face was smeared in egg yolk and her feet propped up in the chair as she painted her toenails red. This was her Friday night.

The phone was balanced between her ear and shoulder as she tried to speak below the sounds that came pouring out of the television. "I just think it would be better for her. She's getting older now, I think she needs a change of scenery."

I wanted to lower the volume but that would be too obvious. So I moved as close to the kitchen as possible, tuned out as much of Tina as I could, and strained to hear what my mother was saying. "Well, this woman on my job sends her daughter there every year; she says she loves it."

There was a long moment where my mother grunted in agreement. "Well, we can swing it. Not for both of them, though. Just Kenzie."

More grunting.

"Well, I think Malcolm is still too young. Maybe next year."

I twisted my face. I still couldn't get the gist of what she was saying. I moved closer.

"No, Mama, you don't have to help. Hyman and I can do it."

Silence.

"I know that you can't do for one and not the other but—"

Silence.

"Okay, Mama. Okay."

When Delia came out of the kitchen I was back where she'd left me.

She stood there tapping her foot and singing along with Tina. "What a life. Ain't she the lucky one," she said as she gazed longingly at Tina. "I wish I'd married someone like Ike Turner," she said and sighed.

We'd find out, years later, that she had.

My mother's quiet conversation with Mable came to light just weeks later.

"Kenzie, look at this."

I was at the kitchen table bent over a particularly hard math problem.

"Look," she said again, nudging my shoulder with her finger.

I sighed heavily and peered up at her. She stood grinning before me, a colorful brochure clutched in her hand. "What's that?" I asked and reached out for it.

"It's information on a sleep-away camp. See, it's upstate." She was talking quickly. She pulled up a chair beside me. "See," she said with every page I turned. Her eyes sparkled at the glossy pictures of the tall green pines and shimmering blue of the lake. "Oh," she gasped when we came upon the campfire and canoeing scenes.

I looked up and into her eyes and I saw the memory of her own childhood lingering there.

"What do you think?" she asked and leaned back in the chair. Her eyes were hopeful and she thumped her foot nervously in anticipation of my response.

"It looks nice," I said and also leaned back.

"Yeah, it does." She got up and reached for her Newports. She bounced the pack of cigarettes up and down in the palm of her hand. "You know, I wish I could send you down home. I mean, so you could be with family instead of strangers." She was talking slowly and staring out the window. "Those pictures remind me of my summers down south. Down home." She breathed out and leaned her hip against the refrigerator.

I saw her cheeks rise with the smile that followed her memories.

"Shoot, growing up down home was like living in summertime all year long." She laughed and stuck a cigarette between her lips. She turned to the stove and then remembered the book of matches resting on top of the refrigerator. "I wish you could go spend a summer there, but all the old people are gone and my cousins are living just like me. Working and wondering where their babies are going to spend their vacations at." She laughed again. "Things just ain't what it used to be."

She lit the cigarette and inhaled. She blew off perfect circles of smoke and then turned to look at me.

"That used to make you laugh when you were little, Kenzie. Those little circles of smoke . . . You thought it was so funny," she said sadly.

I smiled and nodded my head in agreement to a memory I could not recollect.

"Well," she said and took one last drag on the cigarette.

"Well," I mocked her and tried to make light of the hefty moment we were having. She smiled and came to sit beside me again.

On July 1, Malcolm and I stood beside my mother and grandmother amidst hundreds of other children and their relatives. At least sixty coach-style buses lined the street outside the Port Authority. Each bus had a sign posted in its front window that declared its destination: *Camp Chicahow, Camp Pocahontas, Camp Good Hope, Hickory Camp for Girls,* and so on.

Me, I was going to Camp Crystal Lake, set at the foot of the beautiful Adirondacks. Well, that's how the brochure described it.

"If you need anything, you know I'm just a phone call away," Delia said as she nervously twisted and untwisted a magazine that she had brought along with her. She had never had us more than forty minutes away from her, and now we would be more than five hours away in a place she had never been.

"It'll be okay, Delia," Mable said in exasperation and gently pushed her aside. "Kenzie is a big girl and she'll watch out for Malcolm. Won't you, Kenzie?" She ran her hands across my corn-braided hair.

"Yep," I responded and smiled assuredly at Mable.

"Malcolm, you're going to be a good boy, right?" Mable bent down and tweaked Malcolm on his nose. My brother just nodded his head in response. His eyes were wide with excitement as he looked at the hundreds of kids who surrounded us.

"Oh—" Delia moaned. Her eyes were moist and she thumped her foot rapidly on the pavement. Mable shot her a look. "Stop it, Delia," she sang and looked down at her daughter's tapping foot.

"This will be the best summer of your life," Mable said and pulled us to her. "We'll come up and visit you in two weeks," she added and then stepped back.

Delia moved forward and embraced each of us. "I'll miss you guys," she said and wiped at the corner of her eye.

We were off. Me, Malcolm, and many other laughing children. I sat and watched as the towering buildings and smoky gray horizon of New York City was quickly replaced with stately evergreens and a placid blue sky. I pressed my nose against the window to take in the sprawling emerald pastures and dozens of grazing cows and horses that seemed to fly by us as we traveled down the road.

The wide-open spaces and clear blue skies unlocked something in me—a place not even Foch Boulevard had been able to reach. I felt free for the first time, I felt absolutely and completely free.

I leaned back and thumped Malcolm on the side of his head.

"Ow," he whined and rubbed at the spot I'd violated. I smiled at him and reached over and hugged him hard. He smiled back and let me.

Malcolm was homesick for the first three days. He cried for Delia and wet his bed twice. I talked to him and cooed and cuddled him as I had seen Delia do, but my heart wasn't in it. On the third day I became frustrated and dragged him into the wooded area behind his cabin.

I stood before him, my hands folded across my chest, and glared down at him. His eyes were bloodshot from lack of sleep and crying and he had his thumb stuck in his mouth.

"Take it out, Malcolm," I said sternly.

The other children had already started teasing him about his habit. They called him a baby and a pissy mama's boy.

"Listen, you better pull it together or they're going to call Delia up and have her come for you."

His eyes brightened and I realized I had said the wrong thing. I changed my strategy.

"But Delia won't be the one to come for you. Hy-Lo will come and get you and he'll beat you in front of all of the other campers for having him travel so far. Then he'll beat you again for being such a sissy thumb-sucking baby."

Malcolm's eyes widened again, but this time in fear. He popped his thumb back in his mouth.

"Then he'll beat you all the way back home," I continued. "But you know the worst part of the whole thing, Malcolm?"

He raised his eyes and waited.

"He'll beat Delia for having sent you to begin with, especially after he told her not to."

Malcolm just stood staring, mulling the information over in his head.

I pressed: "Do you want Delia to get a beating, Malcolm?"

He shook his head slowly back and forth.

"Well, then you better stop all of this crying and bed-wetting or else that is exactly what's going to happen." I slammed my fist rapidly into the palm of my hand for emphasis. The hard punching sounds reverberated through the woods behind us.

Two weeks went by quickly. I was having the time of my life. I mailed a letter a day to Glenna describing the new friends I'd made, the activities that went on, and more importantly, the man I'd met.

He was a man—much more than a boy. Tall and light-skinned with hazel eyes and long, wavy black hair that he kept pulled back in a ponytail. He told me his father was black Irish and his mother was just plain black. He was eighteen years old and I was twelve.

"How old you is?" he asked one day as I dumped the

contents of my food tray into the large garbage can. I had seen him around—emptying garbage cans and clearing the ground of fallen leaves. He was a young black girl's dream man. A man who would certainly father a pretty baby with good hair. We all swooned in his presence.

I was frozen. Was he speaking to me? I turned my head to look behind me and met the wide surprised eyes of one of my peers.

"Hey?" his voice came again. His tone was gentle and teasing. He reached out and brushed the top of my hand with his fingers.

I jumped and answered, "Twelve."

His eyes went wide and then slanted. "You ain't no twelve. Why you lying?" His hazel eyes rolled the length of my body and then back to my open mouth. "You look more like fifteen."

There were soft giggles behind me. I straightened my back and pushed my small bosom out. "Blame my mama for that," I said, suddenly feeling grown. Suddenly feeling powerful.

"Umph," he sounded and shook his head.

It was over so quickly. The sound of lunchroom chatter and clanging trays became loud around me, pulling me back into reality. Someone pushed a tray into the small of my back. "C'mon," an annoyed voice came with the nudge and I moved along, wondering if the exchange had taken place at all.

"What's his name?" I asked Mildred. She was a small, dumpy girl who could barely walk a mile, much less run one. She had been coming to Camp Crystal Lake since she was five years old and the counselors were as familiar with her as she was with them.

Mildred was the water girl and the cabin monitor; there wasn't much else she could or would do. Her world was locked away in her comic books and that's where they left her. She glanced up from her *Josie and the Pussycats* comic book, pushed her glasses back up to rest on the bridge of her nose, and squinted at me. "What?" she said and blinked.

"What's his name?" I repeated and nodded at the tall figure dressed in white shorts and black T-shirt who was making his way across the grounds toward the recreation hall.

"Oh, um, that there is Mousy," Mildred said and returned to the comic book.

I watched him until he disappeared into the building. "Mousy. What kinda name is that?" I asked, not expecting a reply, and Mildred did not offer one.

I found out that this was Mousy's second summer as an employee of Camp Crystal Lake. Before that he'd been a camper, but he'd always been the object of affection.

Every single female there wanted him—campers and counselors alike. Of course, the female counselors wanted him in a way that our young bodies were not ready to handle. Our eyes had caught glimpses of those acts in R-rated movies and our minds had replayed those scenes late in the night as our fingers rubbed the small pointed flesh between our legs.

"You braid?"

Our second encounter came four days later. The day had been rained out, making outside activities impossible. After breakfast we either retired to our cabin to play jacks or read, or headed over to the recreation hall to play board games. I was seated at the old piano, my fingers lazily picking over the black and white keys as I stared absentmindedly out the window.

"What?" I turned toward the voice.

"Hair?" He had extended a long thick lock of hair toward me. It gleamed beneath the room's fluorescent lighting.

I was flustered and nodded my head yes. He considered

me for a moment and then cocked his head and turned to walk away. I looked around and saw that no one had noticed the exchange, and furthermore, there were no counselors present. I stood on legs of Jell-O and followed him out the door into the gray wet day.

The "green room" was really a solarium but served as a lounge for the counselors. It was connected to the dining area, though its windows had been covered with black cloth to keep out prying young eyes.

My stomach jerked and pulled inside of me as we stepped over the threshold. I was nervous at the thought of being alone with him and I was scared at the thought of being caught—alone with him.

"Be careful," his voice came to me in the dark. I couldn't see him, but I knew he was close. I could feel the heat of his body and smell the light scent of Ivory soap as it sailed off of him and assaulted my senses.

The light came on. I found myself standing in a small room that was made even smaller by a large brown couch and six milk crates turned on their sides scattered here and there. They were makeshift tables that held ashtrays, magazines, and empty soda or beer bottles. The air was musty with the smell of pubescent sweat, cigarette smoke, and the lingering aroma of marijuana.

"Sit down," he said and I did.

He came and stood in front of me. His muscular frame stretched out long before me. I shivered even though my body was on fire. I crossed my legs at the ankle and averted my eyes to the wall behind him.

"You ready?" he asked, his voice laced with seduction.

I had forgotten why I was there or how I had even arrived at that soft, worn place on the couch. I stared blankly back at him and nodded yes.

"You sure, now. I've got a lot of it, you know. It's long and thick," he said and took a step closer to me. His crotch was six inches from my face and I could see clearly the faded place in the material where his penis rested.

Suddenly I heard my mother's voice calling to me from somewhere way in the back of my mind. It was a shrill sound warning that danger was near. I stood up quickly and tried to take a step forward on one wobbly leg.

My eyes must have looked like those of a deer caught in headlights because he laughed a small laugh that got lost in the four corners of the room, and then reached into the back pocket of his jeans and pulled out a black, thick-toothed comb. He held it up before me and smiled.

It was then that I remembered why I was there. I slowly sat back down.

"Damn, I forgot the radio. You want music?"

"Well, only if you do." I tried to make my voice sound like a teenager. I tried to get my body to relax and slump comfortably against the couch like a sixteen-year-old. What would Marcia Brady do? I asked myself, and stared down at my hands.

"Nah, it's all rainy and my cabin is too far away." He turned and plopped down on the floor in front of my legs and then began to slide backward.

I panicked; my knees were locked and refused to part. I mentally commanded them but they only pressed tighter and then his back brushed against them and they magically disengaged. My thighs spread wide open, allowing him to slide comfortably between them. I shuddered.

For an hour, I combed, parted, and plaited his thick locks while he hummed the melodies to his favorite Al Green tunes. The sound of his singing and the easy way the comb slid through his hair lulled me into a comfort I had never known before. My body relaxed and my thighs closed in around his shoulders. He looked up at me and grinned.

I felt heat brewing in the base of my stomach and a fire spread through my body, making it hard for me to breathe.

He felt it too and ran his hand down the length of my calf. His fingertips were as hot as the fire that stirred within me and a sound escaped my mouth that seemed older than my twelve years. He looked at me and grinned again as I wrapped the last thin plait around my index finger. "Done," I said and was surprised at how foreign and grown my voice sounded.

He didn't move and neither did I, we just remained that way, him humming and me wrapping his hair around my fingers while the rain tapped at the roof above us.

Afterward, he did not thank me or tell me how pleased he was with my work. He patted my behind and told me I had a nice ass. He said he would stop by the pool the next day to see what I looked like out of my clothes.

"Promise?" I said, feeling dizzy from his touch and the words that had followed it.

"Yeah, sure. I promise," he said and smiled a smile that shook my insides.

I giggled and handed him back his comb before I half-walked, half-ran between the raindrops toward my cabin and the pale pink stationery that awaited the words I would use to describe to Glenna my first step into womanhood.

I walked into my cabin and my heart sank. There, sitting on my bed, legs crossed and smiling smugly, was Hy-Lo. I stopped and thought that I would drop dead right there on the hard wood floor. I heard thunder boom in the distance and then the sound of the rain coming down heavily on the roof above me. I couldn't speak; all I could do was gulp at the air.

He stood up and walked toward me. His face shifted as the wild thing inside him struggled to get out. I could smell the liquor and the gasoline grime from the highway and I knew he had drank all the way up with the windows open, his feet easing up on the gas just long enough to get past the state troopers who lay hidden off of the shoulders.

"No hello for your father?" he said and took a step closer to me.

I stepped backward. "H-hello," I answered and my eyes moved around the cabin in search of Delia.

"What about a hug for your dad," he said and stepped closer.

I swallowed hard. I had never hugged Hy-Lo; the only physical contact we ever made with each other was when he hit me. He moved in and embraced me. I stiffened and all the blood in my body ran cold and drained down to my feet, numbing them. I held my breath and waited for it to be over.

I felt his heart thumping against my chest and then he let go.

"Get your stuff together, we're going home." He moved away and cleared his throat, embarrassed at his effort and my resistance, and turned to walk out. I saw the imprint of the pint of Smirnoff in his back pocket as he moved through the door. "Don't keep me waiting, Kenzie," he said as he skipped down the steps and tried to duck the rain that fell in buckets around him.

I jammed my belongings into my duffel bag and tried hard to fight the tears back. I heard the horn blow between the cracks of thunder and the announcement that was being made over the PA system: *"Field day has been canceled due to the weather. All campers should report to the recreation hall for fun and games."*

My life had been canceled due to Hy-Lo and I was reporting to a green Oldsmobile for a trip home. What a fucking life!

I looked out the window and saw Mousy leaning against the wooden post of the recreation hall. He was talking to a counselor, but his eyes were on my cabin. I watched him for a long time before I shoved my remaining items into my bag. He would be a sweet memory; that's all Hy-Lo had allowed.

The horn blared again and I grabbed my bag and hurried

out into the rain and toward the car. Hy-Lo was tilting the bottle up to his mouth when I swung the car door open; Malcolm was huddled in the backseat, his eyes wide and confused. Delia sat up front beside Hy-Lo, her face like stone, her eyes staring straight ahead.

"Hi," I said. It came out small and lifeless.

"Hi," she said and turned her head a bit to look at me. Her eye was swollen and the skin was cut at the bridge of her noise. I looked at her and shook my head in disgust, then leaned back into the hard leather of the seat and turned my face away from her eyes.

"You always sorry," I muttered to myself as Hy-Lo took one last swig from his bottle before shoving it between his legs. He turned the radio up and backed the car slowly out of the parking space.

"Say goodbye to the country, kids," he laughed as we did ninety toward home.

I rolled my eyes and shot him the finger behind his back, Malcolm giggled in his hands, and then we settled back and watched the trees fly by until they were gone and we were home.

Chapter Eight

Hy-Lo stirred and groaned as if reading my thoughts. He did that on and off for some time, his groans coinciding with the howl of the wind outside the windows.

Death was close now. I could feel it in the room. Waiting. Just like me. Waiting.

I had been waiting for Hy-Lo to die my whole life, not knowing that my whole life I had been watching him die. Every drop of liquor he ever drank had put him a step closer to where he was today. And somehow he'd managed to take me along with him.

What the hell was I doing there, so close to him after spending a lifetime trying to avoid him?

I looked at him, his open gaping mouth and swollen purple tongue, and willed him to speak, to offer a few words of solace and a lifetime of apologies that would finally, maybe, make my life normal.

He just lay there, taking. Still taking.

"You are so selfish," I muttered angrily and slammed my leather-gloved fist down onto my thigh. "You won't die and you won't let me live. Why?"

I left without getting an answer, not that I expected one, but I desperately needed one. I roamed the streets for two hours, maybe more. The winter night was dark except for the snow flurries that shattered the darkness and littered the sidewalks by the time I arrived at the school.

The muscles in my legs thumped against the forced exercise I had imposed on them and my sweatshirt was soaked through under the arms. I didn't care; no one in that room cared whether I was sweaty or not. What they cared about was getting better.

I stood behind ten people who'd lined up for coffee. I was beginning to recognize the faces, able to place their stories with their eyes. I was still an enigma to them, I could tell by their greetings. "Welcome," someone would say and then squint their eyes and search their memory to find me. But they couldn't and so I was always a new face to them.

But that would change tonight.

I filled my cup with the hot, bitter black liquid and moved to the front of the room. The chairperson was a young Korean girl; her hair was dyed green at the ends and her face was covered with angry red pimples.

"Hi," she greeted me and stuck her hand out. I took her tiny hand in mine and she shook it and pulled me toward her. "You ready now?"

My eyes went wide with surprise. She knew me. "Yes," I replied and turned to face the crowd. She smiled and patted me on the back.

"Welcome," she said, and for the first time I finally actually felt welcomed.

"Hello, my name is Kenzie and I'm an alcoholic."

I said it and my heart went light—a weight had been lifted with those few simple words. I took a breath and began at a place in my life where the hurt was personal and the reality all too genuine for a child just becoming familiar with her teenage years.

When I turned fourteen years old I got a cat for my birthday. She was a black-and-white pure-bred Persian, with large round eyes the color of ebony under moonlight. We were immediately taken with each other and she, like me, avoided my father as much as possible.

I named her Pricilla, because at the time I thought that

was the most beautiful name in the world and she was the most beautiful thing in my life.

She loved to lie on the windowsill of my bedroom and bask in the warm sunlight, and at night she slept at the foot of my bed, her head resting contently on the sole of my foot.

Pricilla was smarter than any cat I'd known and her strength was equal to that of a small dog.

Hy-Lo was as cruel to her as he was to us. When she did happen to stumble across his path he would grab hold of her and drag her across the carpet by her tail, or sometimes hold her by her neck and singe her whiskers with his cigarette.

She would get him back though, but for a long time Malcolm and I took the blame.

"Wasn't there two chicken wings left on this plate?"

"Who was in the refrigerator? There's milk everywhere!"

"Damnit! Who ate the last pork chop!"

Malcolm and I were constantly accused of leaving the refrigerator door half-open, knocking over containers of milk, and taking meat out of frying pans and not placing those pans to soak in the sink.

We would stand at attention in front of Hy-Lo or slouch before Delia and accuse each other of the crime or just swear on our young souls that we knew nothing of the offense that had been committed.

Hy-Lo called us liars and sent us for the belt. Delia would shrug her shoulders and shake her head in disgust and send us to our room, where we would sit and scratch our heads and wonder if there were a ghost living among us. All along it was Pricilla.

Her hiding place was in the hollowed-out underside of my father's record player. It was a beautiful piece of furniture— long and sleek, running nearly the length of the wall it rested against. A deep mahogany with four claw feet, my father kept it gleaming with wood oil and Pledge.

The left side was a case that held his old 78s and newer

33s, while the right side held the turntable. None of us were allowed to touch it and we'd better not even look at it too hard.

I'd spotted Pricilla on a number of occasions slipping beneath its belly and disappearing from sight. I'd lay my body across the floor and move as close to the player as I dared, expecting to see her glowing eyes staring back at me, but they were never there.

It was a long time before I got up the nerve to slip my hand beneath the player. I patted the air for her soft fur and moved it slowly across the carpet in hopes of colliding with her. Nothing.

I pulled my hand out and sat up and scratched my head in bewilderment.

"Oooooooh!" Malcolm's voice rang out like a human siren. "I'matell Daddy you messing with his record player. Ooooooooooh!"

The bond that held Malcolm and me together was rapidly losing its adhesive. With every birthday we celebrated we moved further and further apart. After all, I was nearly a woman and he was still a child.

"Shut up!" I hissed at him. "Stop sneaking around like a little snake."

Malcolm had become a sidler, often entering a room without making a sound.

"Hy-Lo gonna beat you good!" He taunted and teased me until I couldn't take it anymore.

I flew at him and grabbed him by the collar of his shirt. "Shut up!" I shouted in his face, and spittle covered his forehead. I shook him until his head resembled the plastic dolls that bounced their grinning heads in car windows.

Malcolm tried to pry my hands loose but I had a death grip on him. I saw the quick fear that passed across his face and it made me feel superior. I flung him against the wall. He stood there for some time whimpering and examining his torn shirt. "I'matell Mommy!" he screamed and stomped off to the bedroom.

I laughed out loud at his dramatics. "Make sure you do!" I yelled and shot up my middle finger at his retreating back. My adrenaline was still pumping and tiny beads of sweat covered the space above my nose. I considered jumping up and following him, grabbing him again and slamming him around some more. I smiled at the thought and the power of my strength over him.

I turned my attention back to the record player. I lay on my back and slid my head beneath it. It was dark and dusty. I opened my eyes and almost screamed. There was Pricilla looking down at me.

The record player was old. Made in the '40s—they didn't make them that like that anymore. The whole underside was hollowed out and made for a great hiding place.

Pricilla blinked at me and then hissed. I pulled myself out and waited until my heartbeat slowed. I moved in again, easing my hand under and up until I felt her fur. I moved my hand across her stomach and stroked her there until she purred contentedly.

I laid my palm flat against the warm wood and slid my fingers along the unfinished edges. My mind wandered and I closed my eyes against the dusky light of the living room. Pricilla shifted and moved away from my hand. I reached for the warm comfort of her fur but instead my hand found the cold steel of a gun.

I believed he was planning to kill us. Murder us as we slept. One bullet to the head, just like in the movies.

Their arguments and fights became more than just violent confrontations. They were now the opening acts to a scene I was sure would end with Delia clutching at her heart while blood, dark red and hot, spread across the bodice of her dress. She would look at me for one last long moment, mouthing the words I love you, and then her eyes would roll up into her head and she would be gone, leaving me and Malcolm to be raised by my father.

I couldn't tell anyone about what I'd found. It was Pricilla's secret and mine, and who would she tell? The alley cats that watched her as she rested on my windowsill?

My secret ate at me. My stomach knots got knots and I had trouble keeping my food down. I lay awake at night afraid to close my eyes and surrender to my dreams because they were filled with gunshots, blood, and caskets. I was afraid to go to sleep because mothers got killed deep in the night when a lonely cloud blocked the moonlight and children slept curled up in their beds.

"You feeling okay, Kenzie?" Delia held my chin and tilted my head left and then right. Her face was etched with concern.

"Uh-huh," I answered quickly and even forced a smile. It took a lot of energy and the act of bending my lips made me tired.

"I dunno," she said and she eyed me suspiciously.

My clothes began to hang off of my body and deep dark circles formed under my eyes. I was as worried as I was weak. I did not have the strength to jump double-dutch or sit on the park wall with Glenna and hiss at the neighborhood boys. And even if I did, I would still have chosen to remain confined to my bedroom, door slightly ajar, watching and waiting for Hy-Lo to make his move.

Weeks passed and their arguments were contained to short blasts of loud angry words, the yelling and screaming never escalating beyond furious words and slamming doors. It was as if Hy-Lo knew I knew and kept the wild thing within him at bay.

It was the bottle of rum that did it, a gift from a coworker who had taken a trip to Jamaica. White rum, overproof. I remember reading the label over and over again. *Overproof,* what did that mean? I would find out as the bottle went from full to half empty in a matter of two hours.

I knew from then on that it wasn't going to be a good night. Saturdays hardly ever were. Hy-Lo had no place to go on Sunday. Work would be another day away and church was someplace he passed on the street on the way to the liquor store.

The dawn broke behind large black clouds that kept the day gray and the ground wet. It rained so hard and for so long that we could hear the water rushing into the drainage ditch and the consistent cough and gurgle as the sewers backed up and spewed the water back into the street.

There was no place for us to escape to that day. Saturdays usually found us biking in Prospect Park or teasing the monkeys at the Bronx Zoo. Our only activity today would be to avoid Hy-Lo.

"Kenzie!" The sound of his voice traveled through the small apartment quickly. But the sound of the bottle's lip clinking against the glass was even louder and more threatening than Hy-Lo's voice.

My response was just as swift. "Yes! Coming!" I yelled back and hurriedly shoved my bare feet into my slippers. I moved past my parents' bedroom and shot a worried look at my mother's back. She was stretched out across the bed and had been that way for most of the day.

"Yes, Da—" My words got caught in my throat at the sight before me. Hy-Lo had Pricilla clutched by the skin of her back—suspended in the air before him. She was hissing and spitting, trying frantically to free herself.

I wanted to run to her and snatch her from his grip, but my feet were glued to the floor, my mouth hung open.

"This cat—" He spoke low. "This cat has been stealing food." He slapped her across her nose and she hissed. Her breathing was becoming labored and her tongue hung out of her mouth lapping for air.

"She's been stealing food right out of the goddamn refrigerator!" He shook her with every loud angry word. He shook her and my insides twisted, my heart dropped down to my stomach and then shot up into my throat. I could feel tears stinging at my eyes.

I knew she was doing it. I'd walked into the kitchen one day just as she'd managed to claw the refrigerator door open. I watched in awe as she stood on her hind legs and carefully examined the contents of the refrigerator shelves, finally settling for a slice of baked ham that Hy-Lo had placed uncovered on a plate.

"Daddy." My words were barely a whisper. I extended my hand out toward him unable to say any more. "Please, Daddy, please."

He turned and looked at me, his face creased and bloated, his eyes red. I saw evil living there and my hate for him increased. I thought about running to the record player and getting the gun. I took one step sideways toward the living room.

Pricilla hissed again and twisted herself enough to take a swipe at Hy-Lo. Blood sprouted out of the top of his hand and then oozed onto the floor.

"Damnit!" Hy-Lo yelled and Pricilla dropped with a thud to the floor. She was moving so fast that she was no more than a black-and-white blur when she skidded past me. She took the corner too fast and slammed headfirst into the wall. She recovered quickly and disappeared into the dark living room.

Hy-Lo stood staring at his hand; the deep scratch bubbled up revealing pink and white flesh. I half-expected to see the coat of the wild thing that lived inside of him. A thin stream of blood spilled out and onto the white linoleum. That seemed to make him angrier than his wound and he turned eyes on me that were filled with rage.

Hy-Lo cussed under his breath and moved to the sink; he

turned on the cold water and shoved his hand beneath the rushing water. His face cringed at the sting the water dealt his open wound.

I waited.

He snatched the dish towel from its place on the rung over the sink and wrapped his hand in the soiled cloth. I almost smiled at the infection I was sure would set up there. I had wiped a spill off the floor with it earlier in the day.

"That cat is going the hell out of here!" he bellowed as he moved past me and into the living room. He flicked the light on and began looking behind the couch and the potted plant that he had picked up for Delia after he'd thrown out the small pots of jasmine she'd had growing on the windowsill.

I knew where she was and my heart beat loudly at the secret I held. The deafening sound of it caused my head to spin and I grabbed the wall for support.

"Go and find her!" he yelled over his shoulder as he checked behind the couch for the third time. He was spilling blood all over the couch and the floor. "Damnit!" he screamed and stomped to the bathroom.

"Jesus Christ, what the hell is going on?" Delia was standing in the doorway; the whites of her eyes were tawny and her bottom lip hung limp. Her hair was a disheveled mass and for the first time I noticed that she was wearing the same clothes she had worn the day before.

"Shut the fuck up, Delia," Hy-Lo said as he came slamming back out of the bathroom. His hand was wrapped in a baby blue washcloth, the one with the yellow duck. It was mine. I would have to remember to drop it down the incinerator. "Where is it?" He was looking behind the couch again. "Kenzie!"

"I-I don't know," I said and looked at Delia.

"Who are you looking for?" Delia asked as she stepped into the living room and stood near Hy-Lo.

He stood up, considered her for a moment, and then

pushed past her so hard that her shoulder hit the wall with a loud thud. She grimaced at the pain and then smirked at Hy-Lo's back. He was in their bedroom on his knees, peering beneath the bed and cursing at the shadows and dust bunnies that looked back at him.

Malcolm, who had been in our bedroom, came to the door and looked at me. I shook my head in warning and waved him back. He did not argue and hurriedly returned to the safety of his bed, thumb, and G.I. Joe figurine.

"Look for her, Kenzie!" Hy-Lo slammed into my bedroom and ordered Malcolm out of the bed. "Get your ass up and find that piece-of-shit cat. Now!"

Malcolm scrambled from the bed and dropped to his knees, searching beneath the beds for Pricilla.

Delia looked at me and mouthed, *What happened?*

I stared at her as if she were crazy. Did she really expect me to explain her husband's madness to her? *You lie down with him every night; you tell me what happened.* That's what I wanted to say, but I just shrugged my shoulders and looked behind the potted plant again.

Hy-Lo was in the living room again; the washcloth was soaked with his blood, turning it a dirty burnt-orange color. He peered down at it and his rage increased. "Call her," he said and his voice shook. "Call her," he repeated and spittle flew from his mouth.

I looked at Delia, who had settled herself against the wall. Hy-Lo's head jerked and she bounced upright as if his movement were a quick reminder of how much he hated anyone touching his walls.

I glanced down at the faded brown of his slippers and the tiny drops of blood that lay drying there and opened my mouth and called out her name. "Pricilla." It was barely a whisper.

"Louder, Kenzie," Hy-Lo said and raised his hand in preparation to backhand me if I didn't obey.

"Pricilla," I said again, louder. "Here, girl . . . *psssst-psssst-psssst.*" I knew no matter how much I called her she wouldn't come. She could smell him there and sense the danger.

Delia unglued herself and stepped carefully around Hy-Lo, her mouth dropped open for a split second as her eyes caught sight of the bloody washcloth. Again she looked at me, but this time her mouth did not ask the question that her eyes asked: *What happened?*

She stood there for a moment, her eyes moving between me and Hy-Lo's wrapped hand. Her eyes moved back and forth like the glass eyes of the dolls she brought me as a child.

"Pricilla," I called again as Delia moved by me and into the kitchen.

Hy-Lo slammed his wounded fist into the wall and left a bloody smudge there, before stomping into the bathroom again. I could hear the shower curtain being pulled back and forth on the rod. Back and forth until the pink seashell rings that held it gave way with six pops and the curtain fell crumpled into the tub. The lid to the hamper opened and the toilet seat slammed up and then down again. I knew Hy-Lo had lost it. "Kenzie!" he yelled at the top of his voice and flew out of the bathroom toward me.

I raised my hands to protect my face; he was on me before I could brace myself. He snatched at my arm and pulled me into him. His breath was hot on my face and it reeked with the stink of liquor and Camel cigarettes.

"Find that damn cat or it will be your behind. Do you understand me?" He was sweating and I could smell the white rum seeping out through his pores; it was a sick sweet smell that turned my stomach.

"Pricilla," I called again between the sobs that had started to tear through my body.

"Louder!" he screamed.

"Pricilla!" I matched his deafening tone with my own.

Delia was moving past me again, her features seeming to hang on her face. She wiped at the corner of her mouth as she moved around me; her steps were unsure, and she wobbled for a moment and I caught a whiff of something, but it was gone before I could place it.

"Kenzie!" Hy-Lo's voice snatched my attention away and I followed it into my room, where he was bent over in my closet tossing out toys, old dolls, and worn sneakers. Each item hit the floor with a loud thud that made me jump with each impact. A shoe box came flying out, barely missing Malcolm's leg as it crashed to the floor, the lid propelled through the air, and Malcom's matchbox car collection scattered across the floor like fifty colorful water bugs on the run.

Marbles, Easy Bake oven accessories, and Silly Putty eggs followed until the contents of the closet lay strewn across the floor.

"Throw it all out!" Hy-Lo yelled in a crazed voice. We moved quickly and without question. Both Malcolm and I ran to the kitchen to retrieve garbage bags. That's when we saw her. Pricilla had left the safety of her hiding place and had settled herself comfortably on the kitchen windowsill.

I froze.

Malcolm hadn't noticed her lounging there and had hurried back to the bedroom. I could hear Hy-Lo snapping the black plastic Hot Wheels tracks in two and the shrieking sound of the fire truck Mable had brought Malcolm for his birthday as Hy-Lo's foot came down on its shiny red back.

Pricilla's big black eyes looked into my own and then she lifted her leg to clean the soft fur of her belly.

I thought about raising the screen and tossing her out the window. I told myself that cats always land on their feet. But suppose that wasn't the case?

I was torn and my mind was going too fast for my body to keep up. I moved in slow motion toward her, but by then it was too late, Hy-Lo was standing behind me.

He knocked me to one side and snatched Pricilla up by her throat.

"No!" I yelled. "Daddy, please!" I begged and snatched at his shirt. Hy-Lo shrugged me off as effortlessly as if I had been a fly and I went hurling into the refrigerator, sending the mayonnaise jar off the metal shelf inside.

I followed him out into the living room and then to the small hallway that connected my bedroom with my parents'. He stopped there and swung open the closet door. He kept his coats in there: a brown corduroy car coat with a beige collar and a blue waist jacket he wore in the spring.

I knew I was still begging and pleading because I could feel my lips moving, my tongue hitting against the roof of my mouth, and my throat was going dry and tight, but I couldn't hear my words or any sound around me.

I knew I was begging because my hands were stretched out in front of me, my hands opening and closing—pulling at the air, hoping it would pull at Pricilla too. Her eyes were rolling up in her head and slipping back down to look at me before rolling up in her head again. Hy-Lo's fingers were locked around her neck, cutting off her air; her chest rose and fell, pulling in nothing.

Delia was sitting there on the edge of the bed, cocking her head left then right then left again. Her eyes were cloudy and she couldn't get her bottom lip to stay up. She looked like she wanted to say something, but it seemed every time she opened her mouth to try and do just that, the words vanished from her mind.

Hy-Lo held Pricilla way out from him while he dug through the toolbox he kept in his closet. Pricilla was almost dead by then, her paws moved like she was treading water at the shallow end of a pool—easy-like, without the worry that the bottom wouldn't be there if she had to stand up suddenly.

Hy-Lo pulled out his hammer, a big silver thing with a

black rubber handle; it had only been used once to pound a nail in the wall to hang up a picture of the black Jesus Christ over their bed.

He pulled Pricilla closer to him, shook her once or twice until her tail whipped up and her eyes slipped back down to look at me, and then he raised the hammer way up over her head.

The sound came back then, as if a vacuum were turned on inside my body, opening up my ears, allowing everything to rush in at one time. I heard Pricilla mew like a newborn baby, her eyes rolled over me one last time, and I could swear I saw a tear dribble from her eye and get caught in her long white whiskers. Then the sickening sound of the hammer as it crushed her small skull crawled through me, blood spattered the walls, and I fainted right where I stood.

The room was silent except for the sound of my bones rattling beneath my skin. My fingers were stiff and achy from gripping the podium so hard. Someone said it was okay and then another person said it would be all right. Words kept coming at me until the whole room was offering expressions of solace, and then the Korean girl came up and put her hand around my waist. "You did fine," she whispered in my ear as she guided me toward the back of the room. Someone offered me a Kleenex and I looked at the white sheet of tissue in astonishment, because I didn't even know I had been crying.

I watched as others stood, introduced themselves, and began to tell their stories, but my mind wasn't with them. The rest of the story, the part I'd left out, filled my brain and blocked out everything that was going on around me.

I took another sip of my now cold coffee, leaned my head back against the wall, and let the memory have its way with me. I let it come.

After Hy-Lo killed Pricilla I didn't speak to anyone for

two days. I just lay in bed and stared at the wall. I kept see-ing Pricilla looking to me for help and me unable to do any-thing. The sound of her skull being crushed filled my head like running water, and then there was the gun.

I can remember thinking about it every other minute. I touched the palm of my hand and imagined the cold feel of the metal there. The thought made my heart race.

Malcolm told me that Hy-Lo had wrapped Pricilla in a plastic bag and dumped her down the incinerator chute. He wasn't being mean but I punched him hard in his chest anyway.

On Monday Delia walked into my room and snapped the shade up. "Are you feeling better, Kenzie?" Her voice held little concern and she asked the question because it was her duty as a mother.

She was dressed in a crisp red dress that had a white sailor's collar. Her hair was pulled neatly back into a pony-tail and her lips were painted a cool burgundy.

"No," I mumbled and pulled the covers up over my head.

She stood there for a while. Maybe she was looking at me or maybe she was thinking about not ever coming back to that place once the big clock on the wall of her office struck five.

"Fine," she said and walked out. She pulled the door closed behind her.

I could hear Bugs Bunny outwitting Daffy Duck and Mal-colm's soft giggles sailing in from the living room. I imagined it was just after eight and both he and Delia would be leav-ing soon. Hy-Lo would be home from work an hour later.

My bladder was full and I squeezed my legs together against the pressure. The noise from the television stopped and Malcolm called to me from the living room: "See ya later, pencil-head!"

I rolled my eyes and turned onto my back, waiting to hear the heavy sound of the front door closing and the turn of the lock. I heard the door close but a blaring siren outside my window masked the sound of the turning lock.

Finally alone, I got up and slowly opened the door to my room. The low sound of the kitchen radio filled the emptiness of the house. My parents always kept the radio on—to deter would-be burglars.

I started toward the bathroom, but for some reason my feet led me to the living room. I stood staring down at the record player, convincing myself to reach in and get the gun. I was about to kneel down when I heard the crystal-clear sound of glass clinking against glass.

The blood drained from my head and I could feel my world about to spin. I bit down hard on the inside of my mouth and forced myself to take a shaky step toward the kitchen. What I'd imagined I would see was a man, dressed in black, a stocking cap covering his face with holes cut out for his eyes and mouth. He would have a large sack and would be dumping the silverware Mable gave Delia as a wedding gift into his sack.

What I saw instead was my mother leaning up against the refrigerator smoking a cigarette. She had just taken a sip out of one of the daisy-printed water glasses; her lipstick looked like a bloody fingerprint on top of the pale yellow petals of the painted flowers. Hy-Lo's half-empty bottle of vodka sat open on the stove.

I watched her tilt that bottle three times before she finally closed it up and placed it back on the counter behind the container of sugar.

She ran the water from the faucet into the glass and drank deeply, holding the water and then swishing it around in her mouth before swallowing. She took one last drag of her cigarette before shoving the burning tip beneath the rushing water.

When she turned around I was there with my hands folded across my chest.

She didn't speak for a long time, her face was blank, and that tawny color had returned to her eyes. Suddenly she didn't look so nice, her stature sloped, and her lips needed a fresh coat of color.

"Go back to bed or get dressed for school," she said and then grabbed her purse up from the table. "Lock the door behind me," she muttered as she walked past me and out the door.

Chapter Nine

I was still thinking about Delia's drinking problem when I arrived at Kings County Hospital the next day. She no longer had one, thank God. The hardest thing she drank now was coffee and Pepsi. Delia was the only one of us who had just stopped—no therapy, thirty-day detox, or court order. She just woke up one morning and decided she'd had enough. Delia was the strong one, although it had taken me years to realize that.

She had never really been a drinker, not even socially, but being around Hy-Lo made you do things you would not normally do.

I don't know when she started, but it wasn't long before she needed a drink to get her going in the morning and one to settle her down at night.

"You think it's easy dealing with your father?" she would spit at me every time I walked in on her taking a drink.

Our lives were already hard dealing with one drunk and I wanted to ask her how it would get better with her drinking too. But the alcohol had sharpened her tongue and her patience was wearing thinner each day.

She spent most of her time in bed staring at the television, refusing to take phone calls from the small circle of friends she was able to maintain over the years. When she did happen to answer the phone she lied her way out of a conversation, claiming she was just walking out the door or had only just come in from work.

Our diet had moved from full-cooked meals to TV dinners, Chinese takeout, overcooked burgers and undercooked fries from the diner.

Sunday was the only day she cooked and then it was something that didn't require a lot of time or energy. Those meals were bland and tasteless and usually ended up in the garbage beneath the tin cans and the plastic bread wrapping.

The bickering and fighting continued, and as nasty and violent as I had thought it was in the past, that was no comparison to what it had now come to.

For years my mother accused my father of seeking his courage from a bottle. If I had not believed that statement, Delia's transformation would have proven it without a shadow of a doubt.

She no longer backed away from Hy-Lo's words or his fists. They pounded on each other as often as newlyweds made love. While both of them walked away with battle scars, Delia was the one who took the brunt of the beatings.

Her arms and legs held nasty purple-blue marks that swelled and bulged through her clothes. Her face had been slapped and punched so many times that it started to look lopsided.

Her screams and his heavy breathing broke my sleep as he labored with the strength it took to throw her up against the walls of our apartment.

The Lowe family had become the talk of the building and our neighbors began to look on me with even more pity, if that were possible.

"Pinky said maybe it would be best if I don't spend so much time in your house," Glenna said one day as we walked home from school. Her words came out quick as if a dam in her mouth had broken.

I didn't look at her; I just shifted my book bag to the other shoulder and kept on walking.

"We heard them last night, you know." Her words were

slowing up. "Everybody heard," she added and moved her own book bag.

I didn't want to talk about it. I knew everybody heard. The whole block probably heard. Who wouldn't hear a man screaming and threatening to burn down the building at three in the morning? But even that would have been bearable. People threaten crazy things at that hour in the morning. I'd heard worse from the people across the courtyard. No, his words were the least embarrassing part.

Glenna cleared her throat and then continued. "Um, I heard Tyrone's mother telling Mr. Henry that she saw . . ." Her voice trailed off. She was searching for the right words and a tone that didn't make her sound too eager to know.

Sonia Baker was Tyrone's mother. She lived right across the hall from my family. Mr. Henry was an old Jewish man who owned the vegetable store on the corner.

Glenna jumped in front of me and our heads collided. "She said your mom and dad was fighting out in the hallway— naked?"

I rubbed my forehead and looked deep into Glenna's eyes. I wanted to slap her right across her black face. I wanted to shove her against the brick wall and punch her until she doubled over in pain and her nose started to bleed. At that moment I hated her and the simple life she had.

She was always whining and complaining about her mother never being home. Did she know what I would do to be alone, really alone?

No Malcolm, no Delia, and best of all no Hy-Lo. I would give my left arm and my eyesight.

The anger welled up in me and I felt it pushing through the top of my head. I clenched my fists and walked around her.

"Kenzie!" she yelled after me and then put her hand on my shoulder. I shrugged it away.

Why couldn't she wait for me to tell her the story? Why

couldn't she wait until my shame had withered to warm humiliation and I took her to my room and whispered the embarrassing details?

I would tell her that it had been quiet for two days. No arguing, no fighting, just silence. I would describe how he'd been sick with the flu for most of the week and how the medicine and the liquor were turning his stomach and kept him in the bathroom. He couldn't do both so he stuck with the medicine, knowing that in a few days he would be able to drink again. I would leave out the fact that Delia was doing her own drinking.

I would tilt my head back and take a deep breath before I revealed the time the commotion started. Perhaps I would say midnight instead of two, because midnight seemed so much more sinister.

"They were fucking." I would use that word because nasty words like that were forbidden and would cause us both look over our shoulders to make doubly sure that we were alone. "But something happened, he wanted something else that she wouldn't do."

Our minds would run away with the intimate details we'd read over and over again in the Harold Robbins paperbacks my mother kept hidden in her underwear drawer. We would each pick one illicit detail and imagine it was the one Delia simply would not and could not do for Hy-Lo.

"Anyway." I would wave my hand in the air dismissing those erotic images, because talking about my parents' sexual practices made me feel unclean. "She ran out of the room and into the bathroom. She was crying and he was pulling at her arm, trying to get her back in the bedroom."

Glenna would scoot closer to me and look deep into my eyes as if my words could somehow turn my irises into a moving-picture screen.

"I don't know what happened then. He got mad and hit her hard upside her head. He started yelling at her and accused her of doing *it* with everybody in the building while he was at work.

"She ran toward the kitchen, where he caught her by the hair and dragged her to the front door."

Glenna would have to lick her lips and remember to keep breathing.

"He opened the door and shoved her naked out into the hall."

I would nod my head up and down at Glenna's wide-open mouth.

"She just stood there screaming and crying, trying to cover her private parts."

I would have to take my own deep breath and maybe look down at my cuticles, hoping there would be something there for me to pick at after I told my shame.

"He closed the door and then opened it again because she was screaming her head off. Screaming and crying. Waking up the whole building.

"He called her a stupid bitch and forgot that he was butt naked too and went after her in the hall. They didn't stop until my grandmother came up and pulled them off of each other."

The story would leave us low on sugar and we would have to consume two packs of Now and Laters plus an Italian ice.

That's how it would have been, but Glenna had jumped the gun and ruined our whole routine.

I kept walking and she fell into step beside me. We walked in silence until we came to the front of the building.

"If you can't be my friend anymore, I understand." My words were out before I knew I'd even thought them.

Glenna looked at me and shook her head. She walked in ahead of me and held the door. I stepped into the hall waiting for her response. "See you tomorrow," she said and disappeared up the stairs.

* * *

"That was embarrassing," I heard myself say bitterly,

"'Scuse me?" the man's voice floated around the curtain again. "Miss?" he called out after some time had passed and I still did not respond.

When had I climbed the stairs and pulled up the chair? My last recollection was walking from the bus stop toward the hospital and now here I was facing Hy-Lo once more.

I looked down at the green pass the hospital issued; it was clutched tightly in my hands. I thought my blackout days were over—evidently not.

"Miss?" the voice came again and still I did not respond.

Was he an idiot, didn't he know when he was being ignored? Thank God he didn't have legs or he would have gotten himself out of his hospital bed, pulled a chair up beside me, and invited himself into my world. I pinched my wrists hard at that last callous thought.

"Miss?" He wasn't going to stop.

"I'm not speaking to you," I replied, hoping that would shut him up and it did.

He grumbled something and I heard the drawer to his nightstand open and close. Staticky music filled the room and then dropped to a low hum before anyone could complain. He had turned to his small transistor radio for company, leaving Hy-Lo and me alone again.

Hy-Lo looked the same. Time was not being kind to him. I sat parallel to his toes, even though something foreign inside urged me closer.

"No," I whispered to the air and folded my arms across my chest.

How much longer, how many more days before the bobbing green and red lights that monitored his heart finally went long and even? I wondered.

I peered out the window and waited for some long-ago offense Hy-Lo had committed against me to rise up and fill me with anger. But none came and I nodded on and off until Nurse D. Green came in to check his stats and change his intravenous bags. When she smiled, I smiled back and it was genuine because my sleep, for the first time in years, had been clean and clear of Hy-Lo.

I left him early that day; something pushed me out into the winter air. Some kind of feeling resembling joy took my hand and pulled me out into the cold bright day.

I was suspect of that light airy emotion. Joy. Wouldn't trust it completely if Jesus Himself wrapped it up in shiny paper with red bows and presented it to me on my wedding day. It was as foreign to me as France.

I chastised myself as I walked the length of the block toward the bus stop. The wind was picking up, swirling lost newspapers and candy wrappers around my feet. I whistled to myself for company as I waited for my bus to arrive and smiled at the strangers who looked on me with anxious eyes. I boarded the first of two buses that would take me home. It was just after three and they were filled with rowdy children.

I transferred buses and took the only seat available, between a woman who smelled like curried chicken and a man who smelled like a distillery. I held my breath as the bus snaked its way around the double-parked cars and delivery trucks that clogged Pitkin Avenue.

My stop was coming up and a woman I recognized as a former neighbor threw me a quick glance before abruptly standing up and hurrying toward the opening doors. I don't know what possessed me to call out her name; maybe it was because she'd pretended not to see me or to know me, or maybe it was because she wore that green and white sheer polka-dot scarf like it was April instead of December. She knew it was an April scarf, she knew it because the last time I saw her it was April and I was grieving instead of rejoicing in the spring.

That damn scarf was inappropriate then because of the occasion, it was inappropriate now because of the season.

"Mrs. Fulton . . . Mrs. Fulton!" I yelled her name so loud that even the mangy dogs that sniffed the garbage on the corner took notice.

"Uh, yes?" Mrs. Fulton turned to face me. It had been nearly two years since I'd seen her, and except for the extra weight and the gray hair, she still looked the same. The same thin lips and bulging eyes. The same lingering scent of Jean Naté talcum powder and cocoa butter lotion. Funny how some things never change.

We eyed each other for a long time, she pretending not to know who I was, me wondering how long she would want to play the game before I called her out and embarrassed her right there on Euclid Avenue.

"Oh, um, you Delia's girl, right?" she finally said, squinting her eyes at me. Her shoulders were hitched up in a tense pose and she clasped her hands tightly in front of her. Her eyes looked everywhere but at me. She was thinking about the last time we were face-to-face. Or maybe she was thinking about the time before that. The incident that brought us together and then tore us apart.

All the while I watched her green polka-dot scarf and restrained myself from snatching it from her neck.

"That's right, do I look so different?" I asked and wiped at my face as if I could wipe away the mask that suddenly made me a stranger in her eyes.

"Um, no, not really. Well, a little thinner, I guess, but still the same really." Mrs. Fulton turned and looked over her shoulder, hoping to see someone she knew passing by. Someone to save her from me—but only strangers looked back at her.

We stood there for a long time, no idle chitchat passing between us, just the wind and the chill of what had been lost. I stretched a bit and she yawned daintily into her hand, before pulling at that damn spring scarf and peering down at her shoes.

I wanted to ask how Devon was doing. Was he in college? Maybe going pro after graduation? What had Devon accomplished? I wondered.

"Well . . ." I said instead.

"Well," she repeated and scratched at the back of her ear. "It was nice seeing you again. Say hello to your mom and dad for me," she said and tugged again at the scarf.

"Yeah, okay, I'll do that," I responded and just stood there watching her hurry away from me, the thin end of the scarf flapping hopelessly behind her.

I started not to mention it to Delia but it spilled out of my mouth when I opened it up to shove a forkful of spaghetti into it.

"I saw Mrs. Fulton today."

Delia had already eaten and so she was sprawled out on the sofa watching a rerun of *The Cosby Show*. Her head spun around so quickly that I thought it would rock and tumble from her neck like a broken toy.

"What—?" She picked up the remote and lowered the television volume. "What did you say?" Her voice was filled with astonishment.

"I saw Mrs. Fulton today," I repeated casually.

"Umph," Delia sounded and turned to face the television again. She increased the volume until someone from the next-door apartment banged on the wall and yelled for her to turn it down.

"Mom." Her name was like a prayer on my lips. She turned to face me and I fully expected her eyes to be filled with tears, but they were dry as a bone.

Our eyes held each other for a long time and I realized that every day Delia looked older around her eyes and mouth.

"What she say?" Delia asked, and the eager look on her face told me that she wanted, like I did, to hear that Janice Fulton's son Devon was mangled, paralyzed, or dead. Delia sat up and leaned forward expectantly.

"She asked about you and . . . him."

Him was Hy-Lo; his name became vinegar in my mouth and so I found it hard to say.

"What—" she began and then stopped to draw on the stagnant hot air of the apartment. "What she say about her Devon?"

"Nothing," I replied and dropped my eyes. "I didn't ask," I said to my knees. I could hear Delia sigh and then ease herself back down into the worn sofa.

I punished my mouth for mentioning the incident. I bit my lips until they bled and then I hurt my tongue by licking the bruised blood away.

Delia turned the volume back up on the television once she knew there was nothing left for her to listen for. "Oh," she mumbled and reached for her pack of cigarettes.

I had failed her. I wasn't even able to bring home a bit of news that might have made her life better, or at least her day. I watched her for a long time before I decided that I could come up with nothing that would make it okay for her. Two years, and I couldn't come up with anything that would make it okay.

I moved down the hall toward my room and stopped, as I always did, to straighten the framed photograph of Malcolm. He was smiling at me with his crooked front teeth and dressed in a bright green polyester shirt that was unbuttoned enough to show the dark brown of his chest and the three hairs that grew there like the first green blades of spring grass. He thought he was so cool and so did the girls who chased behind him.

I smiled to myself and ran my thumb across the glass, leaving a wide clean streak through the powder-fine dust. I missed him.

Chapter Ten

It was 1979. I was thirteen years old and rap music had a foothold on the black youth of America. We all dreamed of spinning records behind the Sugar Hill Gang and Kurtis Blow.

But my musical taste stretched far beyond the rhyming rhythms that filled the airwaves and pounded hard out of the boom boxes that sat under park benches or rested on corners while young men spun their bodies at breakneck speeds on their heads or elbows like tops on large pieces of cardboard for change and applause.

Me, I spent hours in front of the mirror singing along with Natalie Cole, Aretha Franklin, and Love Unlimited. The bottoms from my pajamas were on my head, the legs hanging down my back. Flannel hair. In my mind I had long silky tresses and I swung them back and forth to the music. My microphone was a comb or brush and my audience the cosmetics that lined my dresser top.

I was happy in my musical world where I was the star and everybody loved me. In concert I was free to shake and shimmy my body all over the stage, stopping to blow a kiss or catch a long-stemmed rose.

My fans adored me and begged me for more and I gave it to them over and over again until I was breathless or until my mother screamed for me to turn it off. I hated for the music to stop because when it did the apartment would become too quiet. I could hear the roaches moving in between the walls and the soft padding feet of the people who lived above us. I could hear the screaming cry of a police siren ten blocks away and the twisting snap of the cap on the short neck of Delia's vodka bottle.

She had them hidden around the apartment, in the box of Christmas ornaments that sat at the back of Hy-Lo's closet and in the corner of her closet behind the three pairs of worn-out shoes she owned. The ones she had the shoemaker dye over and over to fit with the seasons. The ones that needed new lifts and soles every three months or so. She had them hidden in the pocket of the patchwork leather coat she had been so proud of in the '70s, the one with the fake fur collar and the bell sleeves. The one she couldn't bear to part with even though Hy-Lo had flown into a rage in '78 and sliced it with a straight razor clean down the middle.

I had two to contend with now. Both of my parents lived life from the bottom of a bottle. I hated Hy-Lo even more because I knew he had driven her to it.

I watched Delia withdraw from Malcolm and me. She spent most of her time curled up in bed, too drunk to cook, clean, or talk. I became the caregiver, bed-maker, homework checker, and TV dinner heater-upper. Many a night I shoved the tiny foil-wrapped dinners into the hot oven and thought about shoving my head in right beside them.

Hy-Lo came home one Saturday morning and the sink was full of dishes, there was dust gray and thick covering his stereo and the top of the floor-model television. The bathroom sink was littered with toothpaste droppings, the mirror above it was smeared and speckled, and the white ceramic floor was blotchy with dirt.

He walked from room to room taking in the untidiness that surrounded him. He said nothing but the anger was building behind his eyes. Delia was sitting on the edge of her bed staring blankly at the small black-and-white television. Her hair was a bird's nest and her blue flannel robe was buttoned wrong. She had risen with the sun and had

had two screwdrivers before the garbage trucks came to haul the refuse away.

Hy-Lo looked at her but said nothing. He walked to the kitchen and for a long time there was no noise, just the sound of my breath and the beating of my heart, and then I heard it, the twisting snap of the cap that was to begin the day.

I was thirteen and had been hit by Hy-Lo too many times to count. But he had hit me as a father would hit his child. The blows were hard, but did not carry the full force of his strength. I did not know this was the case until that day, when something in the back of my mind snapped and my small fists found themselves pounding mercilessly on his back.

He had been in the kitchen for more than an hour. My bladder was full but I did not want to move from my bed and walk across the floor to the bathroom to relieve myself. The flushing of the toilet would disturb the peace of the apartment and most likely become the starting bell for the fight to begin. So I pushed my hands between my legs and forced it back up inside me, even though my kidneys ached.

The sunlight crept around the loose corners of the window shades and partially filled the room with its morning rays. Malcolm snored softly from the lower bunk, and the sound of Julia Child's voice seeped through the wall like one of her thick creamy sauces. Delia coughed. Maybe she inhaled too deeply on her Newport or maybe her saliva slipped down the wrong pipe. Whatever it was, it caused a thin stream of urine to break free and saturate my hands and dampen the sheet below me. I cussed beneath my breath, but I can't remember if it was because of my wet panties or the sound of Hy-Lo walking across the floor.

"Delia." He spoke low in that tone that assured you you were going to get a whipping.

She didn't answer. Maybe she didn't even turn her head from the television to look at him.

"Delia," he said again, his voice a bit heavier, the annoyance in his words thicker, more dangerous. "This house is a mess. Get up and clean up. Now."

The "now" is what brought the floodwaters down. My mattress was soaked through; the smell was ripe almost immediately and then came the sound of the slap that threw my mother off the bed and onto the floor.

I don't remember jumping from the bed or even running into my parents' room. Although I can recall quite clearly my father standing over Delia, his arm drawn back, his fist a ball of steel flesh poised in midair ready to descend upon my mother's high cheekbones and Cherokee-African nose.

He struck her and left her curled into a ball beside the radiator. There was blood on the radiator from where her head had hit the metal. And there was blood dripping from her forehead as she whimpered. She looked up at him expectantly. No, actually wanting.

Maybe he saw that look too. Maybe it scared him. Or maybe it was the blood; but I think it was her eyes and the fearlessness that bloomed in them.

I jumped on his back and felt the heat of his body between my wet thighs. I beat at his head and shoulders until he spun around hard enough to shake me free. But I was on him again, like a wildcat gone mad. I beat at his back and kicked at his shins. And then he did it. He hit me like a man hits another man in the boxing ring. He hit me like a man hits another man in the street when they're done with words and only fists will do. He hit me like he hit Delia, and the blow took my breath away and sent me flying into the dresser. There was a crack and then the air became thin, the room swam around me and went black.

I had seen Hy-Lo's face look tired, mischievous, mean, and angry. I had never seen fear. As we waited in the emergency room of Kings County Hospital I watched as fear marched back and forth across his face just as many times as he crossed the cream-colored marble floors of the room.

Hy-Lo's eyes were wide and his tone became increasingly humble with every trip he took to the registration window. "Um, how much longer, ma'am?" I heard him say.

"Ma'am" echoed in my ears and even pulled a smile from deep inside me. How much did it take for Hy-Lo to call someone ma'am? Evidently a broken rib inside the body of his only daughter.

My head was resting in Delia's lap; my legs stretched out on the brown chairs of the waiting room. Her hand stroked my forehead nervously. It did not soothe me, but I knew she found comfort in doing it. Every now and then she would bend her head down and look into my face. "Soon," she would say, and her breath, stinking of Newports and vodka, wafted over me.

My sleep was periodically interrupted by my mother's words and the low hum that came from the sick people around me. Someone would moan, cough, or sneeze and then the moan would come again. I thought Delia should be moaning. Moaning for the gash in her forehead and the pain in her life. But she had found places to put those hurts; they were stored in tiny nip bottles in dark corners and holiday boxes in our apartment.

Before we had left the apartment, as I lay semiconscious on the floor of her bedroom, Delia had taken a moment to fix herself up as best she could. She tried hard to hide the violence that was in her life by ripping up an old dustrag and wrapping it tight around her head. A large dark spot, so red it was nearly black, filled the gray whiteness of the cloth almost immediately. Delia put on a camel-colored tam and pulled it down low over the makeshift bandage, and to complete the disguise she put on her Jackie Onassis shades, the ones she wore when her eyes were swollen. She wore those a lot.

"Lowe. Kenzie Lowe!" The doctor came out with his clipboard in hand and called my name.

"She's right here," Hy-Lo answered for me.

Delia shifted and gently lifted my head from her lap. "Take your time, baby," she said as I slowly turned my body and brought my feet to rest on the floor.

"Ow . . . ow . . . ow," I cried out as the pain shot up my side and my stomach flip-flopped inside me.

"Okay, okay," Delia said and swallowed hard. I stood up and took a step, but the pain brought me down to my knees.

"Nurse!" the doctor yelled out. His voice did not carry concern but annoyance. "Nurse!" he yelled again and scratched the bald space on top of his head. "Get this girl a wheelchair."

A woman in white appeared beside me. "Excuse me," she said, stepping around my mother and grabbing me under my arms.

I screamed out as she settled my body into the worn leather of the chair. Hy-Lo rushed to me; the fear was working overtime on his face, his bottom lip hung nearly down to his chin, and his eyes were open wide, blinking back the artificial brightness of the fluorescent light above our heads.

"You remember what I told you?" His whisper was a tremor of words and I knew the fear had hold of his vocal chords too. I didn't drop my eyes in an obedient gesture or nod my head in agreement. Instead I held his eyes with mine until the nurse wheeled me into the examining room. I was in control now; his fate rested in the hairline fracture of my rib and the soft tissue of my tongue.

The doctor probed and prodded me and then sent me for X-rays. In between Dr. Katz asked questions, questions that made my mother bite at her already ragged fingernails. "So—" The doctor looked at his clipboard, flipped through two sheets of paper, and then said my name. He said it slowly with the uncertainty of a man from the Midwest unused to names with African origins. "Kenzie, how did you manage to hurt yourself?" There was no suspicion in his voice. His question was a required one as stated by the Board of Certified Physicians. He probably asked the same question over a hundred times during that shift alone.

I shot a look at Delia. I caught the spite that flickered in her eyes. She couldn't take a stand. Not yet anyway. The right response would be her first step forward and away from Hy-Lo. She held her breath and waited for me to answer. Waited for me to help her climb out. Her eyes urged me to tell the truth.

"I, uh . . ." I began, the words climbing up the inside of my throat. Tired words that once out would allow me to be a child again. They moved too slowly and stopped often to rest. I blinked at the white curtain that surrounded and separated me from the moans, coughs, and sneezes of the others. My back was to Hy-Lo and I heard him shift behind me. Perhaps he was adjusting his jacket or just scratching the short hairs that had popped up on his chin during the few hours we had been there. But I knew his movement was a warning, a reminder of the lie he wanted me to tell.

"When they ask you what happened, you tell them you slipped in the bathroom. The floor was wet. You tell them that!" he yelled out above my screams of pain as I lay across the backseat of his green Oldsmobile.

"I slipped on the wet floor in the bathroom." I said it, I told the lie he had made up for me and the tired truth rolled back down my throat. Delia almost crumbled and the dim light in her eyes went out.

The doctor nodded his head and wrote something down. "I got two kids and . . ." he started to say, but the rest of his words escaped me, lost in the the folds of the curtain that surrounded us.

Things were quiet in the apartment for days after my accident. There was no bickering, fighting, or the sounds of a bottle being opened, none except soda bottles and the grape juice I loved. That afternoon after we came home from the hospital and picked Malcolm up from Grandma Gwenyth's place, I lay in my bed, my ear pressed to the wall listening to Hy-Lo promise Delia he would never drink again. He said "sorry" more times than I care to remember. And then I cringed because I thought I heard a whimper and it was not the one I was familiar with; it was not Delia's.

Hy-Lo was lying, of course. This was his way of redeeming himself and gaining forgiveness from Delia. He hadn't forgotten the look in her eyes from that night.

Delia did not accept his apology; but the fact that she did not hustle Malcolm and me out of the apartment and straight to the warm comfort of Mable's home must have told Hy-Lo she had forgiven him. He threw in his promise for good measure like the cement around the base of a flagpole. Just in case.

That lie rolled so effortlessly from his mouth that even I believed him. He never apologized to me or promised me anything; maybe he thought his words to Delia were good enough for both of us.

Hy-Lo did his best to avoid me. It was as if we had switched places. He would step out of my way and excuse himself if he needed to pass near me at one of the tight corners in the apartment. He kept the shelves stocked with lime Jell-O and canned peaches, my favorite foods. And he did not harass Malcolm or call him those names that hurt his young manhood and fertilized the hate he had growing inside him.

The change was stressful; it hung around us, thick as an early autumn fog. You could cut it with your index finger and serve it up as pie. We moved around each other as if walking on broken glass, insipid smiles on our lips and cautious glimmers in our eyes. Even though our life now was uncomfortable, we hoped it wouldn't change, but then hope had never been something we counted on.

For a week the brown paper bag that was a usual fixture

beneath Hy-Lo's arm did not accompany him through the door every morning. For a week he drank Pepsi by the liter and smoked so much that a thick haze filled the apartment and clung to the ceiling like an awning.

"How ya doing, kid?" he inquired on my third day of convalescence. His tone was light and carefree. He spoke to me as if visiting a friend in the hospital; he spoke as if he had nothing to do with my being in a brace and in pain.

His words took me by surprise and I responded: "Fine." I gazed at him over my *Teen Beat* magazine.

"Good, good," he said and smiled.

I saw that his face had lost the immutable crimson color and that his cheeks had deflated a bit. His eyes were cloudless and his words came out like crystals, clear and clean.

"Lemme know if you need something." He threw those words over his shoulder as easily as a father tosses a ball to his son just learning to catch.

"Who was that man?" I asked the room aloud.

On the eighth day he came home later than usual, almost twelve noon, and I was reading another stolen erotic story. Jackie Collins had me riveted. I was moist and breathless all at once. I heard the front door open and close but that did not distract me. There was a new man living in my house and sleeping with my mother. He did not raise his voice or his hand and he did not walk into my room unannounced or uninvited. I read on.

It was the silence that followed the closing of the front door. The utter stillness of the apartment, the familiar quiet that always followed the storm. I closed the book and slipped it under my pillow. I pulled the covers up under my chin and shut my eyes. My body began to shake and my mouth went dry. A long while passed before I heard the water glass clink softly down into the porcelain kitchen sink. He was done. How had I missed the sound of the bottle's top?

Hy-Lo crept into my room on the balls of his feet; I could

hear the floorboards squeaking beneath him. I tried not to flinch and then he was standing over me and the air was sucked from around me.

The aroma of alcohol covered me like a wool blanket, my skin began to itch, and I wanted to open my mouth and gulp for air. Instead I lay as still as a rock and waited.

He began to hum to himself, some odd tune he'd hum whenever the mood hit him. It was a mocking tune that I'd hated the first time I heard it. He had hummed it when he ordered me to get the belt from his drawer, to pull my pants down and bend over. "Don't you scream, don't you dare," he had said between notes, and then brought the leather strap down across my behind. I was six years old and had broken a water glass.

He hummed and walked over to the shade and pulled it down, blocking out the sunlight, and then he closed the curtains, pulling my room into total darkness. I kept my breathing steady even though my heart was going wild inside my chest.

He came and stood over me again, hummed once more, and then left. We had switched back.

Chapter Eleven

I didn't know how many days I'd been coming here. Maybe three. Maybe eight. I didn't know for sure. The days melded into each other and the hours disappeared altogether. But I realized as I walked down the street away from the hospital and toward the bus stop that the cold was deeper than the first few days, so deep that it reminded me of the blue ice packs that sat next to the frozen meats and bagged vegetables in our freezer on Rogers Avenue. The ice packs that Delia placed over the swells on her face, arms, and legs after he beat her.

I realized that time had escaped me and Thanksgiving had come and gone without my even noticing it. And now the windows of the apartments in the projects and some homes a block away were filled with flashing red and green lights, and some front doors had gaudy Christmas wreaths and cracked plastic signs with faded Santas that said *Happy Holidays* and *Merry Christmas*.

I couldn't even remember how we spent Thanksgiving Day or what we ate. I didn't even remember if I came to the hospital on that day. I knew that Mable didn't call, or maybe she tried and the computer voice told her that the number had been temporarily disconnected and no further information was available. The phone was turned back on now.

She used to call all the time, but she was old now and tired from trying to scream and cuss some sense into Delia, and plus she was still hurting about Malcolm, and Sam's mind was going so she had to remember to keep the doors locked and the windows closed or he'd wander off down the dirt road that sat in front of their house in Poke County, Georgia. Down home.

So she called only on the holidays and sometimes on the odd Sunday. "There's room here if you wanna come on down," she always reiterated before saying she loved us both and hanging up the phone. She had a double-wide trailer with four bedrooms and two living rooms. A big front yard and even bigger backyard. There were pecan trees and watermelon patches skirting the property. Plenty of country space, good country living, and best of all, no Hy-Lo.

But moving to Georgia would be like moving to the other side of the world for me, and so I wouldn't go unless Delia would, and she wouldn't go and wouldn't say why exactly. So here we remained.

I approached the hospital and saw that two large wreaths had been hung on the glass doors of the hospital entrance-way and behind those doors a brightly decorated tree was now sitting in the center of the lobby. I walked in and there was Christmas music being played over the intercom system but the lyrics were constantly interrupted by announcements.

The hospital gift shop was bustling with people as visitors snatched up premade holiday baskets, potted poinsettias, and plush stuffed reindeer dolls.

I walked through the double glass door and tried to go straight to the Visitors Information window. I tried and failed and found myself standing on line in the gift shop behind two elderly people and their granddaughter.

"Cash or charge?" the pimple-faced cashier asked when I stepped up to the counter.

"Cash," I responded, looking down at the glass ball with the floating snow and smiling St. Nick. I didn't even remember picking it up but I stuck my hand into the pocket of my coat anyway. My fingers moved across bus fare and an old Certs mint.

"Sixteen twenty-four," he said without looking at me as he started to pick at a pimple that was pushing through above his eyebrow.

I jiggled the change and then dug deep into the other pocket. There was nothing there, just a wide hole and the air that pushed through it.

The pimple was picked and was now an angry red dot on his face. "Sixteen twenty-four," the cashier said again. His voice was impatient and I couldn't tell if it was because I had no money and was holding up the line or because his hands roamed his face and could not find another plump subject to burst.

"Yes, one moment," I said as I unbuttoned my coat and dug my hands into the pockets of my jeans. Annoyed whispers floated from behind me just as my fingers curled around a piece of something in my pocket.

I pulled it out and saw that it was a five-dollar bill. The cashier's eyebrows raised and his mouth twisted. "Sixteen—" he started to say again.

"I know," I said cutting him off. I dug into the other pocket and pulled out a dollar. "Look, I left my money at home or something. I'll just take a . . . um . . ." My eyes traveled over the stuffed plush toys and plastic candy canes and then settled on the poinsettia. "That," I said and pointed to the large leafy red and green plant on the shelf behind him.

He rolled his eyes at me and ran his hands through his slicked-back hair. "Nine ninety-nine," he said. "Plus tax," he added and cocked his head to one side.

"Oh," I replied and looked down at the crumpled five- and one-dollar bills I'd thrown onto the counter.

More annoyed whispers, clucking tongues, and the sound of merchandise being shifted from one hand to the other. I was so embarrassed; too embarrassed to pick up my money and walk out, so I just stood there with my head down and tried to keep my tears inside.

"Here you go." The voice came from beside me. I saw a ten-dollar bill hit the counter. The hand was small, brown, and delicate. It picked up the one-dollar bill and placed it on top of the ten. "Here," the voice said again and then the hand pushed the five-dollar bill back toward me.

I raised my head and turned my face to look into the eyes of Nurse D. Green. "I—" I started to say, but she put her hand up and slowly shook her head.

"It's okay," she said and smiled.

The cashier sighed in disgust. He snatched the poinsettia off the shelf and was about to slam it down on the counter, but then he caught the look in Nurse D. Green's eyes and thought better of it.

"Thank you," I said as I picked up the change and the plant, and then I turned to thank Nurse D. Green, but she was gone.

The poinsettia looked out of place on the hospital nightstand. More than out of place, unhappy. It had lost its vividness and its leaves drooped as soon as we entered the room.

I wanted to move it, turn it around to show its best side, but that would mean coming close to him again and it had taken all that I had just to lean over and place the plant down on the stand. I couldn't come so close again so soon, so I left it as it was.

Nurse D. Green came in and commented on how beautiful it was. She looked at it as if it were the first time she was seeing it, as if it weren't her hard-earned money that made its presence possible. Its leaves lifted a bit in her presence.

"Uh-huh," I responded in awe and was about to thank her again, but a buzzing sound from the next room caught her attention and she dashed out before I could even open my mouth to speak.

My mind traveled between the poinsettia, Nurse D. Green, Christmas, Malcolm, and Delia. They were swirling, restless, destructive thoughts, like the twisters that battered the Midwest during the summer. The thoughts made my head ache and I pinched my wrist to try and distract myself.

I watched Hy-Lo and the liquids that bubbled through the tubes and kept him alive. I thought again about ending it all. Just pulling the plug from the wall and putting a stop to the memories.

My hand jerked beneath me and I thought for a moment that I would actually do it, but then I felt shame open up inside of me and spread through me until my body shook with the intensity of it.

I didn't recognize this thing in me that was changing my hate, molding it into compassion, trying to sculpt it into understanding and forgiveness. I shook my head against the thought and cleared my throat against the thick film it left there.

I would force myself to remember the smell of hate, the feel of pain, and the sense of rejection he instilled in me every single day of my life. I would remember and then this feeling of forgiveness that was laying root inside of me would dissipate and the hate would blossom again, like gardenias in spring.

I moved my chair closer, leaned back, and waited. It was the carolers who roamed the hallways of the hospital singing to the sick and dying that helped take me back to Rogers Avenue. It was their small voices filled with Christmas cheer, the way they sang "O Little Town of Bethlehem," and how that song happened to be playing in the background on that horrible December 25.

Christmas seemed to have come quickly that year. Perhaps because all of my energy had been focused on refereeing Hy-Lo and Delia—"Let's keep it clean, guys!"—housework, and school. I'd become withdrawn and distanced myself from Glenna. My bruises were worse than Delia's because I was bruised on the inside where they could not be bandaged or treated with antiseptic.

Snow came two days before Christmas; it covered the ground like a blanket of cotton that came up to our knees and spilled over and into the tops of our rubber boots. I had prayed for snow, so much snow that the city would come to a halt and no one would be able to make it to my house for Christmas dinner. Every year there was a scene, some altercation that required police presence. Hy-Lo slapping Delia, Hy-Lo punching one of his brothers. Always Hy-Lo, always liquor, always police.

I smiled up at the sky and thanked God aloud. My words came out in frosty bits of air that disappeared before my eyes. And then the next day the temperature climbed to fifty and melted it all away. We would have Christmas dinner after all and a new nightmare would be created to fill my adult dreams.

Gwenyth came outfitted in a flowing red dress that was so long it dusted our parquet floors, gathering pine needles and bits of fluff as she moved between the kitchen and living room. I watched her adorned in her fake pearls and glass stud earrings and told myself she was Christmas Past: a specter of what once was.

Mable and Sam came dressed in jeans and matching white sweatshirts with red bows and green fluorescent letters that screamed *Ho! Ho! Ho!* across the front.

They came laden down with shopping bags filled with colorful wrapped boxes that held gifts for Malcolm and me.

Delia had not spoken to Mable for more than two weeks and the air between them was sour. Delia barely brushed her lips against Mable's cheek and only offered Sam a stiff hug and a quiet hello. They were representatives of Christmas Present.

Charlie, Randy, and Charlie's wife Carol had arrived right after Mable and Sam. We heard them in the hall of the

building before they even rang the doorbell. They were rau-
cous and half-drunk when they stepped through the door.
They threw greetings over their shoulders at us and made a
beeline straight to the television stand that had been set up
as a bar for the occasion.

Charlie looked like Hy-Lo but he was taller and heavier
and bald. Randy was the odd one of the three; he was short,
barely five feet tall, and as dark as the deepest summer
night. Carol, Charlie's wife, was tall and sinewy. Her neck
was thicker than Charlie's was and her hands were just as
large as his, but you forgot about her size when she opened
her mouth to speak and her words came out sounding like
Mickey Mouse.

"Where are the kids?" Delia asked as they struggled to
remove their coats with one hand while the other hand held
their mixed drinks.

"Home," Carol said and then, "You got any cherries, you
know the sweet ones?"

"Like the one between your legs?" Charlie said and
slapped her on the behind. Everyone around the liquor
broke into a fit of laughter; the rest of us remained solemn.

Delia rolled her eyes and looked embarrassedly over her
shoulder at Malcolm and me. I shrugged my shoulders at
her; we had heard worse from Charlie.

Mable sucked her teeth loudly. "There are children present!" she said in a stern voice and rolled her eyes. Sam patted her knee and scratched at the top of his head.

Malcolm and I stopped unwrapping our gifts and sat
quietly down on the floor beside the tree, crossing our legs
Indian style and resting our chins in the palms of our hands.
We had been denied the pleasure of the Christmas show at
Radio City Music Hall, but we would have front seats for the
show that was about to take place in our living room.

They ignored Mable's comment and talked loudly
amongst themselves, never moving away from the TV stand

and the six bottles of liquor it held. "Well?" Carol said in exasperation and turned to face Delia, who had positioned herself against the wall.

Delia's arms were folded across her chest and she chewed nervously on her bottom lip. "Huh?" she said.

The glass that Carol waved back and forth before her eyes broke Delia's spell. "Cherries, Delia, cherries," she said in an annoyed voice as my mother took the glass from her hand.

"Cheez!" Carol added and then joined in on the tail laughter of the joke.

They behaved as if we weren't there, as if they still stood among the lowlifes who found themselves on a barstool at the Blue Moon on Christmas Day, instead of on the sofa, sipping cider, surrounded by family.

Gwenyth stood, smoothed her Christmas dress, and took a step toward them. "Randy." She called his name sharply and I saw some color drain away from his face.

"Mother," he said, then stepped forward and planted a loving kiss on her cheek. "Merry Christmas," he slurred and Gwenyth's face contorted against the rankness of his breath.

She said nothing else; her eyes condemned his behavior and dismissed him all at the same time. He lowered his head, and had he a tail he would have stuffed it between his legs. Instead he suddenly became aware that we were in the room and began to move between us, offering greetings and words filled with holiday cheer.

Gwenyth's eyes passed over Charlie and Carol and then fell on the bottles of liquor. She licked her lips and turned her attention to Charlie. He would be more difficult to approach. He was the oldest of her sons and knew more of Gwenyth's life than the others. He held that fact over her head like the sharp blade of a guillotine. "Charlie." Her voice was still sharp but there was an air of cautiousness surrounding it. "Charlie," she repeated when she found she was still looking at his back.

Carol had stopped laughing and turned to look at Gwenyth. She looked her up and down and then her eyes settled on the fake pearls around Gwenyth's neck. She sniffed and became aware of her own clothing. A tattered denim jacket that would not have kept out the slight chill of a spring day. A black scarf covered in lint, fraying in the middle and at the ends. She pulled at her jacket and then touched the beige corduroys that had a large ink spot on the knee.

Gwenyth pursed her perfectly heart-shaped, red-painted lips at Carol and stepped around Charlie, bringing those lips close to his ear. Carol seemed mesmerized by Gwenyth: her clothes, her sheer perfection in a sea of imperfection. Carol's hands went to her hair that was pulled back into a ragged ponytail and then to her face. She was as black as the lumps of coal Hy-Lo threatened to leave beneath the tree for us, but with all of her midnight skin, the darkest blue bruise stood out on her face like a smudged thumbprint.

Charlie's head was bobbing up and down in response to Gwenyth's moving lips. She had managed to rest one delicate hand on his shoulder, and had moved in closer so that she could see the entirety of his face.

We all watched and waited. Delia had Carol's empty glass in one hand and a jar of maraschino cherries in the other. Randy had taken a seat on the hassock nearest to Malcolm and me. Carol had moved away from mother and son and had settled herself on the couch near Mable. Mable had scooted closer to Sam while staring intently at the bruises on Carol's cheek and neck, the keloid scars on the back of her hand, and the worn sneakers that covered her feet. Mable wriggled her nose at the stench of alcohol that seeped from Carol's pores and the sour smell that came from not bathing, which clung to her skin. I closed my eyes and hoped that Carol wasn't the ghost of Christmases to come.

"Mother!" He turned on her and broke the odd tranquillity that had settled around the room. Charlie's eyes were wide and red and suddenly he looked like someone other than the playful uncle who slipped me a dollar whenever he didn't need one from me.

Gwenyth took a step back, anger flashed in her eyes, and for a moment I saw her hand jerk as if to rise up and strike him. "Charlie!" she bellowed back at him but did not recover her spot on the floor inches from her son.

"Um, Charlie . . ." Delia started to interrupt but thought better of it and fell silent again.

Malcolm and I leaned forward, our eyes widened, and we held our breath.

"Where the hell you think you going, Mother? To the fucking Christmas Ball?"

Charlie snatched at the material of Gwenyth's red dress. His words were filled with a spitefulness that liquor alone could not have produced.

"Always trying to show yourself off, like some type of goddamn queen." He looked at her for a long time before he spoke again. "You ain't shit!" he yelled at her and slammed his glass down hard on the makeshift bar. Two bottles toppled over the side and went crashing to the ground.

There was more to be said, but not right then. The story, the one that I was born into and could not escape, would come out later in life when I needed to understand.

Hy-Lo walked in just as the jagged pieces of glass scattered across the floor. It was almost two in the afternoon and the ham was still baking in the oven. The greens were done and so were the yams and the potato salad. The cornbread was the last to go in, he knew that, but the ham should have been done and now there was this mess to clean up.

He stood there and looked down at the glass and the clear liquid that covered his floor and ate through his wax. He did not say anything, just jingled his keys in his hand.

Gwenyth was struck stupid and remained glued to the spot she stood in. She did not want to move. If she even flinched that would mean she would have to look into our faces and see the disappointment that was etched there and it would say: *Three sons. Three sons. All drunks. You must be so proud.*

"Get out, Charlie." Hy-Lo spoke quietly. The quiet words before the loud ones. Always. "Get out now."

Charlie snickered. He thought so many things and so many people were funny. Only Gwenyth got him mad and I guess Carol too. "Hy, man, listen—"

"Out!" Hy-Lo cut him off and at the same time snapped his fingers at Delia to start cleaning up the mess. Mable opened her mouth to object and Sam squeezed her knee and shook his head in warning.

Charlie snickered again. And then, to everyone's surprise, he looked at Gwenyth and bowed, bowed so low I saw my reflection in the baldness of his head. "Merry Christmas, Mother," he said and then saluted her. "C'mon, Carol," he ordered and started toward the door.

Now the apartment smelled like the belly of the Blue Moon, the part behind the bar where the floor was always sticky and wet, where the dirty lipstick-stained glasses waited to be relieved of the soggy cigarettes that floated dead at their bottoms. Hy-Lo must have felt at home for the first time since we moved in.

Gwenyth was shaken and did not want to remain on center stage. The bottle of rum that sat on the kitchen table in the dark of her own apartment was calling to her now, telling her she did not have to remain here and be subjected to this type of treatment. "I'm going home," she announced. Her hands fiddled with the fake pearls around her neck, pulling them away from her throat as if they had suddenly shrunk and were cutting off her air supply.

"Make Mother a plate," Hy-Lo ordered Delia as he walked into the bedroom and closed the door.

"I don't believe this shit," Mable hissed beneath her

breath. Not even the soft touches and gentle nudges from Sam would sustain her tongue for much longer.

Delia looked up from her kneeling position on the floor, broom in one hand and dustpan in the other. "Okay, Hy-Lo," she said helplessly and stood to do what she had been told.

Finally, we were assembled around the table. It was a disappointing unveiling. Delia lifted the ceramic turkey-shaped cover to reveal a turkey that had been victimized. The right and left drums were gone as well as a large portion of the breast. Gwenyth would not stay long enough for us to bless the meal and cut the bird. "No, no, I need to leave now," she had insisted when Delia asked her to stay just until Hy-Lo had changed his clothes and washed his hands.

Mable rolled her eyes for the twentieth time that Christmas Day, but said nothing. Delia pretended that nothing was wrong. But then that was her life. Pretend.

I said the grace. Some meaningless words I learned at Sunday school years earlier. Words that never seemed to help me and so I had packed away the memory of them deep inside me and struggled to reach them when Hy-Lo said, "Kenzie, you say grace."

He was drunk too. His posture was unsteady and his steps unsure. I imagined he'd had quite a few Christmas cocktails between work and home. Had probably had a few with Charlie, Randy, and Carol before sending them on ahead of him. "I'll be there. I'm going to have one more with Paul. Robert. Jefferson. The man on the moon and anyone else who walks through that door. Y'all go on ahead."

He had a drink in his hand. The third drink since he walked through the door and threw Charlie and Carol out. He set the glass down close to the edge of the table and then lifted the knife to slice into what was left of the turkey. He sliced a piece off the breast and plucked it up with his fingers and popped it into his mouth. It was tradition in our home, one he had created.

He chewed slowly and then lifted his glass and drained it. We waited.

"Delia," he said, and her name was a low groan in his mouth. "This turkey is dry."

Delia dropped her eyes and said nothing. Intermission was over; the second act had begun.

"I said the turkey is dry, Delia."

Delia's fingers came to her mouth and I started pulling at my cuticles.

"Get my coat, Sam," Mable said and folded her arms across her chest. "Grab Delia's too. Kids, get your coats." Mable had had enough. She was clearing out the house. "What type of Christmas is this for your wife and your kids, Hyman? Your brothers come in here all drunk and insult your mother." Randy flinched at her words and looked up at the ceiling. "You come home just as drunk," she continued, her voice growing, filling the kitchen. "It's Christmas, for God's sake." Mable shook her head in disgust and ran her fingers over Malcolm's head.

"Delia and the kids ain't going nowhere. You, well, you're welcome to go."

"Delia, is this how you want it?" Mable was staring at her daughter with an intensity I had never seen.

"Mama, I—" Delia wasn't able to utter another word. She threw her hands up to her face and began sobbing.

"Shut up!" Hy-Lo screamed at her. "Shut up now, Delia!"

I felt my own tears push forth. I wanted to go. I wanted Delia to come with me and leave this apartment forever.

"Delia, I did not raise you this way." Mable spoke softly as if to herself instead of her daughter. "I did not raise you this way." She turned to retrieve her coat.

I peered up into my grandmother's face. My eyes pleaded for her to stay. I wanted her to stay so that my Christmas would not end with my father choking my mother until she coughed and gagged for air. I did not want my Christmas to end with Delia locked in the bathroom, wailing, while Hy-Lo sent me and Malcolm off to bed so that we would not see him removing the bathroom door from its hinges with his trusty screwdriver. My eyes said, *Please.* So loudly that Mable almost handed her coat back to Sam, but then Hy-Lo spoke again.

"And you don't ever have to come back here again. Ever."

That was it. Mable snatched her coat and stormed out of the apartment. No final words, no rolling eyes, just heavy quick footsteps and slamming doors.

"The turkey is dry, Delia." We were back at the middle and Hy-Lo waited for an answer. "Stop your sniveling, Delia!" He turned to her and plucked her on her head, atop the healing gash on her forehead.

Malcolm and I jumped at the sound, the thick timbre of it as the back of his fingernails made contact with her skin.

"Ahhhhh!" Delia wailed and grabbed at her head. "The turkey is dry, Hy. The turkey is dry, Hy!" She moved with a swiftness that I'd thought she'd lost a long time ago and pushed past him with a strength he thought he'd beat out of her long ago. She grabbed up the ceramic container with the mutilated turkey and moved to the window. "The turkey is dry the turkey is dry the turkey is dry." Her words ran together like a Gothic chant.

Hy-Lo folded his arms across his chest. His face looked bored. "Delia!" His voice rang through the apartment; my ears began to ache.

Delia stood in front of the window, and with a force she must have pulled from deep down in her gut, she flung the ceramic container that held the turkey out through the closed pane. Glass went flying everywhere. End of act two, scene two.

The cold blew in and around Delia. The bitterness of it pulled her back to her senses. She stopped chanting and turned to look at us. Malcolm and I had our mouths open so wide that we could feel the cold pulling at our teeth.

Hy-Lo said nothing. His eyes held mild amusement. "Well, kids, see what your meathead mother did?" He looked at us and for some reason he sounded like the teacher in my third period science class, as if he were explaining the basics of biology. "And the ham is still not done." He shook his head and unfolded his arms, preferring to shove his hands in his pockets now.

Delia just stood there braving the cold amidst the flapping sound of the ravaged miniblind. I was waiting for the pounding to begin, but Hy-Lo had been struck sober by my mother's crazed act.

He stepped around the table and past us. We still did not move, half-expecting he would send us to our room, but he said nothing and then he was heading past us, coat in hand and out the door.

We didn't have turkey that year. But we had ham and all of the rest of the trimmings. After Delia composed herself she threw on her black wool coat with the embroidered collar and went to the store and bought a box of big black plastic bags. She took the broom and broke out the rest of the splintered glass from the windowpane and then taped up three bags over the opening.

We had dinner in the living room. We sat on the floor around the tree, eating dinner and drinking cider. The television was on in the background to help fill the silence that fell around us every once in a while.

We watched *It's a Wonderful Life* before we went off to bed and Delia cried at the end. I knew her tears weren't for the characters, but for herself and us.

Chapter Twelve

I left Hy-Lo and went home to search through old pictures, looking for the periods in my life when I was happy. Black-and-whites, colored photos, and bent and ragged Polaroids lay scattered around me. We had boxes of pictures. Endless squares of memories that marked each year of our lives. I snatched up picture after picture and put aside the ones that showed me smiling. Out of the hundred or so that lay around me, I was only smiling in fourteen.

I looked at each one carefully, searching for a trace of real happiness, but after more than an hour I found only three where my smile was genuine. The others held smiles that had been asked for. "Smile for the camera." "Say cheese, Kenzie."

Even the pictures of my time spent away from our home showed unhappiness. By then, though, I had been unhappy for so long that it had penetrated my features and had taken hold of my character.

I looked again at the younger me surrounded by my classmates. Them grinning, me grimacing. I stood up and looked at myself in the mirror, still grimacing, still sad, still unhappy.

Mable was the one who had suggested it. I had no idea that anything like it really existed outside of the movies.

Boarding school.

She had a book full of them. Schools all over the country. Schools that had classes that would enrich the lives of young adults. That was their line. The small black-and-white pic-

tures in the book reminded me of the colorful glossy brochure I had from Camp Crystal Lake. Laughing children.
Most of the faces were white. Others were Asian. Very few
were black.

"You remember Jessica Nettles from around the corner?"
Mable was talking fast and low as if someone would walk
in at any moment and catch her sharing a secret with me.
"Well, she went to one of these schools, she loved it, and
now she's in college somewhere down south. Black college,
I think."

She moved to the kitchen and grabbed the dish towel off
its hook. Nothing needed wiping; she just needed to have
something in her hands, something to twist and curl. "They
have classes that you wouldn't get in regular schools. They
do things these city schools don't do."

I listened to her go on and on as if she were the national
spokesperson for boarding schools. I flipped slowly through
the pages of the book, through Arizona, Colorado, Delaware.
There was at least one school in every state.

"Could I come home on the weekends?" I asked, cutting
off Mable's continuous babble.

She stopped midword and looked at me. "Why would
you want to, baby?" she asked without even a hint of humor
behind it.

She was afraid for me, afraid of who I might become living with Hy-Lo and Delia. She was afraid for Malcolm too,
but would have to deal with us separately.

"Well, it's just that some of these schools are so far away
from home. I mean, could I come home when I wanted to?"

What I wanted to ask was, could I come home if I *needed*
to. If Hy-Lo hurt Delia real bad and I needed to stand up in
court as a witness to past assaults. If I needed to come home
and be with her in the hospital to make sure the nurses were
treating her well, keeping the life support unit well-oiled
and working.

Mable knew what I meant and nodded her head yes. "Sure. Of course, Kenzie."

We looked through the book for a long time, folding the corners of pages that held schools that looked interesting to me. Folding the corners of pages that held schools that would not place me too far away from home.

There were applications to be filed, fees to be paid. Who would help me do that, who would pay the fees? Better yet, who was going to pay the $5,000-a-year tuition costs?

"You're going to apply for every scholarship ever created. Sam will help you write the essays. We'll pay for the application fees. Don't worry, you'll get in and won't have to pay a dime. You're a smart girl, Kenzie."

Our plan became like *Mission Impossible:* scary and exciting all at the same time. I spent most of my weekends with Mable. Delia was there too, but she was mostly curled up on the couch staring at the television, regaining her strength for Monday through Friday.

Mable, Sam, and I would sit for hours, huddled over school and scholarship applications. I wrote so many essays that I developed writer's cramp in my hand and had to soak it for hours in warm water and Epsom salts.

Mable wrote check after check for application fees and kept a book of stamps handy for my sole use.

"He'll never go for this, Grandma," I said one day after I had licked the tenth envelope and sealed it shut with a smooth movement across the flap.

The winter sun was setting, selfishly taking with it the meager warmth it had offered during the day. January wind howled outside the window and beat visciously at the sides of the house, offering me little comfort that I would ever see the bright warmth of spring.

Mable glanced down at me, her first grandchild, who looked so much like her only child, and her heart must have thumped hard in her chest. I saw the pity that welled up in her as she gazed into my eyes. There was no light left there. Her hands moved to my face and traveled lovingly over my hollowed cheeks.

"Don't worry about that." Her voice was sad. And I could tell that even with all of our planning, scheming, and plotting, she did not have a clue as to how she would convince Hy-Lo to let me go away to school. "Don't you worry," she repeated and then turned to leave. She walked away slowly, her age suddenly wearing down on her.

That night I lay down in my bed and listened to the cold winter wind rattle my bedroom window, not knowing that a solution to my problem was just a few days away.

"You have some mail here, Kenzie." Mable's voice was an excited whisper.

I pressed the receiver closer to my face. "From one of the schools?" I asked in the same whisper.

"Uh-huh," she replied. I could hear the sound of the envelope as she turned it around and around in her hands.

"Will you bring it?" I asked and looked over my shoulder to see if anyone had snuck up behind me.

"Tomorrow," Mable replied, and then came the soft click of the line as she hung up.

It was a warm Saturday evening, warm for early April. The winter hibernation was coming to an end and the streets started to come alive again with the sounds of playing children, laughter, and adults leaning out their windows to share gossip with friends.

Hy-Lo had been in and out of the apartment for most of the day. He was splitting his time between the men he drank beer with in front of the building and harassing us about the dust on the moldings and the grease that stuck to the wall behind the stove. My hands were wrinkled and raw from the ammonia and water, and by eleven o'clock I had scrubbed the bathroom and kitchen floors until they sparkled against the sunlight.

Malcolm was on his hands and knees plucking at the fine bits of lint that remained lodged in the new carpet that covered the living room. It was dark red and speckled with black. Its presence seemed to soak away that last bit of light Hy-Lo had been unsuccessful at keeping out. Malcolm wheezed and sneezed as he crawled around plucking and pulling at the dirt and dust the vacuum cleaner had missed.

Delia had risen early, dressed, and left the apartment before eight o'clock. I did not hear her moving about, or the soft clinking sound she made with her spoon as she stirred the sugar into her Maxwell House coffee. I did hear the sound of the front door being closed and the clank of the lock when it turned in its metal casing.

My heart sank. This would be the third Saturday in a row Delia would leave Malcolm and me alone to fend for ourselves. When she did come back home, it was usually very late at night, Hy-Lo would be passed out on the living room floor, and we would be in bed or getting ready to go to bed. Delia would come in and step over him as if he were a piece of dog shit on the sidewalk. She did not offer an explanation as to where she had been even if we asked, and we didn't bother to ask anymore.

I didn't need to ask, I knew.

I had been with her when they met. A tall man, the color of sandalwood and nutmeg. His eyes were hazel and his hair was a tight mass of brown and blond curls. He had a wide smile that remained even when he spoke, and he smelled like the scent Glenna's mother sprayed her bedroom pillows with when she happened to be between men and felt lonely.

"Hello." The word came out his mouth like bright sunshine and Delia smiled in spite of herself but kept walking. "Delia Hawkins?" he called out again, strong and sure he had the right person.

We both turned around and Delia said, "Yes?"

He was so tall and his legs so long that it only took him

two steps to cover the six we had made away from him.
"Jonathan Hall." He extended his hand and I saw that his
fingernails were clipped, clean, and buffed to a shine. They
looked better than Delia's and I blushed with embarrassment for her.

Delia shook her head in bafflement. "I—I don't think—"

"Bookie. Bookie Hall from down home. Blue and white
house, round the bend from the dairy farm." His eyes sparkled and he licked his lips.

"Oh my goodness!" Delia screamed. The sound was familiar yet so unfamiliar. I heard Delia scream all of the time.
Scream in anger; scream in pain and frustration. But this was
a scream of delight.

"Bookie Hall! Oh my goodness!" She couldn't seem to
find anything else to say. Her hands were up to her mouth,
hiding her bruised smile. Her lips had had an unfortunate
encounter with Hy-Lo's fists two nights earlier.

"You look good, Delia," Jonathan "Bookie" Hall said and
opened his arms and took another step forward. Delia almost did it. Almost stepped inside, and then she stopped,
looked around like a frightened cat, and then extended her
hand. If he was surprised or offended he did not show it.
Without missing a beat his hand took hers and they shook.

"How you been, Delia? How's your mama doing? It's
been so long." He hardly let Delia get a word in. The words
spilled from his mouth like music from a flute and Delia
couldn't stop smiling and blushing. It seemed like forever
had passed before he noticed me.

"This must be your girl, huh? She look just like you!" He
extended his hand but I opened my arms and Delia's mouth
almost dropped off and hit the sidewalk. Bookie laughed his
musical laugh and hugged me. My head pressed against his
chest and I inhaled as much of his scent as possible.

That's why I knew how Delia was spending her Saturdays. She came home with that scent clinging to her skin.

"This is my daughter, Kenzie. I got a boy too, his name is Malcolm." She was speaking slowly, looking from me to Bookie, unable to believe what I had just done.

"And your husband?" Bookie asked.

"Yes." The word came out tired and remorseful. "Hyman. My name is Delia Lowe now."

"Uh-huh, what a lucky man," Bookie said, and his eyes settled on her bruised lips before moving over to the scar on her forehead and down to the blue-black bruise on her cheek, where she hadn't applied enough foundation. "Can I call you?" he asked even though she had a husband, even though I was standing there.

I wanted to say yes. Yes, you can call her. Her lips started to move and I knew she wanted to say yes, but no came out instead. "Sorry, Bookie, I'm married. You know how it is . . ." Her words sailed off and she stared past him.

There was a moment and then he pulled a card from his pocket. "Well, here's my number. You keep in touch, okay?"

Delia nodded her head yes, took the card from him, and told him it was nice seeing him again, and that's when I realized that their hands were still entwined.

We were done with our chores and Malcolm and I stood side by side as we waited for Hy-Lo to complete his inspection. "Where's your mother?" he asked as he ran his index finger across the wooden surface of the television.

Malcolm and I shrugged our shoulders at his back and then answered in unison, "I don't know, sir."

"Humph," Hy-Lo sounded and turned to look at us. "Don't lie for her, you will only make it bad on yourselves." He stared at us long and hard, his eyes picking over our faces.

"We're not lying," Malcolm said and his eyes narrowed. He was growing up, becoming a man himself; his fear of Hy-Lo was slowly being replaced with loathing.

"*We're not lying*," Hy-Lo mocked him and laughed. "You speaking for both of you now, Malcolm? How do you know that Kenzie doesn't know where your mother is? Do you know? Can your behind take a whooping for both of you if she does know and is lying to me?"

I saw Malcolm's eyes move toward me and then back to Hy-Lo. "I don't know where she is." He changed his statement; we were all enemies in that house and enemies could not be trusted.

Hy-Lo raised his eyebrows and a smirk slowly covered his face. He folded his arms across his chest and cocked his head sideways before he spoke. "Do you know where your mother is, Kenzie?"

I almost laughed, almost spit out the name of Jonathan "Bookie" Hall. I wanted to throw my hands up in the air and do the hokey-pokey, snap my fingers, and sing Jonathan "Bookie" Hall's name until the whole block knew it by heart. "No," I said quietly. I did allow a small smile to cover my lips as I said it though.

Hy-Lo's smirk spread until his whole face became a crooked line. "Who was here last night?" He leaned in toward us, challenging Malcolm and me.

"No one," we responded and then exchanged glances.

"No one?" Hy-Lo repeated. "Go get the belt," he said and waited for one or both of us to move.

We stood stark still, staring at him as if he had lost what little mind he had left.

"Did you hear me? Go and get the belt!" he bellowed and I heard the startled flapping sound of pigeon wings outside the window.

"For what?" I asked. My voice was insolent and filled with malice.

"Don't you question me!"

He had me by my arm before I even knew he'd moved. He was squeezing it tightly and I could feel the blue-black bruise beginning to form and swell. I tried to snatch away, but his grip was like a steel clamp.

"Get off of me!" I wriggled and jerked against his grasp. "Get ooffff!"

Tears, hot and fast, streamed down my face. He was dragging me toward the bedroom, toward the coiled leather that rested in the bottom drawer. "Choose!" he yelled and tossed me to the floor in front of his bureau.

I couldn't see, my tears were clouding my eyes. "No!" I yelled back at him. He grabbed me by my hair and yanked me to my feet and then slapped me across my face so hard I flew across the room and landed on the bed.

"Fuck you!" I screamed.

He didn't move. His face was covered in astonishment as he stared at me. Malcolm stood behind him in the doorway, almost a mirror image of Hy-Lo.

"What the hell did you say to me, little girl?"

Little girl. He hadn't called me that since I was four, when I lifted my skirt up in the street to show his mother my new pair of pink and white ruffled panties.

I said nothing. My words had shocked me too. There was murder in his eyes as he walked toward me.

I tried to get away, scooting backward on my butt, but he caught me by my ankle just before I toppled over the edge of the bed, and he pulled me toward him. The bedspread, pillows, and the white stuffed poodle Delia had won at Coney Island three summers before came with me.

He caught me by my throat and squeezed until black walls started to form at the sides of my eyes.

"Dad!" Malcolm yelled out. "Dad! Dad!" He was on him now, trying to loosen his fingers, pulling them one by one from around my throat. I was gagging, clawing at his face and kicking at his legs.

Finally he let go and I collapsed to the floor coughing and retching. Malcolm looked down at me and then at Hy-Lo.

Their noses almost touched, both of them breathing as if the air had suddenly gone thin.

Hy-Lo seemed to come back, the animal receding back inside of him, but not before he shoved Malcolm hard in the chest. Malcolm was taken off guard and lost his balance, tripping over me and falling to the floor beside me.

Hy-Lo stormed out of the room and then out of the house, leaving us afraid of what was to come next.

I was shaken and tried my best to get myself under control before I called Mable. "Maybe you should come tomorrow," I said, my voice hoarse.

"Why? Kenzie, are you catching a cold? Where is your mother?" Mable's voice rose with each question. "Kenzie?" she said again.

"Yeah," I replied in a listless voice. I was tired of fighting this losing battle called life.

"Kenzie?" Mable had heard that tone before. She'd heard it from Delia numerous times.

I just sighed. My throat hurt and my lips were tired of lying.

"I'll be right there," Mable said quietly and hung up the phone.

Maybe there was traffic on the Belt Parkway, or maybe Sam tried to keep her from coming. I can't remember why she wasn't there within her usual thirty minutes. Maybe if she had been there she might have killed Hy-Lo or maybe he would have killed her, or worse, they would have killed each other.

Delia came in just as I hung up the phone. Her lipstick was worn away, leaving behind a smoky red stain. Her hair was a bit messy and I could tell she had put it together in a hurry.

She walked in with a smile that bloomed when she saw me and withered when she saw the dusky purple marks around my forearm and throat.

We didn't say anything to each other for a long time, but just stared. We were each a victim. One by choice, the other by birth, but victims just the same.

Delia's eyes welled up with her own tears and she came and embraced me. I smelled Jonathan "Bookie" Hall's scent in her sweater and her neck and pulled her closer to me.

"I'm sorry, Kenzie, I'm so sorry," she wept.

That's how he found us.

"Well, well." Hy-Lo walked through the door. "Isn't this nice." He rocked back and forth on his feet and folded his arms across his chest. The smirk was still there and I could see that the spiky black hair of the wild thing that lived inside of him had pushed through his skin and covered his chin and cheeks.

"Hyman, why did you do this? Why?" Delia had released me and pushed me behind her. Her voice was small but her tone was angry and disgusted. "You have a problem, Hyman. You need help."

I don't know where she found the courage to speak to him like that, but that was the first time my mother had stood up to him in years.

The wild thing's eyes were red and piercing, its teeth small sharp points that Hy-Lo bared before he spoke. "I need help? No, you're the idiot bitch, you're the jackass that needs help, Delia!"

He took a step forward; Delia and I took a step backward.

"Go to your room, Kenzie!" He was salivating as if what he was about to do was enjoy a feast rather than pound Delia senseless.

I grabbed her hand and tried to pull her away from him. She resisted, it was fruitless. Where would she go? Hy-Lo blocked the door. She could climb out the window, if Hy-Lo didn't throw her out of it first.

"Go to your room, Kenzie." Delia spoke quietly and wriggled her hand free from my grasp. "Go on." She turned and looked down at me. "Go on," she repeated and then smiled like everything would be okay.

I didn't go to my room, but stepped aside as she turned her back to Hy-Lo and walked toward the bedroom. He followed, bouncing his keys in his hands, the smell of vodka coming off of him with each move he made. He threw me a look, but said nothing. The wild thing's tail trailed behind him as he went.

The front door opened again and Malcolm came in. The dark skin of his cheeks was flushed and he was breathing hard. "I saw him come in," he whispered breathlessly. "He was at the Blue Moon. I—I followed him home." He bent over and sucked in air. "She here?" he asked after looking toward the closed bedroom door. I nodded my head yes.

Malcolm sat down on the floor and rested his back against the wall. The length of his body seemed to have extended overnight. The soft boyhood curves of his features were melting away, leaving behind the sharp stony appearance of a childhood lost too soon.

We waited.

Their voices were low, muted, and rapid. Every once in a while there would be a blast of obscene words from Hy-Lo and Delia's voice would rise, shrill and swift like a flock of birds.

The bumping and knocking came soon after. The labored breathing of one adult snatching, slapping, and punching while the other struggled to block, avoid, and protect.

It went on for some time. Malcolm stuck his head between his legs and pressed the sides of his knees tight against his ears. Me, I listened to everything and watched their bedroom door as it vibrated against the weight of Delia's body.

It was the scream that pushed me forward. The resonance of her cry stood my hair on end and caused my heart to leap in fear. I decided, right then and there, that this would end. I jumped up and walked over to the phonograph, dropped to my knees, and reached my hands beneath its belly.

It was gone. I moved my hand back and forth, dug deep into the emptiness of the hardwood, and clasped nothing but dust and cat hair.

"What are you doing?" Malcolm looked at me as if I had gone mad.

"Nothing," I said. My whole body shook. Where was the gun?

Delia's scream came again and neither of us could ignore it. We burst into the room and found her cowering in the corner; her sweater was ripped almost completely off and there were deep, bloody scratches on her shoulder. Hy-Lo stood above her, the gun in his hand, the nozzle pressed to the center of her head.

Everything moved quickly after that. Like the early black-and-white soundless movies. The ones Malcolm and I watched on lazy Sunday afternoons, right before the Abbott and Costello flicks.

I remember my world becoming silent. The sound of my mother's pleas, my father's enraged words, and my own screams became nothing more than streams of red and orange lights that shot from our mouths and disappeared in midair.

My legs turned from flesh to concrete and I could not lift them or even wiggle my pinky toe. All of the life that was left in me moved to my arms and my hands; I know this because they were flailing about like a fish struggling for air on land.

At least ten minutes had to have passed, maybe more, before I felt a heavy hand come down on my shoulder and pull me backward. I heard the static-filled sound of walkie-talkies and the echo of five pistols being cocked and five strong voices yelling, "Drop it, now!"

I did not want to take my eyes off Delia and Hy-Lo. It was my eyes, welded onto them, that magically kept him from pulling the trigger and blowing her brains across the floor I had scrubbed and waxed earlier in the day.

Dark blue uniforms and shiny badges moved past me as quick as light and surrounded Hy-Lo. He turned on them, the wild thing fully emerged, and once again he bared his tiny, pointed teeth. "This is my house," he slurred while still holding the gun to Delia's head.

"Please, Hyman, please!" Delia screamed more in fear for his life than hers.

"Drop it!" they ordered again and raised their guns higher, bringing them level with his forehead.

"Right between the eyes." I thought I'd thought the words, but the slight turn of two of the officers' heads in my direction told me I had spoken them aloud.

The gun went crashing to the floor and the policemen tackled Hy-Lo, hitting him like defensive linebackers and piling on top of him. Delia was still caught; her legs were under the large mass of men, guns, and batons. I don't think she noticed the weight, she was still in shock.

Malcolm moved next to me. "I called them," he said and gave me a look I hadn't seen since he was six. *Did I do good?* his eyes seemed to say. I wrapped my arms around him and pulled him to me; he was shaking and so was I.

One officer approached us. He was short and stout, his dirty blond hair was cut Marine Corp style and I could see his pale scalp beneath. His face was red from the adrenaline that still pumped through him. "Let's go in here for a minute." It was hard for him to speak; his words came out jagged between the breaths he tried to take.

He touched my shoulder with one hand and pointed toward my bedroom with the other.

"Everybody okay?" he asked once we were inside, away from the million questions the other officers reeled at Hy-Lo and Delia. We nodded our heads yes. "Who called 911?" he asked and his watery blue eyes moved between Malcolm and me.

"I did," Malcolm said, unsure if he should have replied at all.

"Very good, son," the officer said and winked at him. He removed a rectangular leather booklet from his back pocket and began to write. "What's your name, son?"

"Malcolm." My brother moved closer to me.

"Malcolm what?"

"Lowe."

"That your dad in there?"

"Uh, yeah."

"That your mom?"

"Uh-huh."

"Your dad ever do anything like this before?"

Malcolm didn't respond right away. Everything was moving too fast for his nine-year-old mind. He hadn't considered the repercussions of his actions, hadn't thought about what Hy-Lo would do to him if he ever found out who made the call. Malcolm began to shake as the thoughts swirled through his mind. He took a step away from the officer.

The officer looked at Malcolm and then me. "What's your name, sweetheart?"

"Kenzie Lowe. I'm his sister. Those are my parents and they fight all the time. My dad is a drunk and he beats on her all the time." The words fell out of my mouth and then the tears followed. "Take him to jail, please take him to jail."

"Hey, Waters, the damn gun was empty." Another officer was in the room now. He was tall and sported the same type of haircut except his hair was black and gleamed beneath the bedroom light. His badge said *Hernandez.*

"What?" Waters stood up from where he'd knelt down beside the bed to comfort me. "Shit," he mumbled beneath his breath and walked over to Hernandez. "She can still press charges for aggravated assault. She *is* going to press charges, isn't she?"

Hernandez shrugged his shoulders and made a face that told me he didn't think that was going to happen. "Shit," Waters mumbled again and stormed out of the room.

Two officers were speaking to Delia. Her head moved back and forth between them as they tried to convince her why she should press charges. They kept asking her if she understood and when she would nod her head yes, they'd begin again.

They had seen a hundred women like Delia, living, breathing women who were battered physically and emotionally on a daily basis, but who still refused to leave their oppressors. The policemen came to their lavish homes or tiny apartments once a month, sometimes more, sometimes less, and told them over and over again that anyplace was better than where they were.

They left literature behind and business cards for social workers and shelters, and still the women made up excuses why they couldn't leave, why *he* had behaved that way, why it was probably their fault and not his.

"I walk too loud."

"Dinner wasn't ready."

"I didn't clean up behind the kids."

"The meat was too tough. The rice too soft. The bread too stale."

"If not for you, for the kids," the policemen would urge.

"It's because of the kids that I stay and take it," the wives, girlfriends, and Delia responded.

The officers shrugged their shoulders in surrender. They were all talked out and removed the silver bracelets from my father's wrists.

The gun was a souvenir from Vietnam. They left him with his memories of war and blood and us with the same.

Mable came in just as the officers were leaving. A small crowd had gathered in the hallway. "Oh my God, what happened?" Mable pushed through the men and went straight to my mother, who was huddled in the corner of the sofa.

"Delia, Delia." Mable stroked her daughter's hair and wrapped her arms around her shoulders, rocking her as if she were three years old again. Malcolm and I stood by watching as our mother moaned softly into her mother's heavy breasts.

In the end we left Hy-Lo alone, sitting on the edge of the bed, his head resting hopelessly in his hands.

For the next ten days we lived with Mable and Sam. I'd hoped it was for good, even though we were cramped. The space I had viewed as a massive castle when I was young was now a paltry dwelling.

Arms and shoulders brushed in passing, and sounds, like inconsistent music notes, traveled through the paper-thin walls interrupting my studies and breaking my sleep.

Malcolm and I were no longer used to sharing the same sleeping space. I slept as if I were naked in a room full of strangers, blankets pulled up to my chin, one eye open and ears peeled, listening for any variation in Malcolm's breathing as he lay sleeping on the floor beside my bed.

He was a man-child and I was losing trust in him as he got closer to manhood.

Sam spent hours trying to pull me into conversation, card games, or just a seat beside him on the couch. I had a handbag full of excuses and a pocket full of lies that I denied his invitations with. He was a man too, and Hy-Lo's actions had blemished his record and the record of most of the men I would come into contact with for many years following that incident.

On the fifth day, when the March wind had become a stiff wall of cold that stopped pedestrians at corners and sent them reeling backward on their heels, Delia did not ring the bell at six-fifteen p.m. and rush in bringing the cold with her. No, on the fifth day she arrived just before midnight, when the March gale was feeble and the sky cloudless and black.

On that night I heard a car door close and the roll of wheels as it crushed the dirt, grit, and garbage the wind had left behind; then there was the chime of the doorbell.

Mable knew. I saw it in her face when Delia walked into the house. No wind pushing her forward or cold ushering her in, just the dead night behind her and the fading glint of brake lights.

Mable's face curled and her eyes slanted with anger. She bit her lip and slammed the door. Delia ignored her and came to sit beside me on the couch, bending over to pull off her shoes. "Hey, you, how was your day?" she said, her voice sounding farther away than the hem of the couch.

"Okay," I said quickly, glancing over at Mable to check her reaction.

"Where you been?" All three of us looked up to see who had spoken so abruptly. Yes, we had heard that same question, that same threatening tone, a million times in the past.

And now here it was coming down the stairs in Mable's home when we thought we'd left it on Rogers Avenue.

"What did you say, Malcolm?" Delia's voice shook just a bit, enough for me to notice, but then if I had asked him the question, mine would have been trembling too.

It wasn't that she needed clarification as to what Malcolm had said, it was just that she needed to be sure she heard right in how he had said it. Whose voice had been used?

Malcolm became aware of our hesitation and his tone changed.

"I—I—" he stammered before Delia cut him off.

"Out. I was out, Malcolm." Her voice was stern.

She did not want to hear Hy-Lo's voice from the mouth of her young son again. It was bad enough his features were carved into Malcolm's face. What was worse, what she couldn't seem to see, was that the wild thing was living be-hind his eyes too, watching and waiting. I saw it there.

Malcolm was confused and made a face before turn-ing and walking back up the stairs. Delia watched until his shadow disappeared from the wall and then she leaned back into the sofa, shaking her head.

After some time she began to hum, a tune that was un-familiar to me. One that carried a strange type of joy, as if someone had written a wrong note, slipping it into the scale even though it sounded out of place.

I listened and moved closer to Delia, helping her slide her arm out of her coat and even removing a bit of lint that had become entangled in her hair. Delia turned and smiled at me; her eyes were soft, almost dewy.

I leaned into her, snuggling my nose against her neck, hoping that look of love belonged to Jonathan "Bookie" Hall. I inhaled, and instead of the smell of the warm, sexy scent of Jonathan "Bookie" Hall, my nose was filled with the stale smell of Camel cigarettes, Magic Shave, and Ivory soap. I almost gagged.

I withdrew quickly, slamming myself back against the sofa, folding my hands across my chest. I heard Mable suck her teeth.

"What is wrong with you, Kenzie?" Delia asked in exas-peration.

"Nothing." I mumbled goodnight and stormed up the stairs.

Mable and Delia's conversation began as it always did: "But Mama, he said he was going to stop drinking."

"Hasn't he said that before?"

"Yes, but this—"

"But this time it's different? How? But this time he *means* it?" The sarcasm in Mable's voice dripped out like poison. I spat into my hand against the nasty taste that formed in my mouth listening to those words.

"Mama, everyone deserves a chance—"

"How many, Delia? How many—one, two, three hundred, one thousand? He was going to kill you, Delia; do you understand that, baby? He was going to blow your head off and leave your children without a mother."

I shuddered when she said that.

There was silence for a while. Maybe Delia was considering Mable's words or maybe she was just staring at her in shock.

"There weren't any bullets in the gun, Mama—"

"This time," Mable spat.

"He's going to get help—"

"He's going to kill you."

"He's going to—"

"He's going to kill you!" Mable's fist came down on the table and the whole house shook. "How many times can you take his lies and twist them into truths? How many damn times?"

Delia didn't respond. Maybe she was thinking about the silk blouse Hy-Lo brought her after he'd knocked her down in the kitchen and emptied the garbage can over her head. It was red with a pointed collar and heart-shaped pearl buttons. It was a size too small but Delia kept it anyway, choosing to hang it in the closet next to the burgundy wool jacket and red and white striped cardigan he'd bought her after similar incidents.

The jacket and the cardigan were also too small, just like his promises, just like his love for her.

What would he get her now? A hat, a scarf, or maybe a pair of lambskin gloves? What do you get someone you've tried to kill?

"Think about your children, Delia." Mable finally said it. The lone sentence, five small words that carried the force of five hundred. I'm sure Delia had to grit her teeth to keep them from chattering. She would not respond. How many different ways could she say that this was the exact reason why she stayed?

The next day Delia came home at six-fifteen; her mood was solemn and she had little to say. The house creaked against the push of the March wind and the noise filled the uncomfortable silence that surrounded us.

He came sometime around three in the morning. Their whispers floated up to me and tickled my ears with their phantom fingers. I knew he was coming, something inside of me kept telling me so, pulling me from my sleep and forcing my eyes to remain open, staring into the misty blue darkness of the room. I had only just lost the battle and surrendered myself to slumber when their muffled words pulled me back.

I climbed from my bed, careful not to step on Malcolm, and walked over to the wall that stood between Mable's room and myself. I could hear Mable's even breathing and Sam's heavy snoring. They were in perfect harmony with one another; even in sleep they kept a comfortable rhythm.

I eased the door open and stepped out into the small hallway. I hugged myself against the cold air that surrounded me and listened.

"You shouldn't have come," Delia said breathlessly. Her voice was thick and she spoke as though struggling for air. I recognized that sound, that struggle to breathe between words and kisses.

I shuddered at the thought of him touching her, pressing his lips to hers, pulling himself into her, reclaiming his control of her and of us.

"Delia, Delia." He said her name over and over until her name became wet and thick in his mouth. "I'm sorry, I'm sorry."

I heard the heavy metal teeth of his zipper separate.

The night turned scalding hot. I felt my head spin in the heat of the darkness that threatened to burn my skin, its flaming fingers grabbing hold of my lungs and heart, gripping them until they exploded and I was nothing.

I swooned and stepped back to lean against the wall when they moved from the vestibule, walking as one instead of two to the couch and falling down onto its cushions. I did not want to listen but was unable to move. I heard Delia's voice call out his name and Hy-Lo responded with a heavy shuddered breath.

My stomach turned and allowed the bile to rise and clog my throat, my hands went to my mouth, and then darkness overtook me.

They found me sitting on the floor, slumped against the wall, my chin resting in the puke on my chest. "Kenzie, Kenzie." Someone's fingers ran across my cheeks and brushed against my forehead. "Kenzie?"

My eyes fluttered open and stared into those of my mother.

"C'mon," she said, her voice a calm wave. The stench of vomit hit my nose and burned the insides of my nostrils like ammonia and I lifted my head and gulped for air. "Get up, c'mon," she urged again.

With Delia's help I pulled myself to my feet and let her take me to the bathroom.

"Oh," she muttered in surprise. I looked up at her and then followed her eyes. She was staring at the back of my gown. A blotchy red stain covered the thin green nylon. "Well, welcome to womanhood," Delia said with a nervous smile.

Later that day, Malcolm and I sat in the living room; our small overnight bags, busting at the seams, rested against our feet. We pretended to watch television, but our ears were tuned to the conversation that took place a few feet away.

Hy-Lo had come for us. It was almost three when he got there. His eyes were bloodshot and his face unshaven. He'd lost some weight and his clothes clung desperately to his withering frame. He was a pitiful sight.

He smiled at us and patted Malcolm on his back. "Hello, son," he said in a voice that belonged to someone else's father. *Son* was not a term I'd ever heard him use. *Meathead, stupid, idiot,* those were his pet names for Malcolm.

My brother nodded his head and shook Hy-Lo's outstretched hand.

"Kenzie?" It was not a greeting but a question for me to grant his permission to greet me. I rolled my eyes and turned my head away.

Delia laid her sad eyes on me; they asked me to try, to please just try. I ignored them.

They did not sit, Delia and Hy-Lo, but stood like young children being scolded as Mable slammed her fist on the table in between the threats she flung at them.

She waved my acceptance letter in their faces. "She will attend this school, Hyman. If you don't allow it, I swear to God I will go straight to Child Welfare Services!"

I saw Hy-Lo's head bob up and down in agreement. His eyes met Mable's for one brief moment and then settled back on his shoes. Delia stood in the background, quiet as a mouse.

It was done and over. Mable squeezed us tight before we loaded ourselves into the car. "Kids, call me if you need me," she yelled as we pulled away from the house.

I clutched the letter tightly as Hy-Lo barreled down the highway. It was my ticket to freedom.

Chapter Thirteen

We walked into the apartment; it was dark and dreary and smelled like cigarettes and fried chicken TV dinners. Hy-Lo had made a makeshift clothesline by stretching a rope from the curtain rod of the living room window to the floor lamp directly across. His shorts and T-shirts hung there drying.

The refrigerator was stacked with TV dinners and bottles of apple juice. A carton of Camels sat on the table next to the ceramic ashtray overflowing with butts and gray matchsticks.

Delia started cleaning even before she removed her coat. "Help me untie this," she said to Malcolm after she removed the wet clothes from the line. I walked straight to my room and closed the door.

My stomach cramped as my anger began to well up inside of me. I threw myself across my bed and cried into my pillow. I hated being back in that place, under that roof where so much hate and pain lived.

I wanted to stay with Mable. "Can I stay here?" I'd boldly asked when Hy-Lo picked up my satchel and started toward the door.

"Of course—" Mable had started to answer but was cut off by Delia.

"No, Kenzie, you cannot. You come home where you belong." I saw the fear that passed across her face. She needed me there; I was her strength and without me she would crumble and he would win. "You come home, Kenzie, you're my responsibility not your grandmother's."

"She's old enough to decide where she wants to live," Mable responded.

Hy-Lo said nothing; his eyes traveled between Delia, Mable, and me. For a moment he resembled a trapped animal, but then Delia rescued him.

"No, she's not." Delia's voice came from deep within her. She would not let Mable win this one. Mable almost smiled in spite of herself. Perhaps Delia's tone gave Mable hope that she still had some backbone left in her.

"You only got to hang in there for a few more months, Kenzie. September will be here before you know it." Mable spoke to me but her eyes never left Delia's, and the smile, although just a shadow, grew and spread across her face. "Just a few more months."

Delia rolled her eyes. "Goodbye, Mama," she said and took a step back so I could pass.

Back home nothing had changed and everything had changed. I had my Get Out of Jail Free Card hidden in an old sock and stuffed behind my dresser. I prayed that the next six months would pass quickly and without incident. That would be a big order for God to fill, but I hoped against hope.

The summer of '79 would be a season of discovery for me and I would, during those eight sultry weeks, discover the sweet mouth and solid touch of a boy whose youth had abandoned him years before his sixteenth birthday.

I did not worry about the others being interested in him. He was not beautiful and sleek. He was long and lanky; his hands were clumsy and oversized, weighing down his already thin arms. His nose was bent at an angle that ruined any immediate attractive qualities his face held. You had to look long and deep to see the beauty of his brown eyes, the thick supple lids that shone smooth as copper beneath the sun, and the weighty lashes that curled upward eternally praising the sky.

There would be no contest between the Donnelly girls, Hillary, Glenna, and me; they did not have the patience or the maturity to consider him with such intensity. So they just dusted him with their gazes and decided right then and there that he was not anything they wanted.

He and his mother moved into the apartment building across the street from me beneath the backdrop of a Fourth of July evening while the sound of firecrackers and cherry bombs consumed the night and fireworks painted the sky in brilliant blues, reds, and yellows.

His name was Jonas and he was miles ahead of his sixteen years. A full-time student in the daytime and a gas station attendant at night. He had been thrust into adulthood when his father, a two-bit drug dealer, was found shot to death in Tompkins Square Park.

I kissed him the first time we met, because I had missed out on that small intimacy with Mousy and had longed for it ever since. It was a quick and easy kiss that reminded me of his smile and melted my insides and curled my toes around the edges of my sandals.

It was his smile that had turned me around the first day I met him. Not the baritone hello or the feel of his fingertips on my forearm as he reached out for me when I passed him. I didn't even notice his eyes, the odd angled nose, or the beauty mark that sat on his left cheek like a speck of dirt. Just his smile, wide and bright.

Before I knew it I smelled the motor oil that was ground into the grooves of his hands and beneath his fingernails.

"Hi," he said as he waved his hand back and forth in my face, fracturing the spell his lips had on me.

"Hi," I responded. My experience with boys was minimal but I did not feel nervous speaking to him out in the open like that. Right on the corner of Montgomery and Nostrand avenues where everyone could see, including Hy-Lo, Delia, and the old man who owned the pharmacy on the corner.

He smiled and his words were soothing. They sounded as familiar as a bedtime story my mother had read over and over to me as a child.

I walked with him to his apartment building and even stepped inside its cream-colored halls. We remained there in the cool darkness, hidden from the eyes of our neighbors and the scorching rays of the sun, talking about anything and everything, and for moments, nothing at all.

"I can't give you my number," I said when he finally asked.

"Can I give you mine?"

"Yes."

I wrote his number in red ink on my palm. The seven digits seemed to sear my hand and I made a fist to contain the fire.

A woman came down the marble staircase that led up to the apartments. She was singing to herself, loud and off-key. Her shoes clicked hard against the stone, running competition with her clamorous melody.

I made a face and snickered. Jonas said nothing. He shoved his hands deep into his pockets and dropped his head.

The woman's hair was cut so short you could see her scalp and the thin scraggly scars that covered the left side of her head above her ear. Her eyes bulged and the whites looked like aged parchment, yellow and dim. She was short, the color of pancake mix, with a belly that rounded out before her and jiggled beneath her T-shirt when she moved. To me she looked like a bullfrog, but I kept that thought to myself.

"J," the woman said coming to stand before us. "J, listen, go on down to that liquor store, get me a pint of . . ." she slurred and lost her words.

I looked at Jonas. He had extended his hand out to retrieve the crumpled money. His head remained bent but I could see the shame in his eyes and the resemblance he bore to the woman.

"Ahhhhhhhh . . ." She was still struggling to find the words to finish her sentence. She snapped her fingers and looked to the cream-colored walls for the answer.

"Gin," Jonas said quietly and slowly took the money from the woman's hand.

"Yeah, uh-huh." She patted him on the back, twice. "Good boy, my good boy." She never acknowledged me; maybe she thought I was an impression on the wall or a shadow. Whatever the case, she turned and stumbled her way back up the staircase.

I looked at Jonas, this person I'd just met but felt like I'd known forever, and realized that we shared the same pain. I took his chin in my hand and tilted his head up and turned it toward me. I wanted to say something grown, something I'd seen in a movie or read in a book, but nothing would come to me. I pulled him to me and pressed my lips against his until I felt I had kissed that moment away, and then we walked, side by side, to the Beehive liquor store.

We spoke on the phone in the evenings when Hy-Lo was at work and Delia had closed herself behind her bedroom door. I stole time with him at the gas station in the small metal box he called his office. I was more than happy to sit surrounded by grease and grime, as long as I could be near him, hear him, touch him.

We shared stories, about our parents and their problems, as if we were both veterans of some long-ago battle now able to laugh.

I was never really able to talk about things like that, not even to Glenna, much less laugh about it. But now I did, we did, laughed until our sides ached and tears streamed down our faces. And then we held each other and kissed the pain away.

* * *

"Where you been, Kenzie?" Delia's face was screwed up. She was standing over the stove scrubbing the chrome with Brillo. Her hair was relaxed now and hung long and black just touching her shoulders. The kitchen smelled of salmon cakes and french fries. Malcolm sat at the table greedily shoving food into his mouth, but he stopped to throw me a warning look when I walked in.

"I—I—" The words were stuck in my throat. Her question had taken me by surprise.

"Don't come in here with a lie up your ass, Kenzie. Where were you?" It was obvious she had been ranting and raving for some time before I got in. I looked at the clock on the wall; it was after ten.

"I was at Glenna's," I said and dropped my eyes.

"You were *where?*" Delia took a step away from the stove.

"Glenna's." I repeated the lie and stepped backward. My back hit the wall.

"Kenzie." My name sounded like shit in her mouth when she said it. "You lying little—" She stopped herself and reached for her pack of Newports. "You wanna come again?" she said as she lit her cigarette and inhaled deeply.

"What?" I would have to stick to the lie; I was in too deep.

"Glenna called here looking for you not more than ten minutes ago. So where the hell were you!" She yelled so loud my ears rang and Malcolm got up from the table, leaving his half-eaten plate of food behind. He brushed past me and went to sit in the living room. It was just Delia and me now.

The cigarette smoke filled the kitchen and hung around us like a gray net. I wanted to move but I was afraid any movement I made would be interpreted as insolent. So I remained perfectly still, my head bowed, hands clasped behind my back, and the taste of Jonas on my tongue.

"Do I look like I have 'stupid' scratched across my forehead? Do I!" She was moving closer now. The cigarette smoke she exhaled tickled my nose and I stifled a sneeze. "Answer me, Kenzie, goddamnit!"

"No," I almost yelled. "No, I don't think you're stupid," I said lowering my voice.

"So where the hell were you?" She was in my face now. I could see the brown tops of her bare feet, the chipped polish on her toenails, and the corn on her pinky toe.

"I—I was—" I couldn't say it. The words were there, but they were caught in my throat.

"I—I," she mocked me and then turned and walked back into the kitchen.

I breathed a sigh of relief and slowly raised my eyes to meet hers when she turned around.

"I'll tell you where the hell you was. Your ass was across the street in that building with that nappy-headed boy!" She crossed her arms across her chest in triumph and glared at me, daring me to deny it.

I said nothing. My body slumped.

"Let me tell you something. If you think you are going to screw up my life because you couldn't keep your legs closed, you better think again, 'cause I'm raising my children, I ain't raising no more than that!"

It was out, she'd said it. She thought I was doing things I knew I wasn't ready for yet. Sex. Jonas and I kissed and petted, but that was it. I was wounded by her accusation and my eyes filled with tears.

"Oh, please!" she said in disgust when the first tear streaked down my check. "Those tears do not move me, Kenzie, not one damn bit!" She slammed the half-smoked cigarette into the ashtray and then immediately lit another one.

"I oughta tell your father, that's what I should do!"

I shook at the thought. "But Mom—" I began, but her hand came up, cutting my words into shreds of air.

"You know I wasn't all for this boarding school thing,

but now, now I'm all for it." She set her eyes on me and gave me a look that I'd seen passed between women on crowded buses when hips collided and tempers flared. "Get outta my face, Kenzie, and—oh, you are not to leave this house for the next week and no phone calls either."

I stood there with my mouth open. What had I done? What crime had I committed?

I stalked into my room and remained there until the next day.

She must have said something to Hy-Lo, maybe in passing or early in the day when he'd just come in from work, his mind still clear and the seal still unbroken on the bottle of vodka. They were able to converse then, like married couples on television, easy unhurried speech that was sprinkled with light laughter and calm interludes. Or maybe she'd spoken in her sleep, mumbling her anger into the softness of her pillow. Whatever the case, he found out and began to watch me.

The questions didn't begin for a few days, although I knew they were lingering there on the tip of his tongue. And then the day came when the words toppled out of his mouth, sending me reeling.

"Are you still a virgin?" He asked it as if he'd practiced the question in front of his bedroom mirror.

"What?" I said blinking in shock.

"Don't *what* me. Are you still a virgin?" he repeated.

I was wounded. What the hell was with them and this sex thing? I was thirteen years old and didn't know anyone who had actually done it. Glenna almost did, but then she chickened out. At least she'd actually seen a penis; I hadn't seen one since Malcolm had been potty-trained. "What—I mean, excuse me?" I said stupidly, not quite sure how to answer him and make him believe me.

"Are you hard of hearing now?" He was sitting on the

sofa, his cup on the floor beside his foot, a cigarette burning in the ashtray on the end table by the couch.

"Um, no, I just—um. Yes, I'm still a virgin," I blurted. My mouth went dry as the heat of embarrassment spread through my body.

"Yeah, well, I'm going to take you to the doctor to make sure." His eyes searched my face for any tick or shift that would indicate a lie.

My face was a stone block and I turned and walked away.

"I will do it, Kenzie. I will," he said to my back and laughed.

The towels came two days after his threat. Large body-consuming towels that were blinding white. Seven of them, one for each day of the week. I was to use only those towels and no one else in the house was to touch them.

He brought them in two large plastic bags that had the name SEARS in black letters on the sides. "Here," he said and shoved the bags at me.

Delia was there, ironing and folding Hy-Lo's clothes. The only piece of his clothing she didn't iron was his socks.

"Oh, those are nice." She was speaking with a lisp; her lip was swollen.

I didn't even ask her why he'd gone and bought those towels for me. We had too many towels in the house as it was. The cedar chest bulged with towels and face cloths. It was an obsession for him: linens and liquor.

I followed the rules and used one towel every day, until a lightbulb finally went off in my head as I stood drying myself.

I was on the sixth set of towels by then. The others had either begun to fray around the edges or go yellow from extensive washing and overbleaching. These seven were brand new, I could tell by how they felt against my skin and the easy anxious way the fibers absorbed the water beads.

Hy-Lo just replaced them every year. Threw out the old

ones, didn't even shred them for dusting rags like he did everything else, just packed them into one of those large black hefty bags and set them out by the trash.

I wiped at my skin and sang along to a song that played softly from my radio. I wiped at the water beneath my breasts and off my stomach, slowly moving down my thighs and then finally between my legs.

I lifted the towel to mop off some forgotten water from my shoulder and saw the red streaks of blood there. I remembered being more disgusted at having gotten my period just as I was about to go to the beach than at the bloodstains that ruined the snow-white appearance of my towel.

Maybe it was the combination of disappointment and the crimson streaks that finally delivered the answer to a question I had never asked, but I knew then why he had bought me those white towels: that was his calendar, his way of keeping tabs on my monthly.

I stuffed all seven towels in a big plastic hefty bag and set them out by the garbage.

I would never use another white towel, ever.

My week of imprisonment seemed to take a million years to pass. I spent hours staring out my window, running my hand up and down my forearm imagining it was Jonas's fingers, not mine, that gently stroked my skin.

I was in love for the first time and it pained and pleasured me in equal measure. Over that week I decided I did not want to leave Jonas. What would I do without his tender kisses and his soothing words?

We were the same, he and I, and it had taken me my whole young life to find him. I would not let him go so easily.

"Mom." I approached Delia as she walked through the door from work.

"Yes, Kenzie," she responded as she glanced at the clock.

I wasn't sure how to broach the subject. I waited while my nerves took hold of themselves.

"Yes, Kenzie," she said again and looked directly into my eyes. We had not spoken for the majority of the week. No idle chitchat about her job or the people on the block. She had nothing to say to me outside of "Turn down that music" or "Wash that cup."

The mood between us was frigid and Malcolm steered clear to avoid the icy edges that surrounded us.

"I—I was thinking that maybe I—uh, well, I don't think that I—" I was stammering, struggling to pull the right words from within.

"Spit it out, Kenzie, I have to get dinner started." She glanced at the clock again and looked at me in frustration. "C'mon, girl, say it."

"I don't want to go away to school." I blurted it out and my legs turned to Jell-O.

Delia hadn't even flinched at my announcement. She just smiled and shook her head. "And why is that?" she asked.

Something inside told me she knew what I was going to say. "I just don't," I said quietly.

"Hmmm," Delia responded and walked into the kitchen. I heard the strike of the match and then the open and close of the refrigerator door. Cigarette smoke sailed out into the living room and circled my head before fading into the darkness.

"Come here, Kenzie," Delia called to me after ten minutes or so.

When I walked into the kitchen she was seated at the table smoking. Two pots boiled and bubbled behind her on the stove and a head of lettuce sat glistening in the sink. She motioned for me to take the seat across from her.

"I was your age not too long ago. I had very few opportunities. Very few." She inhaled on her cigarette and I could tell she was thinking back. "Anyway," she said and shook her head as if trying to shake those memories away. "You have an opportunity to go away to school, to be exposed to something other than what these streets have to offer."

She said the streets, but I knew she meant Jonas.

"You may feel something for that boy, but there will be a hundred other boys in your life that will make you feel the same way. You are only thirteen, you're still a baby."

Delia's words were soft and her eyes shone with understanding, but with every word she spoke, my heart hardened against her.

"It has nothing to do with any boys, Mom." My voice was filled with impatience. "I just want to stay here and go to school with my friends," I lied.

"Uh-huh, well, I'm sorry, Kenzie, you can't do that." Her voice was still soft but there was an unmistakable hardness around the edges.

"But it's my decision," I said. My whole body stiffened with anger.

"Not anymore, Kenzie."

Our eyes locked and I fought to control the tears that threatened to come like floodwaters.

Jonas and I continued, as though our lives depended on our being together. There was two weeks left to the summer and then I would be gone.

"What kind of school is it?" he asked as we lazed beneath a grand oak in Prospect Park. My head rested in his lap and he stroked my eyebrows with the tip of his forefinger.

I don't know why I lay my head there. Maybe because dozens of couples around me were doing it and I felt a need to imitate it. At first I felt awkward having my face so close to his crotch, but then his words began to fill my ears, and the clouds, soft and full, moved across the sky, and I forgot all about the member that lurked there.

"Private. Girls," I said. I did not want to talk about it; the novelty of it had worn off a long time ago.

"My mom's giving a party on the fifth. Her birthday. You should come, it'll be like a going-away party for you."

I didn't answer right away. I was enjoying the clouds, sun, and the late-August breeze that sent the blades of grass waving. I was thirteen and my whole life was ahead of me. I was thirteen and my whole life was keeping my head propped toward the sky.

"Why not," I said and closed my eyes.

I did not have permission to be there. But I'd told a lie. Lying was becoming natural for me. Where I once stuttered and stammered my way through a lie, those words of deceit now flowed from my mouth like mother's milk. "I'm going to stay over at Glenna's," I told my mother. I did a lot of that too, telling instead of asking.

Delia looked at me, searched my face for fraud, and found nothing. I was a blank wall and my eyes never wavered beneath her watchful eye. "Okay," she said and dismissed me with a wave of her hand and a puff of smoke.

Glenna told Pinky that we were headed to the movies. A bunch of us were going to see a kung fu flick on Eastern Parkway. "Double feature?" Pinky eagerly asked as she dabbed perfume behind her ears.

"Uh-huh." We both nodded our heads and walked out the door.

It was just past eight when we arrived at Jonas's door. Al Green's "Let's Stay Together" filled the hallway. Loud laughter and carefree conversation bounced off the other side of the door just before it swung open.

Ms. Murphy, Jonas's mother, greeted us. "Hello," she said. Her eyes were slits and she held a glass of gin in one hand. "J, your little friends are here."

Glenna stifled a laugh and gave me a comical look. "She looks like a—"

"I know," I said cutting her off.

"Hey." Jonas stood before us. He had on a pair of blue Lee's and a white and blue pinstriped shirt. The crease in his pants probably took all day and half a can of starch to put there. His Adidas sneakers had been scrubbed clean, but he'd forgotten to wash the laces. They were a dusty gray and stood out like an eyesore on the burnished white leather.

"Hey," I said back to him. Glenna said the same thing and then we just stood there for a moment staring at each other.

"You look nice." His eyes traveled over my body. I wore a red tube top and black Lee's with clear jelly shoes that showed off my painted red toes.

"Thanks," I said and Glenna snickered.

"Close my goddamn door, J!" Ms. Murphy yelled from the background.

The apartment was small, just a one-bedroom, with a bathroom and kitchen. The living room was barely the size of my bedroom, yet she had enough people jammed in there to fill two apartments.

"Y'all got jobs?" Ms. Murphy slurred at Glenna and me.

"No," we said together and looked at Jonas.

"Oh, okay, otherwise you'd hafta pay like everyone else." She coughed and then laughed and stumbled away to a tight crowd of people near the kitchen.

Jonas shook his head in embarrassment. We stood there in the midst of the music and paper plates filled with greasy chicken wings, coleslaw, and fried corn. We said nothing for a long time, just took in everything around us.

It was my first grown-up party outside the family gatherings. During those the children were confined to a bedroom, often stretched across an aunt's bed fighting with the guest coats, or shoved into a cousin's dank basement with a bowl of popcorn and a few cans of soda.

Now I stood beneath a blue light while droves of adults moved around me, counting me as one of them, not noticing at all that I could have been one of their own children out on a lie.

The scent of reefer moved through the air and tickled at our noses. Glenna and I smiled at each other and lifted our heads and inhaled deeply. We moved further into the deep blue-blackness of the apartment, sidestepping swaying arms, jutting hipbones, and bobbing behinds. It was like walking into a living cave.

Someone shoved a beer into my hand, and before I could politely refuse it a short bald man with big eyes and a potbelly grabbed my arm and swung me around. "C'mon, sweet thang, you wanna dance wit me?"

I tried to object but he was already pulling me toward the sea of people bumping and grinding their way through "Love Is the Message."

"No thank y—" I was in the midst of it before I or anyone else could save me. I looked desperately toward Glenna and then Jonas, but neither of them made a move.

"C'mon, c'mon." The man before me had my free hand, swaying my arm back and forth as if it had some instant connection with my feet. "How you young people do it?" he said and did an awkward spin.

I laughed and popped the tab to the beer can. My feet began to move, stiff at first, and then I took a sip of the beer and picked up on the rhythm, allowing myself to be carried by the music. My feet shuffled and slid across the tired wooden floor as I allowed myself to let loose.

"Yeah, yeah!" The old man clapped his hands and danced around me to a beat he'd carried in his head since the '50s.

Before I knew it Glenna was on the floor with one of Jonas's bleary-eyed cousins and Jonas had flung me around, stealing me from my dance partner.

Who knows how many hours had passed, or how many beers I had consumed, before I even thought to check the time. I remember once making my way toward the kitchen to do just that when Jonas tugged me back and pulled me into him. A slow song finally came on so the old people could sit down, get something to eat, drink, or lean up against the wall.

There were just a few people left on the floor and Jonas and I were among them. I was thirteen. I had never been held so tightly before, pulled into someone so completely that you became one. Jonas clung to me as if I was his lifeline. I felt him grow hard on my thigh and we both blushed with embarrassment, pulling each other closer still, hiding the secret between us.

It was when I yawned and Glenna followed that I saw the hazy blue of early morning pushing beneath the half-drawn shades of the living room. My heart stopped dead in my chest.

"Oh. My. God." I grabbed Glenna's hand and started toward the door. "I'm going to die," I said as I pushed through the crowd of people.

"Kenzie?" Jonas had no idea what was happening. I moved by him like a bat out of hell.

The streets were quiet and we tiptoed across to the apartment building as if it could veil us from prying eyes. Our hearts raced while Glenna slid her key into the lock of the heavy metal door.

Our breathing echoed through the halls when we crossed the lobby and took the stairwell up to her apartment. Glenna looked at me and made the sign of the cross on her chest before slipping the key into the lock and slowly turning it. We took a deep breath and pushed the door open on its creaky hinges, crossing our fingers, eyes, and toes against the possibility that Pinky would be up waiting for us.

The apartment was dark except for the thin streams of light that found their way through the hole-riddled shades of the living room and crisscrossed the floor.

We stood still and listened to Pinky's steady breathing

and whoever shared her bed that morning. Once sure they were sleeping, we moved like snakes, winding and twisting our way through the living room and into Glenna's bedroom. We closed the door softly and quickly undressed, jumping into the bed, our hearts still pounding hard in our chests, leaving us little air to breathe, much less giggle. But we did anyway, giggled for more than an hour into Glenna's pillow before falling asleep, our arms and legs entangled like thick dark tree roots.

Chapter Fourteen

I left Brooklyn two days before Labor Day Monday. I hugged Glenna and winked at Jonas as he stood on the corner; his head was lowered and his hands were shoved deep into his pockets. He kicked at the dirt around him and smiled at me sadly, blowing me a kiss when Delia's back was turned.

Delia spotted him; she twisted her face and huffed, but kept quiet. Jonas and I had said our goodbyes the night before and my mouth still felt the joy of his lips. "I'll see you in November," I said to Glenna as I climbed into the back of Mable's car.

"Write before then," Glenna said, curling her fingers around the top of the passenger window.

"Okay," I promised and blinked against the tears that welled up in my eyes.

Mable backed the Oldsmobile slowly out of the parking space, Delia rolled her window down and lit a cigarette, Malcolm opened up his Spider-man comic book, and I turned my head to see if I could catch one last look at Jonas, but the corner was empty except for the late-summer leaves that danced in the slow breeze.

My heart sank a bit and I sighed heavily. Mable put the car in drive, Delia turned the radio on, and Malcolm flipped restlessly through his comic book. I turned to look again, hoping that just maybe Jonas would be there. There stood Hy-Lo, arms folded across his chest, cigarette dangling from the side of his mouth, brown paper package beneath his armpit. He smiled; I grimaced and glanced away. "Turn that up, Ma," I said as McFadden & Whitehead belted out "Ain't No Stopping Us Now."

The Addison School was a converted monastery with long, wide halls that resembled bright tunnels. The windows swung out instead of pushed up, and the main corridors were still lit by sconces that held three-inch candles.

The school sat at the foot of the Catskill Mountains in the town of Maplewood, where whitewashed homes flew the American flag and white picket fences enclosed the wide yards that held above-ground pools, wooden jungle gyms, and doghouses.

There was a pond that doubled as an ice rink in the winter and fourteen babbling brooks that were shaded by tiny red and white footbridges.

Time had not completely passed Maplewood by, but it hadn't spent more than a night or two there in the last fifteen years either.

The townspeople snatched quick glances at me on the street. I was one of three blacks in Maplewood: two at the school and a man who owned an art gallery on the west side of town.

My four years spent there were, for the most part, happy ones. I played soccer, skied in the winters, and white-water rafted in the spring. My vernacular lost its street slickness, my rough edges began to smooth, and the gray dreams of my feeble Brooklyn youth took on vivid colors that left me feeling powerful and hopeful.

I avoided home as much as possible, spending most of my holidays with my friends and their families. But as much as I tried to avoid who I was and what I had come from, it still managed to find me and remind me.

I saw remnants of my life wrapped around the arm of my science teacher. Dull green and blue fingers glowed painfully against her alabaster skin. I was familiar with the fear behind her eyes. That was the same look Delia had. I knew she stayed past five to do more than grade papers and put together our lessons for the following day. She stayed late to avoid the man who beat her, and then in the same breath told her he loved her as he dabbed her wounds with antiseptic.

I saw it when I was in Vail on a ski trip with my friend Megan Wolanski and her family. We were seated before the stone fireplace of her parents' winter home, wrapped in a black and red checkered blanket; our faces were flushed from the brandy we had hidden beneath the blanket. It was thick, dark, and tasted like licorice. We sipped and laughed, sipped and laughed until our laughter became loud enough to drown out the angry sounds of Mr. and Mrs. Wolanski as they screamed and cursed at each other.

When the first slap rang out Megan scrambled closer to me, knocking over the bottle of brandy and covering her ears with her hands. I picked up the bottle and took another swig before replacing the cork and returning it to its place in the liquor cabinet.

I eased myself back beside Megan and moved my hand across the gleaming blond of her hair. I did not feel any compassion for her; I searched and searched and could not find any. The liquor had hidden it from me. I moved her hands from her ears and looked deep down inside of myself and found some pity the brandy had missed and coated my words in it. "Everything's gonna be all right," I said and looked back at the liquor cabinet. I could tell Megan believed me, but I nodded my head for emphasis and halfheartedly patted her on the shoulder for further effect. My mind was on the bottle of brandy and how good the thick dark liquid made me feel. "It'll be okay," I added, trying to unwrap my mind from the gold-foiled label.

Megan smiled back at me and wiped at her tearing eyes.

She didn't know I was a longtime sufferer of this war, she just thought I was strong.

Hy-Lo was with me even though he was miles and miles away. He came in different skin colors, read the Bible or just the sports page. He was a social drinker, a weekend lush, a martini-swirling beer-can-crushing vodka-and-orange-juice man who beat his wife and terrified his kids. Hy-Lo was miles away and he was around the corner, in the next room, pumping gas at the Texaco, and leaning over the counter at Iggy's Ice-Cream Shoppe asking me how many scoops of vanilla I'd like.

I recognized him no matter what disguise he wore.

The Addison School offered Saturday Temple for the Jewish girls and Sunday Mass for the Catholic ones. Father Gifford was our priest; he was tall with California sun-kissed skin, sapphire eyes, and silver hair.

He was a handsome man and that helped us sit through his long Sunday sermons. He rambled on endlessly, never quite making or delivering a message. He spoke while leaning on his pulpit, his fists clenched beneath his chin while his elbows rested on the open pages of his Bible.

The girls thought it was comical, but I knew different. I saw the flush in his face, the light pink sheen that traveled from his brow and down his neck, disappearing behind his collar and black suit.

A sip before Sunday Mass and the rest of the bottle later. I knew.

It must have been gin because I never smelled it. He smoked, so it was Merit Lights that sailed off his breath when he raised the host in front of my face and said, "The Body of Christ."

I avoided his eyes and said, "Amen."

I knew that Hy-Lo was with me when I entered the confessional and dropped down to my knees and told Father Gifford that I was the child of an alcoholic. I told him that I had a deep hatred for my father and that, Lord forgive me, I had wished him dead on many occasions.

My knees cracked against the worn red leather of the kneeler as I waited for him to reply. What I heard was the familiar twist of a cap, the light falling sound that liquid makes against the soft tissue of the mouth, and finally the inhale of breath as it unleashes itself into the bloodstream.

I did not wait for him to speak on my problem or to assign me ten Hail Marys. I got up and walked away. Made my escape, just as I did when I stepped into my grandmother's car and we took off for the Addison School.

I had started out for the hospital, but somehow ended up standing in the check-cashing store staring at the boxed black numbers of the large calendar that hung on the wall. I knew it was Wednesday, but which Wednesday? I looked down at the stub of my welfare check; it was dated November 28. I looked back at the calendar; there was a Wednesday, December 5, 12, 19, and 26. I shoved the stub into my pocket and turned to face the long line of men, women, and children who stood patiently waiting to collect their food stamps and cash their welfare checks.

My eyes searched through the multicolored faces and fell on a dark-skinned woman with round eyes and a pierced nose. "'Scuse me," I said and took a step toward her. "What's today's date?" She took a step backward and I saw that she had an infant wrapped to her torso with a brightly colored piece of kente cloth.

She blinked before responding as if I'd pulled her from a daydream. "The twelfth," she said, placing a protective hand on top of her baby's head.

"Thanks," I said and walked away.

I decided that I would try to make it special. I had time to make it special. It was the twelfth of December, thirteen days until Christmas. I picked up a tree; it was small and bald in too many places, but it was a tree just the same. It looked as lonely and pitiful as I felt. I had to haggle for twenty minutes with the Korean store owner.

"Fifteen dollar," he said without looking at me.

"Ten," I said and shoved a ten-dollar bill in his face.

"Fifteen," he said and bent to sift through a box of onions.

"C'mon, ten," I pushed.

"Twelve," he said as he tossed the rotten onions aside.

"Ten dollars and you know you ain't throwing those damn onions out!"

"Look, lady, you give me big trouble. I say twelve dollar, take it or leave it, and don't you worry 'bout deez onions."

"Ten dollars because it's Christmas," I said, still shaking the money in his face.

He snatched the bill out of my hand. "You take tree and get out. You big trouble for me, lady," he said and his good eye sparkled with amusement.

I had decided that I would not let Hy-Lo steal Christmas, not like he'd stolen Thanksgiving.

Once I got the tree into the apartment, I pulled out the old Dewar's Scotch box that held the Christmas tree trimmings. Most of the green, red, and gold balls were cracked, missing hooks or whole tops. I used what I could and discarded the rest. I dug deeper into the box, pulling out old Christmas cards, forgotten gift tags, and finally a dusty, half-empty bottle of vodka.

I froze and almost dropped the bottle to the floor. It could have been one of Delia's. Maybe the last one she'd bought before she decided to stop drinking. Or maybe it was one of the last ones I'd bought. I couldn't remember. My body began to shake and I could feel my mouth filling with water as my mind urged me to unscrew the cap and just take one swallow. Just one.

I shook my head against the thought, knowing full well

that one drink would not be enough. I jumped up and ran to the bathroom, convincing myself to spill the liquid down the toilet and flush it away. But what of the smell? I couldn't trust myself, the scent alone could force me to surrender.

Halfway to the bathroom I turned on my heels and ran back into the living room. I looked left and I looked right; were the walls closing in on me?

Just one sip.

"Oh my God!" I screamed, trying desperately to keep that voice in my head at bay.

If you take just one, I'll go away.

I could feel my resistance splintering; I heard the crack as my commitment to sobriety began to come apart in the middle, and then there was the shattering sound of my sanity as it came crashing down around me.

The walls moved closer.

I threw my hands up and began to cry. I looked down at the bottle and saw my life floating at the bottom. I wanted so badly to get rid of it. I wanted so badly to drink from it.

The air thinned.

I started to unscrew the cap, telling myself, like I had so many times in the past, that I would just take one sip, just one. Just enough to silence the voice and fill that black hole that took up so much space near my heart. The top shifted between my fingers and my mind moved backward with each orbit the top made around the clear rim of the bottle.

Like a film, my teenage years and early twenties appeared before me. Those years were lived in a blur of drugs and alcohol. I tried everything and anything: uppers, downers, blue lights, black beauties, mescaline, reefer, cocaine, dope. I tried it all, but in the end I always came back to the bottle.

I drank to numb myself against Hy-Lo. I drank to numb myself against the voices of my professors. I drank to get my head straight before going to work. I drank to wind down before coming home.

What was it my boss said, "You are sick, Kenzie, you need help"? I think those were her words.

My head was in the guacamole at the time and the client, Mr. Mayamoto, and his sales team were clicking away with their sleek silver cameras. I don't know if I actually heard her correctly over the noise of the digital flashes.

"You're fired!" she screamed when I asked if I could just have one more drink. Just one for the road. Then I turned and puked on her Italian leather pumps.

Their loss, I thought to myself as I stumbled home. Shoot, I was the best account executive they had, at least that's what the vodka and orange juice told me every morning before I went to work.

Then there was Mr. Thierry, with his thin red nose and crooked toupee. He shook my hand, indicated for me to take a seat, and then said, "Kenzie, tell me a little bit about yourself." And I did, I rambled on and on about my experience and why I would be the best candidate for the position, and then I noticed that Mr. Thierry had his face screwed up so tight that his top lip covered the openings to his nose.

I tried to ignore the look on his face, I kept on talking and concentrated on how good I looked. I had on my finest, sharpest suit. The one that showed just enough thigh to be considered aggressive but not sluttish.

But then he opened his mouth and I wasn't sure I'd heard right. "You smell like a distillery," he said to me ten minutes after I walked into his office.

"What?" I replied, smiling and leaning forward, showing just enough cleavage to be considered powerful but not easy.

"Ms. Lowe, have you been drinking?" He snatched a quick look at the cleavage I presented him and his face went beet red. He rolled his chair backward. "Have you?" he said and then screwed his face up again.

"Drinking?" I played stupid. "Like coffee and tea?"

Mr. Thierry's face kind of undid itself and I would have expected his features to soften, but they didn't, they just looked undone and irritated.

"Do you really think I could consider you for this position?" And then he laughed. "You, a drunk?"

I laughed too, laughed until my sides hurt and security came and removed me from the building.

Then there was that thing William would always accuse me of—what was it? Oh, yeah: "The only time you want to have sex with me, Kenzie, is when you're half-drunk, and then you can't even participate in it."

That's when sex was at its best for me. I needed to have a few drinks in me; without it I was as passionless as a log. I never really wanted sex unless I was drinking; it was as if the liquor reminded me that I was a woman.

"Funny how you never make that comment before the sex," I would mumble and roll away from him.

"Why don't you ever let me hold you?" he'd ask. I could feel his eyes looking down on me and I knew he was trying so much to love me, but found himself hating me more and more each day.

"Because I needed to be fucked, not held," I would say and I knew, even in a semidrunken haze, that those words belonged to Hy-Lo. I couldn't remember the exact age I was when I first heard him utter those same words to Delia, but I remember thinking that the sound of it reminded me of smoke and ashes.

That was it for William, he'd had enough of me. The numerous one-night stands he'd heard about, the public drunken outbursts. "Get out, Kenzie," he said late one night in a low even voice. I could still see him, propped up against his pillow, one hand searching the nightstand for his fashionable tortoise shell–rimmed glasses, while the other hand wiped at the tears in his eyes.

William had put up with me for a long time, nearly a

year. They need to make a trophy for a guy who still kisses you full on your lips after you've had your head in a public toilet.

A national award should be instituted for the man who brings his girlfriend home to meet his mother and doesn't even blink in embarrassment that the woman drinks his dad and two older brothers under the table before passing out in the lounge chair in the backyard.

Why isn't there a certificate of recognition for a man who loves a woman who can only love him after she's had a bottle of wine and two after-dinner cordials?

I tried to love William, but my efforts were as fleeting as the seasons and paled and withered as quick as fall leaves.

"Drop dead," I said to him and slammed out of his apartment with nothing but a gallon of vodka in one hand and my pocketbook in the other. Butt naked, I stood on the corner of 90th Street and Columbus Avenue at four in the morning, trying to hail a cab.

That's how I ended up in the G building with four doctors peering into my eyes, ears, and nose with penlights, pushing white cards with funny-shaped ink blotches in my face, asking me about my childhood, my mother, and if I'd ever thought about killing myself or anyone else.

I was sober by then; the cold steel stool against my exposed behind, the large bright lights, and the crisp white walls of the room had shocked me back into sobriety.

"Do you know how you got here . . . miss?" one doctor questioned and folded his arms across his chest.

I wasn't sure. I sort of recalled a policeman approaching me; he was bent forward a bit and he took large steps like he was trying to avoid stepping on a crack in the sidewalk. His arms were stretched far ahead of him and his hands moved slowly up and down as if he were bouncing two basketballs in slow motion. His mouth was moving but all I could hear was my own voice screaming, "Taxi!"

The next thing I knew I was worried about getting frost-bite on my ass.

I spent ten days there. They would have let me go after three, but I started talking to the air around my bed and smiling at the thick black bars of the windows, and my doctors thought better of it.

Glenna brought me tulips; who knew where she'd found them so late in November. She told me that the washed-out gray of my hospital gown did nothing for my complexion and made my butt look big. It was supposed to be a joke, but neither one of us laughed.

We sat across from each other, our eyes moving over each other's faces, taking in as much as possible, storing it away just in case it was the last time. Just in case. Glenna had stuck with me through everything—the times I yelled at her for taking me home before last call. Through each lost job and boyfriend. She never gave up on me. Our fingers linked at some point during her visit and we cried.

We held each other for a long time when she got up to go. The other visitors, patients, and staff probably thought we were lovers. I could hear the snickering at my back, and I pulled Glenna closer to me. I wanted to tell them, those people who laughed and pointed, that we were the best of friends and loved far beyond the physical plane.

When Delia came to see me, her eyes were red and her shoulders slumped as if she were coming to visit a criminal instead of her sick daughter. I smiled when the orderly led her into the visiting room.

We didn't say much, just shared a cigarette and watched the other patients visit with family and friends. I hugged her when she got up to leave and I told her that I was staying because I needed the rest.

Delia surveyed the room and then came back to me, and for a second I thought I saw envy flash there. "Uh-huh," she said and moved her hand across her forehead.

* * *

Bottle in hand, I moved to the door of the apartment; my hand shook as I grabbed the doorknob. "God, please," I begged as I took the first step out into the hallway. I could feel the cold wrap around my arms and hear the wind as it slipped in through the open windows of the corridors. "Please, please, please," I prayed as I moved down the hall, closing my eyes against the black and white block pattern of the floor. Those blocks bucked and writhed beneath my feet like an angry ocean and I had to stop every so often and press my back against the wall for balance.

I moved on until my fingers wrapped around the wooden handle that would open up the heavy iron door of the incinerator.

"Please, please," I begged as I dangled the bottle between my hell and the fiery one below. The wind mocked me and called me weak while it whipped through the hall above me and started down the stairs. I moaned because it hurt somewhere inside of me in a place so deep I couldn't reach it, and then the wind laughed and slammed my apartment door back hard on its hinges.

I thought once more about taking a sip before turning the bottle loose, thought about the feel of the glass mouth against my own before the liquid streamed out, but then I heard music come in off the street and for some reason I remembered the pain that was dying in a hospital bed across town.

My fingers uncurled and let the clear glass bottle slip free and down into the flaming blackness.

After that I thought I would need air so I took a walk, but found myself back beside him again, closer now. My chair centered with his knees. Some type of understanding shadowing my hate.

I believed I'd won a battle that day; the war was still raging, but I was making progress.

"You never won the battle, Hy-Lo, did you?" I asked in a whisper while my fingers fiddled with the hem of the sheet that hung off the bed. "You gave in to the laughter of the wind, didn't you?" I asked his sleeping face.

His foot flinched a little and I knew his answer was yes.

"Hello," Nurse Green chimed as she poked her head around the curtain. "How are we doing today?" she asked, her face glowing, her white starched uniform still whiter beneath the sunrays spilling in through the windows.

"Fine," I answered and for the first time held her face with my eyes.

The act must have thrown her off a bit because her eyes widened and she stammered her next word. "G-good," she said and her smile broadened. She stood there for a moment, smiling and looking from me to Hy-Lo and then back to me as if she was waiting for something else.

"Good," she said once again, patted my shoulder, and left.

When I returned home I sat alone on the couch for hours staring at the Christmas tree with its thin branches and empty spaces. Someone fired a gun off in the distance and somewhere in the building a dog howled long and sad.

I wiped at my eyes and expected my hands to come away moist and salty, but my eyes were dry. I moved to the window to stare out into the blue-blackness of the night. There were a few people moving up and down the sidewalk, stepping over the garbage that swirled and spun in the wake of the wind pushing at their backs and messing with their hair. They moved around the garbage that stood on the corners— those two-legged pieces of trash that pushed dirty hands into their faces and begged for spare change.

Hy-Lo had become that type of rubbish, the type that lived and breathed and asked for change from good and decent people. "Can you spare a quarter?" "Got a nickel for me, brother?" "Spare a dime?"

He was jobless and would have been homeless if it weren't for me. He had lost much of his mind with Malcolm. Then he lost his house, whatever spirit he had, and his dignity followed soon after; that's how he ended up on the street begging for change.

I would feed and house him best I could because I hated the look I saw in Delia's eyes whenever I put the dead bolt on the door. "Your father is still out there," she would say to me and her eyebrows would come together.

Yes, I fed and housed him best I could, but I would not buy his liquor, so he turned to the street and the kindness of strangers.

He wasn't the only one, there were a few of them— gray-skinned men with dirty jeans that bagged at the knees. Their eyes were bloodshot or jaundice-colored and their faces gruff with a five o'clock shadow present at any hour of the day. These men, including Hy-Lo, smiled most of the time, and the times they didn't, they sang. But they could all be found in front of the liquor store or at one of the two corners the liquor store sat between.

"*Youuuuuu send me. I know youuuuuu send me.*" That was Hy-Lo's favorite song. "*Darling, you do, darling, you do,*" he would bellow out off-key and do a little James Brown kick-and-turn after each chorus. He would almost always lose his balance and end up falling into a pedestrian, who would either shake their head in disgust and move on or cuss him and then give him a violent shove for good measure.

He would stumble backward and put his hands up in apology and ask, "Got a dime?" and then laugh like an old man, even though he was only forty-eight.

Alcohol pulls your youth from you in layers. I know for a fact that it does because at thirty-four I have counted more than 145 silver strands that have sprouted up in my head like gray weeds and I have to dab concealer on the puffy skin beneath my eyes. Sometimes my body shakes for no reason, and then there is the forgetfulness.

When I look in the bathroom mirror at myself I realize that I look the way Hy-Lo did all of his life. And sometimes I see my reflection in the glass of the window and see Delia's face in mine, the way she looked those years she tried to drink away the pain.

Chapter Fifteen

When I graduated from high school I came back to our small apartment and found that the rooms were bare except for the brown boxes that were stacked one on top of the other.

"Surprise!" Delia exclaimed when she saw the expression on my face. "We bought a house!"

I'd never seen her happier. In fact I'd never seen her happy.

The house Hy-Lo purchased with his VA loan and the money he had saved over the years was a small one-family structure on Autumn Avenue, a tree-lined street way on the other side of Brooklyn in a neighborhood that bordered the borough of Queens. It was a sixty-year-old, two-story white brick with old pipes and solid walls. The house had three bedrooms and a basement that would always reek of dog and mildew.

The neighborhood had turned over four times in forty years. First, the Italians moved in and the Jews moved out. Then the Garcias and Lopezes of Puerto Rico and the Dominican Republic arrived with their salsa music and roast pork, sending the Italians running for the safety of Queens and Staten Island. Now here we were, with the East Indians at our heels.

Hy-Lo and Delia were older now and for a short time we were able to keep the violence hidden from the neighbors. We tucked it behind our smiles and buried it deep beneath the cinnamon brown of Delia's Cover Girl foundation.

Then just two months after we moved in I had to call the police, and everyone on Autumn knew we were less than perfect.

Delia was a nervous mess; her thin orange housecoat was ripped at the front, exposing the worn curve of her breast. Her lip was still bleeding where Hy-Lo had punched her, and a black space beamed where her front tooth used to be.

Hy-Lo had fled before the police arrived. I imagined him lurking behind a tree or in the back of our neighbor's yard, inhaling fiercely on cigarette after cigarette and pacing nervously until the cruiser pulled away from in front of our house.

"What does your husband look like?" the bored police officer asked.

He had twenty years on the job and could care less about the woman before him. I stared at him with his fat cheeks and knew he was thinking about food rather than Delia's bleeding lip.

"What was he wearing when he left the house?" he asked in the middle of a yawn. His partner seemed embarrassed. I couldn't tell if his embarrassment came from Delia's appearance or the lack of concern his partner showed her. He kept shifting his weight from one foot to the other until I threw him a look that made him stop and lean motionless against the sink.

"Has he ever done this before?" the white cop asked and then turned his deep dark eyes on Delia. She looked at me and then down at her hands. I opened my mouth and then closed it again.

"N-no," she lied without glancing up.

The embarrassed cop looked at me and I mouthed: *Yes.*

"Uh-huh," the fat cop said and stared at the top of her head. "Was your husband drinking, Mrs.—" He had to flip through the sheets of paper to find her name before continuing. "Mrs., um—Lowe?"

The embarrassed cop looked at me again and I nodded my head yes and mouthed: *Always*.

"N-no," Delia said again, still peering down at her hands.

"Well, do you want to file charges?" the fat cop asked as he got up from the chair. He already knew what the answer would be.

I bit my bottom lip and pulled at the ragged collar of my T-shirt. "Mom?" I said hoping my voice would push her.

"N-no," Delia responded without lifting her head up.

The fat cop shrugged his shoulders and shot the embarrassed cop a look that said, *I told you so*.

Malcolm, who had been pacing the small hall space outside of the kitchen, turned, punched the wall, and slammed out the front door.

"Have a good night," the fat cop said behind a heavy breath and turned to leave.

"Um . . ." The embarrassed cop started to say something, his cheeks flushed cherry, and then he thought better of it and instead said goodnight and followed the fat cop out the front door.

I wonder now where Hy-Lo spent those nights. Six weeks of heavy dark twilights. We thought he was at work; I think now he must have been at the Blue Moon drinking away his shame, anger, and his life savings.

If it wasn't for the phone calls we would never have known.

"May I speak to Mr. Hyman Lowe?"

"Um, he's not here right now. This is his wife, may I help?"

"Mrs. Lowe, this is Mr. Hagerty from Pendant Mortgage Company and I'm calling to find out when you plan on sending in your past due payments—"

"Past due payments?"

"Yes. Three months past due."

"Are you sure you have the right Lowe? I mean my husband . . . three months past due?"

"Yes, we will be starting foreclosure proceedings on your home in a matter of—"

"I don't understand, three months past due? Three months?"

Delia confronted Hy-Lo. Quietly at first—she chose her words carefully and picked through her range of tones until finally settling on one that was soft and timid. "Hyman, the mortgage company called, they said that we're behind on the payments . . . they said three months . . . three months past due . . . ?" She was speaking to his back as he rummaged through the top drawer of his dresser. "Hyman—" she began again after he continued to ignore her.

"Shut up, Delia," he said without turning around. He slammed the top drawer closed and snatched open the second one.

Delia stood there for a while, waiting for him to find whatever it was he was searching for so frantically. He had opened and closed all five drawers of his bureau before finally turning around to face her.

"Hyman, I want to know—" Delia started again and Hy-Lo cut her off again, visciously this time.

"I said shut the fuck up, Delia!" he yelled and stormed past her. Their shoulders connected and she stumbled backward.

She did not approach him again, not for at least two weeks, not until after she grew frustrated and tired of the bill collectors.

She began to search, digging through his drawers at night when she thought he was at work. She found stacks of overdue bills, white and gray envelopes that held threatening pieces of paper with angry red letters stamped across them that screamed: *FINAL NOTICE.*

She found them tucked beneath his neatly folded undershirts and boxer shorts, the ones she had spent her Saturday mornings washing, starching, and pressing. Delia's heart must have sunk and her hands must have shook as she moved to the next drawer and found more of the same. In the third drawer she found an unemployment check and in the fourth she found the letter that told her that her husband had been terminated from his job. Terminated.

The apartment was hot and the heat fueled the anger my memories brought on. I laughed aloud, forgetting that Delia was in the back room.

"What?" she called to me.

"I was talking to myself," I responded and sat down again on the sofa.

I looked back at the Christmas tree; it had slumped to one side like a trampled old man, like Hy-Lo when his pride had become nothing more than backwash in the bottles he drank from.

I got up and went to the kitchen to fill a glass with water to pour into the green and red tree stand. The apartment was hot and so I cracked the window and allowed the cold to filter in, giving the tree some air and a chance.

If only that would have been enough for Hy-Lo. A glass of water and some air.

"Ha," another bitter laugh escaped, and I covered my mouth against the troop of laughter that piled up at the base of my throat. I swallowed hard and forced it back inside of me.

I sat back down and leaned into the couch, flicking through the TV channels, faster and faster until the pictures moved across the screen in a blur. Finally my thumb tired and I settled on channel eleven. The news was on and I leaned my head back and closed my eyes while I listened.

In today's news Ellen Fable consults the president about black political America and where the African American community stands . . .

I sat straight up and rubbed my eyes. Ellen Fable had been in quite a few of my classes at Marymount College. She was a large girl, at least a size twenty. The relaxers just didn't seem to take to her hair and so she wore it pulled back into a puffed ponytail that attracted lint and dust like a magnet. She had one pair of shoes whose seams had split open to reveal the small bend of her pinky toe.

Ellen Fable had nothing, less than nothing, and we pitied her behind her back as she moved through the halls like a great whale through the sea of students that made way for her. "She gets welfare, you know," people said when Ellen was out of earshot. "She lives with her grandmother. She's blind, you know, the grandmother."

"Where are her parents?" I asked one day.

"They're dead. Both of them."

"Oh my God. How awful. How?"

"Drunk driver."

"Oh! A drunk driver hit them?"

"No, her father was the drunk and he drove himself and her mother into the back of a gas truck. Ellen was eight years old."

Ellen Fable with her missing tooth and lazy left eye, Ellen Fable who had nothing, less than nothing, and still ended up having more than me.

"Oh, shit," I mumbled as I moved closer to the television. Ellen Fable smiled broadly while the cameramen took snapshot after snapshot.

She had a mouth full of teeth now and the lazy eye was hidden behind a fashionable pair of lightly tinted glasses and Ellen Fable had slimmed down to a respectable size twelve.

"Oh, shit," I said again and moved back into the sofa as Ellen's face was replaced by the drab features of the weatherman.

Ellen Fable had come from nothing and had everything. I had come from Delia and Hy-Lo and had nothing.

* * *

I needed to walk. I was gone before Delia rose the following morning. Christmas was just a week away and the streets were filled with Saturday-morning Christmas shoppers. I mingled amongst them, trailing behind mothers and their children, coming up alongside whole families, trying to stand close enough to feel a part of something joyous.

Some noticed and clutched their pocketbooks closer to them, others gave me dirty looks and walked quickly away, while a few smiled at me as if they knew that's exactly what I needed.

I ended up, as I did on most days now, at Hy-Lo's bedside. He had not changed, he didn't look worse and he didn't look better. I had bought a Christmas card at a five-and-dime store on my way there. It was flimsy and the ink was cheap. On the front was a brilliant Christmas tree, the colors faded in places and dark and bold in others. On the inside it read: *Wishing you a Joyous Holiday and a Very Happy New Year!*

I sat the card down beside the poinsettia, the colorful side facing Hy-Lo. For some reason I needed this space to be full of something other than his sickness and my sadness.

I moved my chair up a bit, just past his knees until I was parallel to his groin. I felt uncomfortable there and moved up a bit more to his stomach.

The room was filled with visitors and I looked around at the faces in the beds and none of them was familiar to me. Change, it was a constant in that ward; whether it was for better or worse, things kept moving on. I pulled the curtain around us and blocked out the rest of the world.

I had taken my jacket off and laid it across my lap. My gloves remained on my hands and my head remained covered by my hat. I was still cold, but it was nothing like the cold that had overwhelmed me during my earlier visits. This was more like the unbalanced chill of a late April evening, the kind where winter still claims the nights even though the tulips have pushed up through the earth and nests made by tiny brown birds dot the tree limbs and lampposts.

It was that type of warmth and cold mixed up wrong that gripped that day they found Hy-Lo's brother Charlie in a stall on a toilet in a halfway house, his head lolled to one side, foam seeping from his mouth, his pants down around his ankles, and a bottle of gin resting on his lap.

I was at his apartment when the call came. His wife placed the phone back in its cradle and said to no one in particular, "Charles is dead," and went back to dusting the furniture. I could have sworn I heard her let go a sigh of relief as she moved the candy bowl and the imitation porcelain dogs to the side of the table that had already been dusted.

His children, five of them, looked up from what they were doing and stared at each other. It seemed as if they were waiting for a cue. Some emotion from someone that they could imitate and build on. But it never came and they went back to what they were consumed by before they'd heard the news of their father's death. I grabbed my coat and left.

That had shaken Hy-Lo, but not enough for him to stop drinking, not enough for his eyes to mist with grief, just enough for his head to dip while the minister spoke over Charlie's dead body.

Gwenyth had taken it hard; after all, he was her child, even though they had not spoken to one another for more than three years. She pretended that the distance and the silence didn't bother her, but we all knew it did because she clung even tighter to her youngest child, Randy. She would have turned to Hy-Lo, but he was like Teflon, so what would be the point in trying?

A year later, as if on cue, the phone rang just as I was thinking about Charlie because his son had called from jail and wanted me to send him sneakers.

No, I think I was thinking about the sneakers when the

phone rang and I picked it up and almost said "Nike" instead of "Hello."

"Yes, may I speak to Hyman Lowe, please?" The voice sounded clinical.

"He's not here, this is his daughter, may I help you?"

Hy-Lo was there, but he was passed out in his chair in the basement. I could hear his loud snores through the floorboards and I stomped my feet even though I knew he didn't hear me.

The voice paused and then cleared its throat. "Well, I suppose I can give you the message." I rolled my eyes because I had just come in from my night job. I had only four hours left to sleep before I had to head back to the city to take my place behind the cosmetic counter at Bloomingdale's. I stomped on the floor again, harder this time—because that is what Hy-Lo had made my life: harder.

"Um, his mother," the voice came again, "Gwenyth Lowe expired this morning at four-thirty."

The voice went dead and I took it as a gracious act in order to leave me a space to voice my grief. But I had none and so I said, "Do you need him to come in and identify the body or something?"

Silence seeped into the room from the other end of the line.

"Thank you for the information, I will let him know," I said without giving the voice a chance to respond.

Gwenyth had been admitted into a nursing home just six months after Charlie died. Her mind had snapped in two despite how close she kept Randy to her. Maybe if she'd had both of her sons to hold on to, her mind would only have bent against the loss she suffered instead of coming completely apart in the middle.

Gwenyth's life was reflected in the sparse number of people who attended her funeral: one or two people I didn't know, five grandchildren, an old friend from her childhood, two daughters-in-law, her remaining sons, and Glenna. We felt ashamed of the emptiness in the small room of the funeral home the service was held in, and so we spread out, attempting to fill the lonely spaces and catch the echo of the minister's words as they bounced from the dark wood walls.

Glenna sat beside me, fidgeting and whispering apologies in my ear. "It's okay, Glenna. It's okay," was all I could offer her. My mouth was like cotton and my insides were hard and cold like my grandmother's body.

Gwenyth lay before us, dressed in a smart burgundy wool suit, her hair a mass of tight silver curls, her makeup impeccably applied. She looked the same in death as she did in life: perfect.

The preacher invited people to stand up and say a kind word about Gwenyth Lowe. There was a shuffling of programs and then the creaking of chairs as people eased themselves deeper into the aluminum frames. But no one stood or spoke. The preacher looked embarrassed. His mouth puckered in bewilderment and then he cleared his throat and once again invited someone to stand and speak. "Is there anyone who would like to say something? Anyone at all?"

"I'd like to say something," a voice called out from the bank of chairs on the left side of the room. Someone gasped in surprise and all heads turned toward the woman who stood up. It was Uncle Charlie's first wife, Evelyn, the one we weren't allowed to mention in the house. Evelyn was dressed in a red suit with a fur collar. There was a man sitting next to her, who I assumed was her new husband. Evelyn raised her hand and moved a perfectly curled lock of hair from her forehead. That's when we all saw the ring—so disgustingly huge that it didn't just sparkle, it glowed.

Evelyn was rich now and she had taken the time to drive in from her home in the Hamptons to pay her former mother-in-law her last respects.

"I'd like to say that Gwenyth was a bitch on wheels,"

Evelyn said and smiled broadly. Someone chuckled and Delia pulled air between her teeth. "And I know a lot of you
here agree with me, whether you care to admit it or not."
Evelyn's eyes rolled over the faces that watched her. "She
ruined my marriage to her son and for that I owe her a debt
of thanks." She smiled maliciously, nodded her head at the
preacher, and sat back down.

The room was reeling from her words. Even the preacher
was speechless for a long time, he just kept looking down
at his Bible and then back at Evelyn. "Any—uh—hum . . .
anyone else have anything they'd like to say?" he asked
cautiously.

I searched within myself and found no bits of remorse
or intimations of grief that would inspire me to speak over
Gwenyth's body. She had never really been a grandmother to
me; she was always Hy-Lo's mother, Mrs. Lowe.

Hy-Lo's head dipped lower at this loss and his chin
rested on his chest throughout the service, but he did not
cry and his shoulders did not heave. He handled the death
of his mother as he did everything else in his life: he climbed
deeper into his bottle.

I sighed at the memory and felt a pang of pity for him. My
hand moved up and rested lightly on the fragile skin of his
arm. I expected my body to shake with disgust and my hand
to recoil against the feel of his flesh against mine, but none
of these things happened and so I left my hand there until
the early-winter evening glowed purple through the window and I was confronted with a memory so blanched with
time that it was almost unrecognizable to me.

"I don't want to go."

"C'mon, Kenzie."

"No."

"C'mon, please?"

"I say no!"

"Okay, if you come out I'll buy you an ice cream."

"No, no, no! Chocolate?"

"Uh-huh."

"Sprinkles?"

"Rainbow."

I must have been three years old, maybe younger. Hy-Lo was searching for me, yelling my name through the apartment. "Kenzie! Where are you? Kennnzzziiiee!"

It was a game we played when my mother went out and left us alone. Before he moved from beer to vodka, before he stopped simply yelling and started slapping.

I had hidden myself in Delia's closet and placed my sneakers on the wrong feet and had horribly knotted the laces. My coat, an Easter lightweight that was pink with a white collar, covered my head and blocked out the blotchy darkness of the closet. I felt well hidden, but he found me anyway, pulling me from the closet and hoisting me up in his arms and then spinning me wildly through the air.

We laughed together, father and daughter, and afterward I rested my head in the smooth curve of his neck and delighted in the feel of his rough whiskers as they brushed against my forehead. Chocolate ice cream danced in my mind and I felt safe wrapped in my father's arms.

The memory moved me to tears and my forefinger traced the length of his arm until it reached his wrist and finally the creased back of his hand.

I waited, hoping that his hand would flinch and jerk until finally turning over and welcoming my fingers into his palm. I waited and watched his face for any change. I waited and realized that my hand had enclosed his and his fingers had bent to oblige.

Chapter Sixteen

I made the eight o'clock meeting on the second floor of a three-story building in a space Genie Carpets once occupied. It was a bright and airy location with floor-to-ceiling windows and whirling ceiling fans. Even in the early darkness the room made it seem more like early spring than the dead of winter.

Bolts of carpet were stacked like colorful logs in the four corners of the room and *Going Out of Business* signs lay in neat heaps on the windowsills. Large fluffy pillows with mosaic designs had been strategically placed around the floor and the lingering scent of myrrh curled through the room. I smiled a bit and looked around at the flustered faces of some of the older women who were trying to figure out how they were going to sit on the floor without embarrassing themselves.

I took my place in what I thought to be the coffee line, behind a large white woman with red hair and black eyebrows. She turned and offered me a smile; I returned it and then dropped my eyes. I didn't need to make friends; I just needed to find some peace.

The line moved past cookies, donuts, and brownies. "No coffee?" I asked as I stood at the table blinking at the clear water the woman behind the table had just poured into my cup.

"No." The woman laughed at the surprise in my voice. "Just herbal tea." The meetings always had coffee. "And no smoking in the room," the woman added and turned her teapot on to the next cup.

"Oh, okay," I remarked and made my way further down the table toward the multicolored boxes. Green tea, chamomile, Red Zinger. I was dazzled by the array but all I really wanted was coffee. I closed my eyes and stuck my hand into the first box my fingers found.

This was a women-only meeting run by a lady named Fatima, who had been clean for nearly twenty years. She was almost sixty, but didn't look a day over forty-five. "Welcome," she said, and her Jamaican voice boomed across the room grabbing your attention by the chin. "Hello, my name is Fatima and I'm an alcoholic."

"Hello, Fatima."

I had pulled my pillow as far away from the crowd as I dared without someone calling me out. I sipped my herbal tea and listened as the stories rolled on like meadows after a war, trampled flowers, torn trees. That's who we were, war-torn meadows on the verge of new growth.

"Well, ladies, it's almost ten o'clock, would anyone else like to share?" Fatima asked, her large dark eyes searching through the sea of female faces.

Heads turned and swiveled, hands pointed, pushed, and pleaded, but no one would take the last call. How ironic, I thought to myself; in our drinking days, we all would have jumped at last call.

"Well, thank you for coming and have a blessed evening," Fatima said and flashed her brilliant white smile.

My coat was halfway on, one empty sleeve dangling mercilessly behind my back as I attempted to grab at it with one hand while balancing my cup of herbal tea with the other. For a moment or two I looked like a cat chasing its tail.

"Here, let me help you with that," a familiar voice said, so I stopped and allowed the delicate hand with the simple gold wedding band to help.

"Thanks," I said, turning and coming face-to-face with Nurse D. Green.

I was struck dumb for a moment or two; my mouth was working but nothing came out except the clucking sound my tongue made against the roof of my mouth. "How are you doing?" Nurse D. Green asked, rescuing me from saying something stupid.

"F-fine," I said and blinked a few times.

"I like this meeting, is this your first time here?" There was that smile again, the one she wore like a badge all day long. She looked terribly normal at the moment: her hair was wrapped in a colorful kente cloth, her lips glowed warm with a cinnamon gloss, and large hoop earrings dangled from her tiny ears, giving her a pure Afro-Caribbean look, something her starched white nurse's uniform camouflaged.

"I—I didn't know you—" I started my question and stopped just as abruptly.

"Of course you didn't, how could you, that's what anonymity is all about."

"Yes, yes," I said because I had nothing else to say—but so much I wanted to know.

"Well, it's late . . ." Nurse D. Green started to say and then she let her words float for a moment while her mind worked with something else. "Can I give you a lift?" Her eyes sparkled and I saw that her offer was genuine.

"Oh, I'm way out in East New York . . . It's a good trek . . . I can catch the bus . . ."

"Oh, it's on my way, really, come on."

I found myself strapped into Nurse D. Green's red Jeep Wrangler. She'd had it for twelve years and had bought it used, a large hole was wearing in the floor beneath the gas pedal, and I could look down and see bits and streaks of the black tarred roads we traveled. The trip was bouncy and the tea ran through my system and settled uncomfortably in my bladder. I held it for as long as I dared.

"Um, you know what, I've got to go to the bathroom," I said over the sound of the engine, the creaking gearshift, and the Bob Marley cassette tape that had probably sounded nice three thousand plays ago, but Bob was dragging through "Redemption Song" and now it sounded like crushed glass to me.

"Oh, okay, let's pull in here." Nurse D. Green made a sudden and vicious right turn from the left lane into the parking lot of a McDonald's. My heart was in my lap as I waited for someone from one of the cars she had cut off to pull up beside us, snatch us both out of our seats, and beat us unmercifully. "C'mon," she said as she hopped out of the Jeep, ignoring the horns and screams of obscenities that came at us from the street.

"Something to eat?" she asked as we exited the ladies' room and headed toward the glass doors.

My stomach was aching, but I didn't have more than two dollars in my pocket. "No, I'm fine," I said and pushed the door open.

"Oh, I need a Big Mac," I heard her say and turned to see her positioned in line behind two teenage girls who should have been in bed on a Tuesday night instead of hanging out at the local McDonald's.

I let the door close and walked over and sat down at one of the white Formica-topped tables. I hoped she was getting it to go. My eyes were beginning to hurt against the bright lights of the fast food place and I actually began to long for the darkness of the Jeep.

"Here, I got you a chicken sandwich, french fries, and a coffee." Nurse D. Green plopped down across from me and placed two orange trays down on the table.

I looked at the food and my stomach growled. I quietly reminded myself of the two dollars that sat folded in the back pocket of my jeans. There was at least five dollars' worth of food in front of me.

"Hey, eat up . . . it's on me," she said and dumped three packs of sugar into her cup of coffee.

"Thank you," I said and tried not to seem too eager as I unwrapped the paper from the sandwich. We ate in silence for a while, our eyes playing tag and then dropping down to our food. I was dabbing a french fry in a glob of ketchup when she finally broke the quiet.

"You don't remember me, do you?" she asked and popped the last bit of her Big Mac into her mouth.

My mouth fell open, "Of course," I said trying to keep the annoyance out of my voice. Did she think I was an idiot or something? Did she think I took rides from strangers? Of course I knew who she was. "From the hospital," I continued and tried not to screw my face up.

"No." She laughed. "Not the hospital . . . before that."

I examined her face, the rosy cheeks and small button nose. There was some hazel in her round eyes and her skin glowed the color of gold holiday ribbon. "No, I'm sorry, I don't remember you from anyplace else but the hospital."

"Well, maybe you were too young, I mean I would see you at least once a week with your mom and brother; how are they?" she asked.

"F-fine," I lied and left it at that.

Nurse D. Green tilted her head a bit and seemed to look through me. "Oh," she said, and I knew she knew I was lying.

"Well, I was dating your Uncle Randy for a while, but before that, you know, we were all friends. Hy-Lo, Charlie, Randy, and me. I grew up with them on St. John's Place." She took a sip of her coffee and I thought that it must surely be cold and then I thought about how small our world really was.

"You grew up with Hy-Lo?" I knew I sounded like an idiot but I couldn't help it. I had never met anyone who grew up with Hy-Lo, not counting his siblings. I thought that Hy-Lo had killed off all of his friends so no one would ever know anything about him.

"Uh-huh," she said and nodded her head. "My mother and your grandmother Gwenyth were good friends. We were at her funeral," she said and then her eyes went soft. "I'm very sorry," she added.

I wanted to tell her that there was no need for her to be sorry, because I wasn't. "Thank you," I said instead. Her eyes moved over my face and I knew what her next set of words were going to be. I braced myself.

"How are you handling . . . um . . . your dad's . . . um, condition?"

I took a deep breath. "Fine," I blurted out and knew that my pitch was too high, making it sound happy instead of sad. I felt ashamed and cleared my throat and avoided her eyes.

"It doesn't surprise me, really. I mean, not that I can judge or point fingers . . . I'm not attending AA meetings because I like that type of social scene." She laughed and then continued, "I've been going steady for five years now. But those Lowe boys could really put it away at an early age; you know what I mean? They drank like grown men when they were just fourteen and fifteen years old."

She laughed at the memory and glanced at her watch. "But I suppose you know all of that. I mean, he is your father."

She started to clean up her mess, tossing used napkins and coffee stirrers onto the tray. Another glance at her watch. I didn't move. "No, I don't know anything about my father," I said when Nurse D. Green started to rise from her chair.

She looked at me for a moment and then slowly sat down again. "I—I thought you two were close because you're there so often. I mean, all day and late into the night." She stopped for a moment and then said, "No one else comes, but you. Just you."

"I don't know why—" I started, and then my words got caught in my throat. I bit my bottom lip. "I don't know why I come," I continued as the tears began to well up in my eyes.

"Okay, okay," she said, patting my hand. "Let me get some more coffee." The tears fell then, rolled down my cheeks and onto the debris of my tray; I let them come and my body heaved with relief.

Some stories start out happy, go bad in the middle, and end up happy at the end. Still others start out bad, get worse, and still end up happy in the end. Hy-Lo's story started out bad, curdled and soured in the middle, and ended up worse.

I listened to Nurse D. Green (finding out during our time together that her first name was Dianne) as she told me of the abuse Hy-Lo and his brothers had suffered. The times Gwenyth beat them across the bottoms of their feet and then had them stand barefoot in the snow, or barefoot in the summer on the black tarmac of the street, as punishment for some childish misdemeanor or failing grade.

There were locks on anything that held food. Heavy link chains looped through the handles of the kitchen cupboards and stretched across the blue and white linoleum floor like a silver boa constrictor until finally closing around the belly of the refrigerator and locking tight with a padlock.

Goose bumps rose on my skin as I recalled the food rules in our house. Malcolm and I could not go into the kitchen cabinets or the refrigerator without asking first.

"She never locked up the liquor, though; the liquor would stay out in the open right on top of the kitchen table," Dianne said in between sips of coffee. "I learned how to mix a Tom Collins, screwdriver, and martini at the age of fifteen right there in Gwenyth's house. She warned us that if we ever told our parents, she would deny every word of it. And she would have too, and who knew what else she would do to us. We saw the marks she left on her kids."

I began to shiver. "She really beat them?" I asked and began to rock.

"Beat them? Umpf, that's an understatement." Dianne

stopped and placed her hand over mine. "Oh God, you're like ice—"

"Please," I said and moved my hand away.

"Are you sure you want me to go on?" Her eyes were filled with concern and something bordering on fear.

I forced a smile and stopped rocking because I was afraid she wouldn't tell the rest of it. "Please," I said again.

Dianne licked her tiny lips and glanced at her watch. The manager had been circling our table like a hawk, sneering, making faces, and sweeping at invisible bits of dirt near our feet. Dianne straightened her shoulders, threw him a look I didn't think she could physically back up, and then continued.

"Gwenyth didn't just beat those boys, she fought them like she was a man—slamming them up against walls and choking them into unconsciousness. Randy was the youngest and the smallest; she hung him out of the bedroom window by his throat one day. I remember that, I was so scared for him, I really thought she was going to drop him. They lived on the fourth floor, he wouldn't have been able to survive a fall like that."

We both shivered at the thought.

"She had those boys scared shitless." Dianne leaned in and dropped her tone. "I mean, they were really scared of her and I think they were scared of her until she dropped dead."

My eyes bulged.

"Did you know my grandfather?" I asked and hoped.

Dianne shook her head back and forth. "No, they all had different fathers and none of them knew who they were. Only Gwenyth knew and she didn't tell a soul." She swallowed hard and then went on: "I remember Randy saying that Gwenyth told them she wished they were never born. Called them devil children, oh, all sorts of things." She waved her hand at the memory.

I felt my mouth tremble in anger.

Dianne, realizing that she had probably said too much, pulled back and tried to clean up the mess she was making of me. "Y-you have to understand though, Kenzie, that Gwenyth was like you and me. Like Hy-Lo and his brothers . . . I mean she was an alcoholic, and all of her actions stemmed from her disease . . . just like ours . . . just like your dad's."

She leaned back and waited for her words to have some type of effect on me.

"Who the hell am I supposed to blame or hate . . . Hy-Lo or his mother? The chicken or the fucking egg! Who?"

My abrupt and angry explosion caused Dianne to jump backward in her chair; someone in the back dropped a tray and the manager cleared his throat.

"I—I'm sorry, I'm sorry," I said and wiped at my tears.

"Okay, you needed to do that; you needed to get that out of your system." Dianne cautiously leaned in again. "There is no one to blame, not even yourself. This is the life you were dealt, but you can change your hand, you don't have to continue playing with the same bad cards. You know what I mean?

"It hurts, I know it does, but you have to work toward curing that pain and conquering the hurt. Don't keep holding on to the pain and carrying it around with you because, believe me, you'll eventually pick up the bottle again or something worse. Let go of it here and now and take the first *real* steps toward your recovery."

"I've been in recovery for nearly six months and I—"

"You have not been in recovery, you have stopped drinking. Maybe you've taken a hiatus from the liquor and once in a while you drop in on a meeting to fool your mind into believing you're actually in recovery, but your heart knows different and you can't fool it into ignoring the pain and that empty space that's growing right next to it."

I almost fell out of my chair. How did she know about

the empty space near my heart? Did she know I tried to fill it with alcohol, did she have one too?

"How—" I started to ask, but she cut me off again.

"That anger, that pain and hurt that you lay down with at night and wake up with in the morning, that's the weight keeping you down; you're not going to be able to move forward as long as you've got anger for your lover."

The lights began to dim. "We're closing up, ladies," the manager announced.

"You'd better let it go or you will end up like your father, and any kids you ever have will come to visit you on your deathbed and not know why they come either. End the cycle now."

We stood, leaving our trays on the table, and walked out into the cold night. Dianne's words bounced around in my head like balls as we made our way to her Jeep.

"Hey, why did you and Randy split up?" I asked before climbing into the vehicle.

"We were both drunk and got into an argument," she answered. "He threw me down a flight of stairs and broke my collarbone. I decided that if I could go two weeks in the hospital without a drink then I could go forever without one, so I went on the wagon. Randy chose not to. That was almost fifteen years ago."

"When was the last time you saw him?" I asked, wondering if they ever got together as friends.

"I see him every Wednesday and Sunday when he comes in for dialysis," Dianne said and started the engine. She turned and looked at the surprise that covered my face. "Oh, shit, you didn't know that either?" she asked, exasperated. "I guess you guys aren't really a close-knit family." She said it with some humor but the truth in it was too real to ignore.

"When was the last time *you* saw him?" Dianne asked.

"At my grandmother's funeral, he and Hy-Lo got drunk, got into an argument, and he tried to throw Hy-Lo down a flight of stairs." I felt a giggle rising in the back of my throat like a gas bubble. "I guess Randy's got a thing with the stairs," I said and began to laugh hysterically.

Dianne just smiled and let me have my madness. I laughed until I cried and then I laughed again.

"Thanks for everything," I said and wiped at my eyes as she let me out at my door. "I mean it."

"I know," she said. "See you soon." She smiled, winked, and drove off.

Chapter Seventeen

For two days I stayed away from the hospital, choosing instead to bundle myself up, brave the cold, and roam the streets in search of solace. On the second day I found myself moving quickly down Nostrand Avenue, past the fruit and vegetable markets, the West Indian bakeries and roti shops. This was my old neighborhood and it should have been familiar to me, but instead I felt like a stranger in a foreign land.

The buildings had aged and looked as tired and worn as the empty black faces that moved in and out of their broken doorways. Twenty-four-hour bodegas littered every corner and liquor stores etched a place for themselves in between the Jewish-owned meat stores and the East Indian ninety-nine-cent shops. Every block I walked mirrored the block before.

The streets were teeming with people who had no other choice but to brace the winter chill to run their errands. The ice-cold of winter would not stop life in Crown Heights.

Music blared from the open windows of overheated apartment buildings as well as from the gleaming new cars that pushed through the crowded streets. It looked more like a Saturday afternoon than an early Wednesday evening.

I made a left on Empire Boulevard and the wind caught me by surprise, slamming into me like a steel door, holding me hostage, and then shaking me until I broke free. I pulled at my coat collar and hunched over to fight against the sudden gusts that came at me in sevens and snatched at my breath.

No matter what, I was going back to where it all began. I wanted to end the battle I had been fighting within myself for so many years. The wind wrapped itself around me and laughed aloud at my effort. I laughed back and moved on.

The memories began to flood my mind as soon as I stepped into the halls of 245 Rogers Avenue. Nothing much had changed; the walls were still cream and the floors were still covered in cheap black and white octagon-shaped ceramic tile. The lock to the second door was missing, and someone had stuck toilet paper in the round space where the lock should have been.

I pushed the door open and walked into the main hallway. I had spent so many of my childhood days playing in these halls. Hide and Go Seek, Hot Peas and Butter. We ran through at breakneck speeds, our laughter laboring to catch up with us.

I had seen a lot of good times in these halls.

I moved to the right and walked toward the apartment where Gwenyth had lived. I expected the door to be closed, but it was wide open and the smell of paint floated from its insides. I inched closer, straining my ears to listen for whoever might still be inside. Nothing.

"Hello?" I called as I stood at the open door. Cold air and the smell of turpentine rushed out, but nothing else; I stepped in.

As a child, I hadn't been inside Gwenyth's apartment very many times. Children, no matter that we were her grandchildren, were not her favorite beings, and so we were hardly ever welcomed. "They're nasty, little dirty things that misbehave and break things." That's what she told Malcolm and me one day when she came up for a visit and we had three of our cousins over. She didn't even sit down, just looked at us, shared her words of wisdom, and turned on her heels and left.

I stood in the middle of the living room for a long time waiting for something to happen.

I waited until the sun slipped beneath the dark blanket of dusk and the superintendent came and chased me from the apartment with a broomstick.

I went searching and thought I had found nothing except an empty apartment with newly painted white walls and refinished hardwood floors. Not even a memory of Gwenyth lingered in the air, and why would it? She had lived there so long ago. How many people had come and gone since then?

The superintendents just kept repainting the walls, coating the memory of the previous tenants away forever, reinventing the space for the new people and the memories they brought.

That's the way life was. Ongoing, ever changing, with a fresh coat of paint.

So I realized, as I boarded the bus to head home, that I *had* found something. I found that I needed to sweep away the pain, open up the windows, and air out the hurt; let in some joy and patch that space up near my heart, apply a fresh coat of paint and move on with my life.

When I arrived home that evening I found Glenna sitting in my living room, her feet propped up on the hassock and a cup of soda resting on the table in front of her. She turned and offered me a grin and a wink. I smiled back, but said nothing. She had been in the middle of a sentence when I opened the door, but now her lips were pinched together; her eyes darted from me to the kitchen and then back again. She had been talking about me.

Delia was in the kitchen. I couldn't see her but I could hear her voice above the sound of the hot grease as it jumped, bubbled, and browned the chicken and french fries she was cooking.

"Kenzie's here," Glenna sang out.

Delia said nothing for a long time and then she responded, "Oh?"

A light veil of smoke filled the apartment as Marvin Gaye's voice floated in off the transistor radio, asking the world: *"What's going on?"*

"Hey," Glenna said, after I still had not spoken.

"Hey," I replied. "Back from Europe so soon?" I added and then raised my eyebrows a bit and cocked my head so that she would know I was aware that they had been discussing me. Glenna ignored me.

"Well, should I leave?" she asked when I started toward my room instead of coming over to greet her.

"Oh, please, Glenna, gimme a minute to put my coat down."

Her eyes dropped and her smile wavered, but just for a moment. "Okay," she said and turned back toward Delia. "Kenzie's grumpy!" Glenna yelled and then laughed in her very best good-witch voice.

"She's always grumpy!" Delia said and then she laughed too, but her laughter got muffled in the smoke of the frying chicken.

I walked into my room and placed my coat on my bed. I sat down and unlaced my boots. I just remained there for a minute or two, trying to compose myself. It wasn't working but I went back to the living room anyway.

"Hey," I said again and leaned down and kissed Glenna's cheek. "Happy holidays." I sat down beside her.

"Uh-huh," Glenna answered and gave me a sideways look. "So I see you put a tree up." She pointed at the sad piece of timber that barely filled the small corner of the living room.

"Yeah," I said and wished I had a magazine to flip through. I didn't want to look at her.

"Trying to call up some Christmas cheer?" Glenna's eyes dared mine to look right at her.

I couldn't and so I kept looking at the tree.

"So where ya been?" Glenna asked and turned her body toward me. She rested her elbow on the back of the couch and cocked her chin in the palm of her hand.

"Out," I said and started to get up. I didn't want to do this.

"Out where?" She grabbed at the end of my sweatshirt, pulling me back down to the couch.

I didn't say anything else; I just turned and gave her a look.

"Uh-huh," she sounded and released my sweatshirt.

I stood up again and walked toward the Christmas tree. I needed to do something with my hands, so I fiddled with the ornaments, moving them from branch to branch.

"Kenzie, get that can outta the freezer for me," Delia said as she laced a plate with paper towels to catch the excess grease from the golden-brown chicken parts. "Okay, Glenna, the chicken is ready and so are the fries. I got ketchup and hot sauce."

"What you got to drink?" Glenna called back to her.

"Um, Kenzie, look and see if any more of that Pepsi is left in there," Delia said and scratched at her head.

"Yeah, a little bit," I replied as I peered into the bare refrigerator. That was basically all that was there. A half-empty bottle of Pepsi, a stick of butter, and a loaf of bread. The first of the month was still two weeks away and I only had twenty dollars in food stamps left.

"You need me to go out and get something?" Glenna said as if reading my mind.

"No," I snapped.

Delia looked at me with wide eyes and I heard Glenna mumble something under her breath.

"What's wrong with you, Kenzie?" Delia asked and shook her head in disgust.

"Nothing," I said in a quiet voice. What was wrong with me?

We settled in the living room, balancing our plates of chicken and french fries on our laps, eating with our hands, and licking our fingertips instead of wiping them with the cheap paper napkins Delia had placed on the small living room table.

The conversation was light and broken in places by the sound of the television and the music that moved in from Delia's bedroom. Random gunshots from the street or loud talking in the hallway outside our door took up the large open spaces left between our words.

It wasn't noticeable right away, not during the first fifteen minutes or so, but the closer we came to the reddish-brown bone of the chicken we ate, the less we found to say to each other. Instead we looked to the bowl and the remaining tiny wing parts and scraggly french fries that rested at its bottom.

We wanted to keep our mouths filled with food so the real words, the hurtful ones that moved around the dark corridor behind our tongues like specters, did not drift out.

I swallowed hard and glanced over at Glenna. I could see she was uncomfortable. I could tell by the way she felt the need to giggle behind every other word she spoke and the intense way she listened to Delia ramble on about her Saturday-night bingo games and how the person sitting next to her, beside her, or in front of her always seemed to win the jackpot instead of her. "I just ain't got no kinda luck," Delia said and shook her head pitifully.

Glenna's head bobbed up and down with interest and agreement, but her eyes darted around the apartment and her mind studied the poverty Delia and I had fallen into, or, rather, had been dragged into by Hy-Lo.

A roach crawled up the wall and Glenna shivered at the sight of it. We didn't have roaches when we lived in the apartment on Rogers Avenue or in the house on Autumn Street. At those addresses we had had almost everything a middle-class income could buy. Here on Sutter Avenue, on the first of the month we collected money from the state, lived in a government-run housing project, and paid for groceries with food stamps. We had roaches here, and not much else.

"You need some lights on that tree," Glenna said as she leaned back into the cushions of the couch, watching the roach as it kept moving up the wall. "And what happened to the star?" she added and looked at me.

I shrugged my shoulders and smirked at her. Delia rolled her eyes and said, "I don't know why she even bothered putting that thing up." Her tone dug at the anger growing inside of me.

"Well, because it is Christmas," I spat without looking at her. There was silence for a long time before I spoke again. "And we always had a tree before . . ."

My words hung thick in the air around me. Delia turned her head away and rested her chin on the back of her hand. Glenna cleared her throat and ran her hands over her hair.

We would leave the space void of words, but we each knew what the others were thinking.

"Well, we just always had a tree for Christmas," I said, trying to fold the corners of that void, creasing it and smoothing the middle before tucking it away.

The Cosby Show came on and Delia gave it her full attention. Glenna kept snatching glances at her watch and tapping her foot to some song that played in her head. She wanted to go, but wouldn't be the first to make the suggestion, even though a blue smoky evening was quickly snuffing out the dim light of the afternoon sun.

"You remember how Dad always brought home the biggest Christmas tree he could find? I mean, they were always at least six feet tall and the branches were so long and wide . . . upmf! Those were some big trees." The words just tumbled out of my mouth and the smile that followed topped it off like a cherry on a sundae.

Glenna's and Delia's heads spun around on their necks so quickly that a snapping sound followed.

I dropped my eyes and kept on talking even though I did not know what was compelling me or why I felt the need to go on. "Oh, and then we'd be up till at least three in the morning decorating it."

Delia made a face at me, but her eyes were soft. "Yeah, he always waited until near midnight on Christmas Eve before he went out and got the damn tree," she said and reached for a cigarette. "Always a scene too. The trees were always too damn big, he had to trim the branches down just to get it through the damn door." Delia huffed and smoke came out of her mouth in a big white cloud. "And then he had to saw off the top just so we could stand it up." She inhaled on the cigarette again and shook her head in dismay.

Glenna's face was a mask of surprise. She was familiar with the Lowe family stories, the ones that brought tears to your eyes and made you doubt that you would ever marry or have children.

"Then there was that one time, remember, Mom, when we bought that angel hair—oh, we were up scratching all night long . . ."

I had dragged her into a conversation about a man she had been married to for over thirty years, a man who had abused her for all of those years, a man who she had found the courage to walk away from only after he was unable to walk at all.

"Had to put you and Malcolm in the tub before you clawed your skin off!" Delia laughed and then her face went slack. She had said his name and brought the small joy that floated around us crashing down to the ground.

"Yeah, I remember," was all Delia's quick misery allowed me to say and then I looked down at my hands.

The small smile that had moved across Glenna's face faded, she stretched her arms above her head and forced a yawn that would clear the way to her leaving. "Well, I gotta—" she started to say, but Delia cut her off.

"Christmas just don't mean much anymore without Malcolm. He was the one always put the star on the tree." She stood up and walked over to the Christmas tree and grimaced. "Why you had to go and get a tree, Kenzie, why?"

I avoided those eyes of hers and stared at her feet instead. The house was filled with the saddest type of quiet for a long time. I supposed Glenna was holding her breath because she was seated right next to me and I didn't hear a sound coming from her.

"I just wanted it to be like it used to be," I said without looking up.

"It used to be bad," Delia said and looked back at the tree.

"And you call this better?" I asked.

"I call this different."

"Well, I call this worse," I said and leaned back into the couch. My shoulders brushed with Glenna's and she jerked.

"Worse? Humph. So you mean to say you didn't mind seeing my face and arms bruised and banged up? That was okay with you?"

She'd never spoken about her abuse, not openly like she did now, as if it had been on the front of the *Daily News* or announced on the six o'clock evening news, and certainly not in front of Glenna. She had never spoken about it aloud and maybe she'd thought not saying the words would make it less real.

My mouth fell open, and before I could answer Glenna touched my knee. I pushed her hand away. "That's not what I mean, Mom . . . Of course . . . I mean I hated that you allowed him to—" My words were getting all mixed up.

"*Allowed*, Kenzie? Is that what you call it?" Delia laughed bitterly and bowed her head before lifting it again to look at me. Her lips were curled into a smile that made me feel terrible. "You think I allowed your father to beat on me? Well, if afraid to stay but more afraid to go means I allowed it to happen, then you're right."

She walked past me and went to grab her pack of cigarettes off the table.

"If trying to make a home for my children—I mean a good home for my children—means I allowed it, well, I guess I damn well did!" She lit a cigarette and sat down.

Glenna twisted her behind further into the couch and raised her hand to touch my knee again, but changed her mind and laid her hand to rest on her own knee.

I wasn't through yet, and did not know why I even continued, but I did and things just got worse, when all I wanted to do was make things better.

"You think that we had a good home, Mom? I mean with him beating on you and then beating on me and Malcolm—you thought that was a good home?" I had my hands stretched out in front of me, palms up, pleading for some type of understanding.

"Did you ever go without, Kenzie?"

"Mom, I—"

"Did you ever go without? Without food, clothing, shelter?"

"I—"

"Did you?" Delia's voice was low. Her voice, even and mean.

"No," I said quietly. I could feel my eyes melting, becoming soupy. I was able to look at Glenna now, but she was disgusted with me and avoided my eyes.

"I didn't have a father, Kenzie, and I went without everything. Every goddamn thing. You think it was easy for your grandmother and me? We had a room, one bed, and one goddamn pillow. I had to share a fucking pillow!" She threw her hands up in the air in exasperation. I could see tears sparkling in her eyes, but she blinked them away. "Me and her for years. Cooking on a hot plate, wearing hand-me-down clothes. We didn't have nothing or no one but each other and it just wasn't enough!"

She stopped, bent over, and stubbed her cigarette out in the ashtray. She looked at Glenna and her eyes were apologetic, but she kept on anyway.

"There were nights when I had to stay alone, nights when Mama had to work overtime, double-time or triple shifts so we could have shoes or a coat or just a new pair of drawers. Humph, I was six or seven, maybe even younger, and I was always alone. Me—" She slapped her chest loudly. "In a rooming house filled with strangers—a child. Alone."

Glenna lifted her eyes and quickly moved them between Delia and me before dropping them again. She reached for her glass of Pepsi, lifted it, and realizing the glass was empty cradled it between her hands. She kept her eyes lowered.

"You and Malcolm had everything that I wouldn't have been able to give you without him. New bikes, roller skates. Oh, and let's not forget the clothes! Did you ever not have the latest style?" She raised her eyebrows and waited for me to answer.

I just shook my head.

"What about that private school you went to, Kenzie, what about that? Yeah, I know your grandmother paid some and you had your little scholarship money, but where do you think the extra money came from, the money that paid for the ski trips and camping equipment? The plane and train tickets to Colorado, Martha's Vineyard, and wherever else you begged to go with those rich white girls—what about that?"

I couldn't find the words to respond to her accusations, so I just hung my head.

"Uh-huh," she said and pointed at me. "I didn't want my kids to have to do without and you didn't! I did without so you didn't have to. I did without a normal happy life so you didn't have to live the way I did before Mama married Sam!"

She reached for another cigarette and then took a deep breath before lighting it.

"Every day, every goddamn day I told myself that when I had children, they would have a father and their own fucking pillows!" That last sentence came out entangled in the white puffed smoke of her exhale.

We were all quiet for a long time.

"Afraid to stay, but more afraid to go," she uttered again and inhaled on the cigarette.

Glenna and I stood on the corner, our backs against the wind that slapped angrily at our coats. We didn't say anything, just tried to keep warm by dancing in place. The streets were almost deserted except for the occasional police cruiser. We'd been out there for about half an hour and not one taxi had passed.

"You got a cell phone, right?" I said above the sound of the wind.

Glenna's face twisted and her eyes stretched wide. "You think I'm going to pull my celly out around here?"

"You think these drug dealers want your two-year-old cell phone, Glenna? Please! Even the crack addicts got cell phones around here!"

Glenna didn't laugh at first, she just rolled her eyes and shook her head. But I laughed, I needed to laugh to push away the evening's events, and I did until the tears turned to salty diamonds on my cheeks and my teeth chattered from the biting cold.

Glenna joined in just as a white Caprice Classic pulled up. "You need taxi, ladies?" the man behind the wheel asked.

"Yeah," Glenna said and then turned to me. Her eyes moved over my face, she looked at me the same way Delia had—as if I'd suddenly become a stranger.

"Later, girl, okay?" she said and gave me the peace sign

before opening the door and climbing into the backseat. I knew she had so much more she wanted to say, but the icy wind had made it hard to think of anything else but trying to get warm, and now the brown plush of the seats and the sweet stink that floated from the inside of the car rocked her worse than the cold and she put away her words until we would meet up again.

She let the door hang open for a long moment, maybe to air out the car or lend light to the murky darkness, or maybe just to look at me again and make sure that I was her friend and not the stranger my mother thought I'd become.

"C'mon, lady," the driver called out over his shoulder impatiently. We both threw him a look and rolled our eyes in classic B-girl style.

"Yeah, later, girl," I said and pushed the door closed. There would be time later to tell her what I had learned and who I was becoming.

If it wasn't for the wind and the cold, I would have walked off down the block and away from the apartment building. But the cold had numbed my fingers, toes, and the lobes of my ears. It had beat at my breast and pushed at my back like a school bully until I turned away from it and toward the building.

The wind followed me in and howled its way through the stairwells and hallways. I could feel it pushing at the bottom of the elevator as it climbed toward the eighth floor; even as I stepped into the hallway and started toward the apartment, it taunted and teased me.

I walked in and almost slammed into Delia.

"You think I don't know where you go every day? You lie to me and say you're making meetings, you lie to me and say you're visiting with friends or just taking walks. But I know what you're doing and I want you to stop!"

Her eyes were wild and flaming.

"I—" I started to explain, to plead my case.

"I know you sit beside his bed watching him die a comfortable death, while we live an uncomfortable life. You go every day wasting money on bus fare, money that could buy eggs or bread. Giving your time, your precious, precious time, when you know that if the shoe were on the other foot, he wouldn't even think of giving you the same. You know it's true—didn't you even see it in him with Malcolm?"

She said it and the hairs on the back of my neck stood straight up and I listened hard for the sound of Malcolm's picture sliding lopsided against the wall, but all I could hear was Delia's angry voice.

"You want to forgive him and I'm saying that even though he's your father, no one deserves forgiveness less than he does." The words felt like a blade. "Don't you forgive him, Kenzie, don't you dare!" Delia screamed. "Don't you dare forgive him," she repeated and her words echoed into the empty hallway behind me and danced away with the mocking sound of the wind. She swayed her index finger in my face before turning away and walking toward the couch.

I closed the door and removed my coat. The apartment stank of Newports as ribbons of cigarette smoke moved eerily around the bare lightbulb sitting in the center of the cracked and peeling ceiling. She must have smoked at least ten cigarettes during the time I was gone. I wanted to open a window, dump the used oil from the frying pan, and scrub away the burnt bits of meat that stuck to its silvery insides. I had a need to empty the ashtrays and then maybe sweep the floor. I didn't want to talk about forgiveness with a woman who seemed to have forgotten that she'd forgiven her life away and mine right along with it.

"He don't deserve it, uh-uh, he don't deserve it." Delia shook her head back and forth, speaking more to the stale air around her than to me. Her hands searched across the litter of old magazines, candy wrappers, and the outdated

TV *Guides* that covered the living room table. "I know I had another pack of cigarettes here, damnit," she muttered to herself, temporarily forgetting about me.

There seemed to be more gray hairs around her temples, many more than this morning, and the skin beneath her eyes looked darker, the space it colored etched deeper than a few hours ago. Delia had been old for a long time but it was really beginning to show and I felt guilty because I knew I was causing it.

I walked over and sat down beside her. She moved away from me; it was a quick and disgusted movement as if I had something clinging to me that could soil her. Her hands continued searching the table for her cigarettes. I got up and went into the kitchen; she always kept at least one pack in the refrigerator. I opened up the egg-colored door and stared into the bright emptiness.

Delia was flinging things off the table; her frustration was pushing toward a breaking point. I listened to her mumble and cuss under her breath and knew that most of her rage had nothing to do with her missing cigarettes.

I flipped up the plastic cover on the inside door that said *Butter* and there was a new pack of Newports.

"Here," I said, handing her the pack. She snatched them from my hand, and like a fiend began tearing the clear plastic wrapper away.

"Lemme tell you something, Kenzie," she said breathlessly as she stuck a cigarette between her lips. "There are things you don't know, things you couldn't know." She lit the cigarette and inhaled deeply.

I did know things, always had, things Delia would drop dead from if she knew I knew. Things she preached against but had, in her private past, succumbed to.

I knew about the thing that found her near forty, pregnant and unhappily married. Things that found her up on a cold steel table, legs propped up in stirrups while a doctor had his whole hand up in her, probing and jabbing. "Seven weeks," he said and pulled off the plastic gloves that covered those angry fingers. He didn't just pull them off; he snapped them off so Delia could feel the disgust he had for her. He hadn't seen the blue-green marks on her arms and back, he just assumed that she was careless and forgot to take the pill or that she was too lazy to get up and put in her diaphragm. He didn't know that Hy-Lo had thrown all of those things away, including the douche bag that hung on the back of the bathroom door.

"Are you sure about this, Mrs. Lowe?" the doctor asked after he saw the tears forming in her eyes.

Delia moved her head up and down yes—before the question was out of his mouth because she did not want to be *sure* about it, she just wanted it to be over and done with.

She breathed in the anesthesia and her eyes fluttered once, twice, three times before the big blue eyes of the doctor disappeared and she was sucked into a blackness that was so sweet, she would long for it the next time Hy-Lo hit her.

When Delia woke up she was on her stomach and her arms were by her sides, her hands palms up. She was in a warehouse of women wrapped in white sheets on steel gurneys. They were lined up one after the other, three columns and six rows across. Head to head and toe to toe. Delia thought about the green accounting sheets at work and stifled a laugh. And then she thought about the slave ships and the cargo they carried and she bit her lip so she wouldn't cry.

The women filled the white-walled room and they looked like poultry beneath the large silver light fixtures that hung from the ceiling. They were all faced down and distinguishable only by race, girth, and hair color. Lawyer, teacher, clerk—their titles melded to form the only title that mattered: woman.

All of them had had a life sucked from the womb and

so this connected them. Delia could see that at least three of them had done so for the same reasons she had; the purplish blue that stood out like streaks of paint on their arms, calves, and shoulder blades told her so.

For some reason this made her feel better, less guilty because she saw that she was not the only one. She formed an alliance with these women in her mind and even smiled at the nurse who came to check on her.

I knew things.

"But Mom—" I tried to speak, and her finger was up again, swaying back and forth in my face, chopping my words into nothingness and dismissing them just as easily.

I closed my mouth. I knew she felt like I had abandoned her, and even though there was only twelve inches of worn tweed fabric between us on the couch, I was miles away from the daughter she'd raised or even the woman she'd seen this morning.

I wanted to tell her that the change in me started a long time ago, shortly after I stopped drinking, but I didn't know it for what it was then. It wasn't until the other day when I found the bottle and the wind found me and taunted me, reminding me that I was a weak woman, that I was just a child of an alcoholic. The wind told me that people would expect me to bend and break.

I wanted to take Delia's hand and hold it tightly and tell her that even though everything was against me, I let go of that bottle instead of drinking from it, and when I did, a light broke through the dirt and grime I had been carrying around inside of myself ever since that summer day on the sidewalk when I was five and the clothes rained down around me.

I wanted to pull Delia close to me and cradle her in my arms, tell her about Hy-Lo's childhood, ask her if she'd ever noticed the scars on the bottom of his feet or the fear that shone behind his eyes when he was in Gwenyth's presence. That fear made him stone-blind to love. Did she know that?

"You just don't know," Delia said again before she exhaled. I moved closer to her.

"He had a hole near his heart," I said.

"What?" Delia asked and turned to look at me. "What hole?"

"Right here," I said and placed my hand near my heart.

Delia gave me a queer look. "Your father has a lot of things wrong with him, Kenzie; I don't think he has a hole in his heart, though," she said and gave me a look that made me think she wished he did have one. "He'd certainly be dead by now if he did," she mumbled beneath her breath, confirming my thoughts.

"No, not in his heart, next to it, here." I patted the place on my chest for emphasis. "Like I do."

Delia took a deep breath and rolled her eyes toward the ceiling. "You have a hole near your heart now?" She spoke to me as if speaking to a three-year-old child, slow and patient.

"The hole where the pain ate through . . . I tried to fill it with the liquor, tried to make it feel better . . ."

"Kenzie, stop—"

"He did the same thing, only it kept getting bigger . . ."

"Kenzie, please stop it—you're not making any sense—"

"Bigger and bigger until all he was on the inside was one big hole and that's what's killing him now!"

"Kenzie!"

We ended on the same high, violent note. We sat there for a moment, breathing heavily, our chests and shoulders heaving.

"Stop talking crazy, Kenzie. What is all of this about holes? What holes your father had in him came from the gallons and gallons of liquor he drank." She wiped at her brow and ran her hands quickly across her lap a few times. "I don't know why you're making excuses for him all of a sudden. I guess you've forgotten all the things he did to us, huh?"

Delia reached for another cigarette.

"I guess you've forgotten the beatings . . . the ones we *all* got?" She lit the cigarette and turned to face me. "It's because of him we don't have a house anymore, it's because of him we have no money, and it's because of him Malcolm is gone, or have you forgotten!"

Delia's body shook with anger and her eyes filled with tears. For a moment she looked as if she would strike me, but she drew on her cigarette instead.

"I guess you've forgotten, Kenzie, huh?" she said as the tears flowed down her cheeks and showered her shirt like a soft spring rain.

Of course I hadn't forgotten. How could I forget that day? Even as I sat watching Delia cry I could hear the sound of their bodies slamming against the walls.

The sound was unmistakable, the bumping and banging. But on that day it was different, harder and meaner. My heart pumped heavily in my chest because I knew Delia was at work and the only other person in the house besides myself and Hy-Lo was Malcolm.

Malcolm was seventeen years old and towered over Hy-Lo. His shoulders were broad and his neck thick. Since Hy-Lo hated having to look up at Malcolm he often spoke to him across a room or at least made sure there was a foot or two of space between them. It seemed as though the taller Malcolm got, the more Hy-Lo harassed him. He belittled him and degraded him every chance he got.

"You're nothing but a stupid idiot," Hy-Lo said one day when he overheard Malcolm complaining to me about a grade he had received in math. "Dummy," Hy-Lo cackled as he stood over us with his hands folded across his chest. "Jackass," he spat and grinned. "Can't count, huh?"

"I got a ninety," Malcolm said between clenched teeth. His hands had balled into fists and his face went red.

Hy-Lo's smug expression faltered and then recovered all in one quick wave, then he said, "Yeah, idiot ass—you couldn't pull a hundred!"

He laughed and half-walked, half-stumbled out of the kitchen, leaving the stench of vodka trailing behind him. Malcolm's eyes watered and I saw hate reflecting off his teardrops as they streaked down his cheeks.

The walls shook again and I remembered moving up the stairs, taking two at a time until I reached the first floor and came face-to-face with the blood that was smeared across the wall. I knew it was blood but something inside of me kept yelling, *Ketchup! Ketchup!*

The house shook again and I turned the corner and found Hy-Lo and Malcolm wrapped around each other. Hands around throats, pulling at ears, punching at stomachs and faces. But the worst thing was the breathing, the heavy let-loose of air that sounded to me like snorting bulls. The house shook again as Hy-Lo slammed Malcolm into the front door. The glass window shattered and cut at their skin. There was more blood now, lighter in color than the blood that spilled from their noses and the sides of their mouths. *Ketchup! Ketchup!* my mind screamed again.

I was afraid to get between them. It would be as dangerous as trying to break up two mad dogs. I began screaming at the top of my lungs, but they just kept slapping and punching at each other. I stomped my feet and begged and pleaded, but the house kept shaking as their bodies bounced off the walls.

Malcolm finally got loose, leaving most of his shirt tangled in Hy-Lo's hands. They stood there bleeding and staring at each other, breathing so hard that they sucked the air in from around me, leaving me breathless.

I guess I was still screaming because Hy-Lo told me to

shut up. He didn't turn to look at me; the words spilled from the side of his mouth with his blood while his eyes held Malcolm's face.

My brother wiped at his nose and his hand came away bloody. He looked down at his fingers and the red that coated them and his chest heaved.

He turned and walked away. His misery moved past me before his hand even brushed against my wrist. I'm still sorry I didn't look into his eyes; maybe I would have seen the future there and could have grabbed at his shoulder and begged him to stay.

The bedroom door of Malcolm's room moved and Devon Fulton stepped out. His head was bent and his hands were shoved deep into the pockets of his baggy jeans. He moved past Hy-Lo without looking at him. He stepped over the blood drops on the floor as if they were potholes that dotted the streets of our neighborhood.

I think he was grinning when he walked by me. I saw a glint of white beneath his nose. He was always grinning like an idiot, everything was humorous to Devon, even the hostility between father and son—the blood on the floor and walls.

I wanted to kick him in the ass as he slithered past me, following Malcolm down to the basement and out the cellar door, but instead I just stared blankly at the blue and green band of his boxer shorts where his oversized jeans slipped from his hips.

Hy-Lo walked past me and into the bathroom, he slammed the door so hard the jagged pieces of glass that remained in the doorframe shook free and shattered on the floor. The hallway looked like a battle zone and all I could think of was cleaning it up and trying to make it right before Delia got home.

I was thinking about how I was going to replace the glass. The blood was gone, but she might notice the clean streaks on the mustard-colored walls. The hall smelled like Pine-Sol and that would be odd for a Wednesday but I could make up something. The glass would be the problem.

I heard the whizzing sound of their bikes as Malcolm and Devon took off down the street. The sound echoed in my left ear, so I knew they were going to the Dip. I licked my lips and wondered where the Yellow Pages were.

I wasn't there when it happened, but half of the kids who lived on the block were. The Dip was the place kids would drop their forties, ditch their weed, and scramble like roaches when the cops arrived. The Dip, some long-forgotten mishap by the Department of Roads and Highways. No one wrote letters in that neighborhood, not even when sanitation skipped a week or the light on the corner of Lincoln and Sutter went berserk and shone all three colors at once: *Stop. Yield. Go.*

So the Dip remained and the children began to utilize it when the playground became too dangerous to play in unless you owned a bulletproof vest.

I think I'd found a company to replace the glass by the time Malcolm and Devon arrived at the Dip. Maybe my finger lingered on ABC Glass Replacement and then moved down to ACME Glass by the time they situated their bikes at the top of the Dip. I decided on ABC Glass Replacement and was probably dialing when Malcolm looked down the black-tarred thirty-foot slope. My fingers got tangled and I had to hang up and dial again when Malcolm turned to Devon and said, "See you on the other side."

I would have wiped at the dried blood around his mouth and assured him that I would see him. But Devon was his friend and not his sister so he just gave him a pound salute and said, "Awright, dog!"

I had been placed on hold by some woman who sounded like she'd been taking orders to replace the glass broken in household disputes all day long. I tapped my finger against the thin sheets of the Yellow Pages and hummed to myself, because there was no hold music.

Hy-Lo was still in the bathroom and I heard him curse to himself over the sound of the medicine cabinet opening and closing.

The woman came back on and told me she would be with me in another minute.

The street that bottoms out at the Dip is a quiet one that's rarely used because it's broken and crumbling. It tears away at car bottoms and snaps axles like shinbones. No one expected a semi to come barreling down the street.

They said Malcolm didn't even see it coming. His arms were outstretched like the wings of an eagle when the shiny silver grill of the truck struck him. He was sent flying just like an eagle over the pavement, but his heart stopped in midair and he lost the gracefulness of flight and landed fifty yards away in a crumpled heap on his side.

I had heard the bellowing howl of the horn right as the driver laid a too-late-hand on its rubber blackness. The sound grabbed my attention, just for a moment, before the woman came back on the line: "I'm so sorry for the wait—this day has been murder with a capital M! Now, how can I help you?"

They wouldn't be able to come before tomorrow. I would have to make up a lie or hope Delia wouldn't notice the missing glass. I thought again about the horn and another sounded off in the distance. Semis traveled Linden Boulevard at all hours of the day and honked their horns at the small cars that got in their way. It was a familiar sound, like crickets on a summer night.

Hy-Lo was in his room. The house was quiet except for the flapping sound of Malcolm's light green windbreaker as it swayed lazily back and forth on the clothesline. It was spring and it was one of those days where the chill in the air came in shreds and slithers between the gliding warmth of the season. It was one of those days.

The bell rang and broke the silence. I looked at the clock; it was almost seven and Delia had still not arrived. Two police officers stood outside our door. I noticed their nightsticks first and then the nine millimeters at their waists.

They removed their hats and their eyes moved between my face and the broken step of the stoop.

"Yes," I said and leaned my head on the wooden frame of the door. I was tired and thought someone had called them to report the disturbance.

They shifted their weight between their feet and chanced a glance at my bare legs and the faded denim shorts I wore. "Mrs. Lowe?" they asked solemnly.

I didn't hear the Mrs. or maybe I was too used to taking care of everything to think of myself as anything other than Mrs., but I said yes anyway and waited.

"Um . . ." the one with the freckles and harelip started, but a car backfired, causing both men to grip their guns.

"Yes," I said again, annoyed now.

"You have a son . . . um . . ." The black leather book, flipping pages, flipping pages. Our information always seemed to be in the back. "Malcolm Lowe?"

"Uh-huh," I said and noticed the police cruiser for the first time. Was that Devon sitting in the backseat?

"May we come in?" the officer with the curly brown hair and thick eyebrows asked.

"No . . . What happened . . . where's Malcolm?" I said, straining my neck to make sure it was Devon. What had they done? Where was Malcolm?

They weren't giving me any answers, just looking at my legs and my bare feet as I stepped out of the doorway and onto the cold concrete of the stoop. My hands were on my hips and I tippy-toed to look over their shoulders to make sure it was Devon, and it was, but he wasn't grinning. Something was wrong.

I looked into the faces of the officers and I knew this was something I couldn't fix before Delia got home.

"Malcolm was struck down by a tractor trailer today on Jenkins Avenue—"

"What hospital is he in?" I asked as I turned around to run back into the house to get some money, my sneakers, and Malcolm's light green windbreaker.

"Well, he . . ."

I didn't even hear the officer's words, I just heard Malcolm's picture slip lopsided against the wall and I knew.

We go to court every day; even Glenna takes a leave of absence from her job to sit between Delia and me. She holds our hands through the proceedings and lets Delia cry on her shoulder. I don't cry. I can't cry. All I am is stone and stone sheds no tears.

On the long wooden bench there is a space where Mable and Sam should be. I touch the mellow-colored wood and think of them every day before the judge bangs his gavel and court begins. They're not there because they don't know Malcolm's been in the ground for three weeks and will have been in the ground for ten before Delia finally tells them.

We smell like gardenias, the three of us. The smell clings to our skin and hair, and even though we shower twice a day, the scent remains. It would have been lilies if we had a choice. If we had money to make a choice. But we didn't and someone had sent gardenias to the funeral home by mistake. The deliveryman wouldn't take them back, even though the name on the delivery slip said *Mike's Auto Body* and not *Cane's Funeral Home*.

"De address—it's de right one, yes?" the man with skin the color of night and teeth bright as day kept saying over and over to the receptionist.

"Yes, but this is a funeral home, not an auto body shop," she repeated for the fourth time in exasperation.

"I leave here, yes? You settle with dem later, yes?" he said and pushed the delivery slip into his pocket. He tipped his yellow, green, and black baseball cap that said *AFRICA* across the top in large black letters and then jumped into his beat-up station wagon and sped away.

That's how we got the gardenias, us and everybody else who had a family member laid out in one of the six rooms.

To me hate always smelled like vodka and cigarettes, but now hate also smelled like gardenias and sounded like a million mothers weeping and was the color and texture of a green silk scarf with black polka dots.

Hy-Lo doesn't come. Not once. Not to the funeral home, graveyard, or courtroom. I think he tried to, almost every day, but before he could shower the bottle called him. And after he combed and patted his hair into place, the bottle called to him again, and when he ran his thumb over the scuff on the end of his shiny black shoe the bottle called him again.

Better he just stays and finishes the bottle and not have to deal with the pain at all. So Hy-Lo doesn't come.

I think he tried. I'm sure he tried.

Every day I sat there trying to listen to what was being said, but my hearing was clouded by the vision of Malcolm laid out on a slab of steel, a white sheet thrown over his body, covering the naked and bruised parts but allowing us to see his face. On that day I think he looks more like Delia than at any other time in his life.

Half the time I can't see the judge or the people around us because I can't stop the movie that's playing in my head. Over and over again I see Delia's legs giving way at the sight of her dead son. I see her head hitting the wall and spewing blood everywhere. I hear her moaning and crying and I see the blood running into her eyes and her shaking hands and they remind me of how Hy-Lo's hands shake on Sunday afternoon when the liquor stores are closed and he has nothing left over from Saturday.

On the last day when the judge bangs his gavel down hard, my hearing comes back and I feel like I'm floating near the ceiling looking down on me. People are moving out of the courtroom. Some come over and say things. Their words sound garbled, but I can tell from the way their lips move and the dewiness of their eyes that their words are sweet and sometimes pitiful. Others lightly touch my hand and Delia's; many grab hold of our shoulders and squeeze. I just nod my head and say thank you.

"Where's your dad at, Kenzie?" "Delia, where Hy-Lo at?" they ask after they make sure they sweep the courtroom good with their eyes. Make sure they don't miss him sitting at the back or by the window.

No one cares if he's there or not because they know how Hy-Lo is and they've already figured out that he had something to do with it, but they're not sure how and what exactly.

They don't care but they put that emotion aside for the moment and ask anyway because it's polite to inquire, and besides, they need something juicy to discuss over their meat loaf and mashed potato dinner that evening.

"He's home," we reply in unison like some off-key duet.

They didn't need to hear any more, their imagination would take it from there. They'd shake their heads and maybe offer a sympathetic "tsk, tsk" and move on.

The driver of the truck is the last to approach; he is a small man like my father, but Mexican. He has written my family six letters, each more apologetic than the last. Delia unclasps her hands and spreads her arms out at her sides, like a bird protecting her nestling, as if his closeness alone could take the life of her remaining child.

His hands are cuffed behind him and there is a court officer on either side of him. His eyes are brimmed red and there is scarlet present beneath his bronze skin. I am familiar with those brimming eyes and the tint in his skin. Even without reading the police report, I knew that this man shared many things with my father.

"I'm sorry," he says. I've read it twenty times in his letters, in between the names of his children and the description of his sod house in the small fishing village of Tulum where he was born and raised. The village where his aging parents remain, eating and surviving on the small amounts of money he is able to send them after he feeds and clothes his family here in the States.

I look at him, but he is not looking at me. His eyes are focused on the six small faces that stare back at him: his wife Maria, four daughters—Diana, Isabelle, Estela, Jacqueline—and a newborn son, Enrique. I know their names well. He has written them in his letters just as many times as he has written, *I am sorry.*

But now I hear him say it and his voice is filled with sorrow and I decide that his brimming red eyes are not from rum, vodka, or tequila, but from the salty tears that streak his face.

His wife falls to his feet, wailing and hanging on to his ankles. Her hair is straight and black and for some reason reminds me of the tire marks her husband's truck left in the street at the bottom of the Dip. And then I think of Malcolm; this man left him there too.

She drops to the floor, screaming and crying. The children follow and they fight to embrace him. Some cling to his waist, others grab hold of his neck. The smaller ones lose out and have to settle for his legs and ankles.

They sob in unison, *"O Dios mío! Por favor!"*

He cries with them and his words are a sorrowful mixture of Spanish and English that says he's sorry and that it was just a small bottle, *Es pequeño.* But they still take him away to serve his three-to-five though not less than two.

Hy-Lo drinks small bottles too, I think to myself, and we all get up to leave.

* * *

The lights went off and then on again in our apartment, and what little connection Delia and I had left disappeared with the sudden darkness.

She grabbed up her pack of cigarettes, wiped at the salty tracks beneath her eyes, and pulled herself up from the couch, stepping over my feet, careful not to touch me as she moved slowly past me and toward her bedroom.

Chapter Eighteen

I went to him that night even as the temperature dropped below zero and the streets went slick with black ice. The weather report called for snow, sleet, and freezing rain. But I went anyway, like some sick junkie needing a fix.

I ran most of the way after jumping off the bus, cutting between moving cars and dashing out against the light, running like something was chasing me.

I've got a death wish, but it's not mine and I need to cancel the request I put in when I was five, so I run like a madwoman through the streets and nearly knock down an elderly couple. I trip over a dog, but I get up and keep going until my chest feels like it will bust open and my heart threatens to give up on me.

I can't stop because I need to see the bottoms of his feet, because he can't answer my questions about the wind so I need to see his feet. I need to know for myself that it's true.

It's late when I finally get there and visiting hours have been over since eight. I make it past the guard because he's too wrapped up in the conversation he's having with the big-breasted nurse. She has long wavy hair and his eyes never leave her chest or the glossy strands that bounce around her face as she laughs at his corny jokes. His eyes never leave her, not for a moment, so he never sees me sneak past and up the stairs.

I take the steps in twos and by the second landing I'm taking them in threes.

"Miss!" I hear someone scream out at my back when

I make it to Hy-Lo's floor. "Miss, visiting hours are over!" The voice screams without even considering the sleeping patients or the scared and dying ones who can't take loud noises or things that scream and go bump in the night.

I don't stop, I just keep moving until I come to the doorway of his room. I don't stop until I'm sitting down next to his bed, so close now that I can hear the very faint sound of his breathing and see the slight rise and fall of his chest.

I remove my hat, scarf, and gloves, take off my jacket, and after a moment or two, I pull off my sweatshirt and sit there in my faded jeans and a thin blue T-shirt with tiny pink bears dancing across my chest. I don't shiver at all; in fact there are small beads of sweat on my arms, across my forehead, and forming on the space above my lip. There's warmth moving through and around me.

I move closer still and my knees knock into the steel leg of the cabinet that holds all of his monitors; the red and green lights blink spastic for a second at the impact and then hold steady again.

"Daddy," I whisper in his ear and place my hand on his cheek. The skin is soft there, soft like a newborn's. "Daddy," I say again and run my hand over his forehead.

He doesn't look as bad as he did all of these weeks I've been coming. He's got some color in his cheeks and he looks like he just might open his eyes and sit up. That scares the shit out of me because I know the suffering is over for him, the pain has left his body and his life is about to follow.

There's not much time left, so I lean in and tell him, "I know why you were who you were. It's the same reason why I am who I am."

I don't really understand it myself, and some small part of me begs me to reconsider my forgiveness. But I don't look at it as forgiving, I look at it as a fresh coat of paint, and then I hear the voice inside me say: *You've got to let go in order to move forward.*

Even so, I look at him hard trying to see the animal that lurked inside of him for so many years. I strain and twist my head this way and that to see if it has hidden itself in the folds of skin. But there is no beast there, just Hyman Lowe, the father I would never know.

I see a shadow cross the wall and I know the end is near. "Daddy," I say again and take his hand in mine and try to pull him away from God's grip. I want so much to take back those times I wished him dead. "Daddy," I hear myself cry and I can't believe my face is wet and I can't believe it hurts so bad inside. "Daddy!" I'm screaming now, because his hand is going cold in mine and the movement in his chest is slowing down.

Dianne found us beneath the steady stream of blue and white morning light that filtered through the window. My head resting on his chest, his arm thrown across my back.

I was sleeping, he was gone.

"Kenzie, Kenzie," she called softly and shook me.

I looked up at her and smiled. Dianne smiled back, but her smile was sad.

"Kenzie . . ." she started and then stopped to compose herself. She ran her hands across the clean white of her uniform and glanced out the window toward the sky before looking back at me and beginning again. "Kenzie . . . your dad . . . he's . . . gone."

I knew that he was. I watched him slip away. I saw him take his last breath and felt his hand squeeze my shoulder goodbye.

My eyes filled with tears and I straightened myself up and looked down into the sallow face of what Hy-Lo's soul had left behind.

"I need to see his feet," I said.

"What?" Dianne responded as she wiped at her eyes.

"I need to see his feet," I said again.

Dianne undid the sheet and pulled it up to reveal Hy-Lo's feet. They were black and shriveled; the soles were yellow and covered with large star-shaped scars.

I sighed and wiped at the fresh tears that formed in my eyes.

"Do you need more time?" Dianne asked.

"No, no," I said and shook my head.

She slowly covered his feet and then pulled the sheet up over his face. "I'm sorry, Kenzie." She put her hand gently on my shoulder.

"I'm sorry too," I said and felt the hole near my heart shrink. "I'm sorry for both of us," I said and looked out into the warm December day.